Reflections of the Past

By

Joan Byrd

Deep Indigo Books
Published by Indigo Sea Press
Winston-Salem

Deep Indigo Books
Indigo Sea Press
302 Ricks Drive
Winston-Salem, NC 27103

For information regarding bulk purchases of this book, digital purchase and special discounts, please contact the publisher at indigoseapress@gmail.com

Cover Design by Pan Morelli
Manufactured in the United States of America
ISBN 978-1-63066-618-7

Dedication

I dedicate this book to Mike Simpson.

I believe God places special people in your life that touch your heart by believing in your God-given talents waiting to be found. I had been searching for someone who would see my books the same way I did. I had no doubt that my God had given me a special gift for writing and I knew the non-stop words that have been pouring out into my listening ear came straight from heaven, through my very talented storyteller Patrick, my guardian angel, as well as the Lord himself.

Before I had my first book published, I read about Mike Simpson's publishing company. They were telling authors who wanted to have a book published to call. There was a photo of Mike Simpson, which came in handy when I met him. After calling, I left my message on voicemail. My answering machine is—or was until I got a do nothing flip phone—an original. I would make singing messages for seasons and holidays. Mike called and heard me singing. Later on, he told me, "Before we met to check out your book, I told my group: I don't know if that girl can write, but after listening to her singing message, I want to meet that girl."

Before we met, Mike told me to look for the short, fat man. When I saw him coming to the door of Panera Bread, I greeted him and shook his hand. He said: "You spotted the short, fat man."

I smiled and said, "No, I saw the man in the photo."

My arms were filled with two very long novels. Mike took the top one and opened it. He read the first paragraph, paused, and looked up, saying, "Joan, you nailed it on the first paragraph. This is a book I want to read."

Sometime later my first book was published. It was appropriately named *A New Beginning*, both from my main character, Reverend Gene Scott, and for my writing finally becoming a long-awaited dream come true. Since that first book, Mike has published twenty-two books for me and reflections of the past makes twenty-three. Three children's books have also been published.

I have always heard that some people go the extra mile and now I can agree. Mike Simpson has always gone the extra mile to support, offer good advice, restart a cranky word processor whenever it claims to be filled up, to lift your spirits with gratitude over doing God's will—which always comes first in my life, and to build me up as a great writer. And he is sincere in his beliefs, always a minister of God in his loving, giving heart.

Mike has met his soulmate in Susan and even though they both stay busy, they always find time for one another. Mike has become more than just my publisher; he is a true genuine friend to me and my husband Ray. In my eyes, Mike Simpson's stature is higher than that of a basketball player. It's what comes from within a person that makes them special. When I first met Mike, I never saw a short man who was fat. I saw a man the same height as my daddy, who never seemed short or fat, and who was looked up to by many people for his talent in carpentry.

So let's be clear, Mike is neither short nor fat, he never was. Mike also has a hint of joking and he cares about everyone he meets. Let's not forget his laughter when something is funny and that big smile he gives when I hand him his Christmas pie! Mike, you are worth every bite you take of that yummy chocolate-pecan-pie! Everyone tries to guess my secret. Mike's pretty close. It is yummy, it is pecan, and a pie.

CHAPTER 1

Natchez, Mississippi, 2019

The sun shone brightly in the big double window that stretched down to meet the upper porch floor. Twenty-year-old Victoria Stanford sat at her commuter filling out her latest solved mystery report. Ever since Vicky was six years old, she loved solving mysteries and declared: "When I grow up, I will be the very best sleuth around! Move over Holmes!"

Living and growing up in Natchez, Mississippi, Vicky learned from an early age how to appreciate history and the charm and majesty of the big homes and plantations, fully restored to their glory days. Even though her family did not own one of the grand homes in Natchez, they were happy and content with their smaller three store bungalow and called it simply, Sunrise. For it luckily faced the eastern sky and the over-sized windows drank in the morning sun light, making a soul feel glad to be alive.

Victoria switched off her commuter and finished getting dressed, for another day, another client, in her small office downstairs on the lower floor. Never charging the poorer clients and lovingly accepting homemade goods, such as freshly baked bread or a strawberry pie, kept Vicky unable to afford rent on a downtown office. So, the young detective was content at home. Hilda, the family help, loved all the fresh fruits and vegetables given to the young detective, when some of the poor farmers came calling, with missing farm hands when the fields needed planting or the hay needed harvesting. Such was her last case, missing…Jimmy Jacks, sixteen, never showed up for hired labor after asking Henry Franks for half his pay up front, so he could buy a new pair of work shoes. Victoria found the young man in the next town with Franky Franks, Henry's daughter, trying to get married. The judge was holding the young couple for forging their parent's names on the marriage license.

Vicky reread the case and laughed softly to herself, then filed it under, case closed. Her thoughts were interrupted by the familiar sound of her mother, calling her.

"Victoria, if you're dressed darling, can you come down. You have a special delivery this morning. It must be important!"

Vicky raced down the steps, brush in her hand, where she had been getting her overnight tangles out of her long black hair.

"Who it from mom? Does it say?"

"The only return is Stanford Hall." Irene Stanford stared down at the professional envelope. "I've been trying to recall where I have heard that name before." Victoria's mother handed her the tan-colored envelope.

"Irene, did I hear you say, Stanford Hall?" Steven Stanford walked from his home office, after overhearing his wife of twenty-two years. Standing six feet tall with black hair and blue eyes, it was obvious who twenty-year-old Victoria took after.

"Dad, do you know where Stanford Hall is?" Victoria felt a new mystery might be in her future and it had something to do with this early morning delivery.

"Yes, sweetheart, I recall my parents telling me about the once grand Stanford Hall Plantation, dating back to the revolutionary war. The one relative that stood out in my memory was another Stanford, named Victoria, same as you, darling."

"Is that why you named me Victoria, Dad?" Victoria had never wondered about her name until that very moment.

"Actually no, she never entered my mind the day you came into the world, precious." Steven bent over and kissed his beautiful daughter's cheek. "It was Irene who came up with Victoria, remember dear?"

"I most certainly do, Steven. You were such a beautiful baby, Victoria, we called you our little princess. So, Princess Victoria came to mind, who later became Queen of England." Being born in London, England, Irene Covington Stanford admired all the royals and had insisted that their daughter would carry one of their names. "Your handsome father swept me away to America after we were wed, and I found my new life here in Natchez, where I've learned to appreciate everything this lovely old town has to offer." Irene hugged her daughter. "There's still a lot of Brit in me, but I think I am more of a southern bell now, just like you are darling."

"You are quite the southern bell mom and I'm proud to say I am very much a bell of the south!" Victoria turned to her father. "Back to this Victoria who lived at Stanford Hall, was she back in the 1700's?" Vicky was getting anxious to read the letter, but she was just as intrigued with old family history she knew nothing about, until now.

"Heavens no child, your Aunt Victoria, three greats back, was born in 1839, before the civil war, 180 years ago." Steven Stanford looked down at the tan colored envelope in his daughter's silky hand. "Go ahead and open the letter. You must see what this letter is all about, Victoria."

With great care, Victoria opened the old-looking stationery and pulled out the folded, matching stationary inside. Opening it, she noticed immediately the letter head. It was sent from the law office of Vincent and Neuman, Castleton, Louisiana. She began reading aloud the contents, while her parents gathered around her, following the type written words.

"Dear Miss Stanford, I am writing to inform you that you have inherited and are the soul, heir of Stanford Hall Plantation, located ten miles from our small historic town, Castleton, dating back to 1773, three years after the great manor house was built on the Stanford Plantation. Completed in the fall of 1770, the stately four-store, pillared manor house, with the complete wrap around porch, sits on one thousand areas. The estate has fine stables, equipped with six black stallions, to attach to stately carriages inside the carriage house. There are big barns, several workmen quarters, where the staff and field hands live, and various outbuildings all over the property. Included in the inheritance is a sizeable bank account to insure the upkeep of the estate and for the owner to maintain a livable lifestyle, for the length of the time you own the property, which must be a life time commitment. Full details when you arrive in Castleton, Louisiana, next Friday,

September 15th, 2019.   Jefferson Neuman, lawyer to Victoria Bell Stanford's estate."

"Good lord! Victoria, you are the heir to a grand plantation!" Irene grew excited over the thought of her only child being named soul heir to a place the family has never seen or been a part of. "Steve, say something! Are you speechless for once?"

"I…I cannot conceive my beautiful daughter being an heir to a place we know absolutely nothing about, except a few memories of my parents telling me about such a place. It all seemed like a fairy tale to me at the time. The sad truth is, I never ask about it later when I grew older. I was still very small when we packed up and moved to Natchez, so as I grew, this place became first in my life.

I cannot imagine you living in Louisiana, the state of my birth, and your mother and I living in Mississippi." Steven took the letter from her hand and reread it to himself. "This letter makes it sound like everything is still the same as it was when Victoria Bell lived 180 years ago."

"Friday, September the 15th is this Friday!" Vicky took her smart phone from her skirt pocket and typed in maps, then Castleton, Louisiana. "It has to be somewhere on this map." Suddenly the screen lit up with the area and Vicky enlarged the small town. "There it is. Approximately one hundred miles from New Orleans. I will fly into New Orleans and rent a car. The roads are rural but they are marked well. There appears to be one service station about fifty miles from the turn off to Castleton. I can top off there in case there's no gas stations in the historic town."

"Victoria darling, we cannot let you travel to someplace you have never been to alone." Steven looked to his wife for an answer when he announced "Irene, I have to go on that business trip for the company. It has been planned for months and William is counting on me. I leave first thing Wednesday morning." His eyes fell on his daughter. "There's no way to get out of it now, Vicky. Irene, how is your week, dearest?"

"Steve darling, you know this is my weekend to be one of the tour guides at Stanton Hall. I missed the last two weekends helping out at the hospital and a third weekend when we took that little trip to Charleston, South Carolina. I made a promise that I would differently be there this weekend." Irene rung her hands. "Janet left this morning on her vacation, and Betty and Suzanne made plans four weeks ago." She gently took her daughter hand. "Victoria, we simply cannot permit you to go alone. How about Sam? Maybe you could give your best friend a call."

"It's short notice mom, but I will see if she is busy." Victoria looked down at her phone as she dialed Samantha Brandon's number, then chuckled when she heard the phone ring. "I am sure Sam will drop everything to tag along with me. She loves to go on all my great adventures."

"Well, this one should prove to be anything but dull, for such two out going friends as you and Samantha." Steven took a relieved breath when he heard his daughter say,

"Great! I will call the airport and make arrangements!"

CHAPTER 2

"This is a lovely drive, Vic. There's quite a bit of rural farm land and wooded areas around here. Very picturesque and peaceful, wouldn't you agree?" Samantha glanced over at her longtime friend, who returned a beautiful smile, then faced the road ahead.

"Yes, it is Sam, very pleasant and quiet after the busy streets of New Orleans. The lady behind the information desk, said Castleton was a restored historic town and it made you feel as though you were stepping back in time when you drove down the smooth cobblestone street."

"It cannot be much different than old Natchez, who has always held the title of the oldest town in the south." Samantha chuckled, being from a well to do family and her family owning one of the oldest houses in Natchez, she felt her manor, Brandon Hall, nestled in a grove of Magnolia trees, whose aromatic bark and scented white flowers, released it heavenly fragrances in the breezes that blew through the vast windows, was as old as anything she would see in Castleton. "I must admit, while our home was built in 1853, this town was started in 1773." Sam read from the pamphlet the airport information desk handed them.

"And Stanford Hall Plantation goes back even further! All the way to 1770, before we even got our independence!" Vicky slowed down when the speed limit dropped to 45. "We are still forty miles away and this speed limit has dropped from 55 to 45. I guess the road is getting somewhat narrow."

"It's not from all the heavy traffic, pal!" Samantha said sarcastically. "We haven't seen another car since we took that turn off toward Castleton. It cannot be much." Vicky's friend stared out the window and saw fields stretching out as far as one could see. "I bet this plantation is dilapidated after all those years of neglect. The windows are probably all broken and heaven knows what sort of gritters are living inside its once fancy rooms!"

Samantha suddenly grew silent as she watched a group of children walked from a patch of woods. She wondered why six young people were out in what appeared to be nowhere, and dressed like they were being filmed for a movie or something. She had not noticed her friend slowing down to almost a stop, until she saw the group of children looked her way. Sam gave them her warm friendly smile and waved, but they all seem to freeze in their tracks.

"Wow! Do you see that?" she couldn't draw her eyes away from the oldest kid, a young boy who seem to be their leader. Maybe, an older brother, she thought.

"Who could miss those silly pigs crossing the road!" Victoria had stopped when several pigs stepped out of underbrush in front of her "Now, why would twelve pigs be wondering out here from nowhere?"

"Pigs? I was referring to those six kids that stepped out of those trees over there." Getting Victoria's attention, Sam continued. "They're right over there..." the kids had vanished. "Now where could those kids have gone. They were standing there as sure as those silly pigs crossing this road. Two boys and four little girls, all dressed like they were on the set of Little House on the Prairie."

Vicky looked passed her and only saw a patch of trees. "What was in that coke bottle you had back there at that service station. Sam?" Victoria laughed, as she watched the last five pigs moving at a turtle's pace across the narrow road. "I can make out six shadows from the tall trees, no children from Little House."

"Go ahead and laugh, Vic. I guess I must either be pretty tired from traveling or getting hungry because we haven't had any lunch yet."

"At the rate we are moving, we might have to wait for supper and pray there is a place to eat in this town." Victoria slowly started moving, when she noticed her friend had practically turned around in her seat, trying to see those woods behind them. Being a detective at all times, Vicki glanced up into the rearview mirror and slowed back down, when she saw the shadows form into six children, just as her friend had described. The oldest boy suddenly stopped and looked directly into Victoria's eyes, giving her an unusual feeling. As the other children seem to fad into the woods, the boy with the piercing eyes, stared at the car as it sped up and continued down the road.

"Well, they're gone now. Probably from a farm not far from here and playing dress up, the way we did when my family opened our home to visitors, touring Natchez on Pilgrim Days." Samantha reached for her pocketbook and started searching though the contents. "I'm glad I picked up that candy bar back there at that service station. Maybe it will keep me from starving." She sat back when she found it and began unwrapping the paper. "Want half?"

"I'll wait, Sam. Just enjoy it." Vicky could not get that boy off her mind. There was something unusually strange about the way he was staring at her. Almost as if he recognized her face. She needed to know more so she casually asked her munching friend. "Sam, did those children see you watching them?"

"They looked right at me, so I smiled and waved to them." Samantha frowned over at her friend to see if she was ribbing her. "Why do you want to know, Vic. I thought you had written it off as another Samantha dream and thought I was only fooling around." She noticed her friend had a serious expression, so wondered if she had also witnessed something she hadn't. "Vic, did I miss something back there?"

"Sam, just answer my question first. Did those children see you wave and wave back?"

"I guess that was the reason I was so dumb-founded. I could not figure them out. At first, they appeared to be looking right at me, but when I waved, I could tell their eyes were focused on something on the other side of the road, as though they were looking straight through me." Sam scratched her head in confusion. "And before you ask, no, they weren't looking in the direction of those pigs."

Victoria passed a weather-beaten sign reading: Castleton, twenty miles, followed up by another speed limit sign, 35mph. The young detective could not get that young boy from her thoughts.

"Sam, how many children did you count back there?"

"I counted six, four small girls, and two boys, about two years apart. The oldest boy looked to be around...oh?"

"Twelve! Raven black hair and incredible intense blue eyes!" Victoria shivered, still seeing his youthful, handsome face.

Samantha stared in disbelief at her smart friend. "Gosh! Vic, I thought you said you did not see them, but creeping turtles, you just describe the same boy I saw. A handsome little devil! Too bad he is so young!" Victoria's friend could not get over the perfect description. "Vic, I know you are a great detective, but seriously, how did you come up with the exact description of that boy. When you never once took your eyes off this road."

"My perfect driving record got a little bit off when I noticed you had turned all the way around in your seat to get one last glance at those children. Let's just say, my curiosity got to me, so I slowed down to look in my rearview mirror to check out what you claim to have seen. Those shadows I saw became six children, and five of them faded into the woods. The twelve-year-old boy stopped and looked directly into my eyes and no, before you ask, he wasn't looking through me. Sam. His stare was so intense, I really believe he thought he knew me. I know that sounds weird, but when I started moving faster, he watched for a few more seconds, then simply disappeared."

"Hopping horn toads! You don't suppose we just saw..." Samantha's eyes grew wide when she spotted another young boy crossing in front of them on an old faded red bike. "Vic, look out!"

Spotting the boy up ahead, Victoria had already started slowing down and coasted to a stop when he road his bike right out into the road.

"Dang! That was close!" Sam took a relieved breath, then reached over to pat her friend on the back. "I am glad you spotted that kid too." She shivered, wondering if this kid was real or would he just disappear like those other children.

Vicky put down her window and called out at the small boy, that appeared to be out there by himself. "Young fellow, where are your parents? You should not be out here near this highway all by yourself. You could have gotten run over if another car had come along speeding and not have seen you dash out like that."

"Shucks ma'am, tant hardly no automobiles come down this here road. Why, the only time it sees a lot of automobiles is during the two big celebrations for both our wars, and the Stanford Hall celebration that brings lots of strangers to our old town." The young boy laughed, showing two missing front teeth. "Why, this here town is practically crawling with city slickers, cramming into the old hotel and neighbor folk's homes. It shore is a sight!"

"You don't say.' Samantha gave a little chuckle at the delightful boy's language. "So, people actually open their homes for people to stay?"

"Sure, ma'am, there be plenty of room for a body to plopped themselves, if'in they got a mind to." The young boy pointed a chubby finger down the road. "Why, that old town is jest down the road there. You can't miss it none. This here road don't go nowhere else, 'cept Castleton."

"What is your name, son, should we have the pleasure of meeting you again while we're here?" Victoria hoped the rest of the citizens of Castleton was as friendly as this small boy.

"My name is Johnny, Johnny Pennywise! I just turned six and this is my new bike. My ma and pa done gave it to me this morning, ma'am, and said I could ride it down our drive way yonder. I was just turning around in the road when you came along." He gave another big smile as he climbed on his old-looking bike. "I shore hope Santa brings me some new front teeth fer Christmas! It ain't easy eating my turkey leg with missing teeth."

"Then we hope Santa grants your wish this Christmas, Johnny. My name is Victoria, and my friend's name is Samantha." Vicky smiled when the little fellow extended his hand. She reached to shake his hand and noticed him staring at her face. "Is there anything wrong, Johnny?"

"I guess there ain't ma'am. It's jest that you look a whole lot like that pretty lady who lives in that big plantation house!"

Johnny broke into another toothless grin. "Are you her kinfolk, come a visiting?"

"I guess you could say, I've come for a visit, Johnny, if the pretty lady you are referring to is my Aunt Victoria, dead some 180 years" Vicky noticed a little frown grease his brow. "Is there anything wrong, Johnny?'

"Someone told you a fib, Miss Victoria. Your Aunt ain't dead, she is as alive as me!" The boy turned his bike toward his road. "I gotta go home now. My ma is probably looking fer me." The old bike flew down the dirt road, leaving a trail of dust behind.

"Crazy crawling cats! What do you make of that kid, Vic?" Samantha laid her head back, suddenly unsure of going on to this strange town, much less an obvious haunted house. "Do you think that kid really believes your old dead aunt is still alive? He seemed so normal, for a back woods farm boy."

"Children can have big imaginations, Sam. His parents probably took him to see the old house and he could have seen a painting of Victoria Bell and remembered it as real." Victoria reached over and patted her friend's hand. "Relax Sam. I am sure the adults will act different than a six-year-old child." She spotted the town up ahead. "We're almost there."

"Then, explain the ghost we saw?" Sam sat up as they moved slowly down the cobblestone street. "Explain the young twelve-year-old boy with dark hair and intense blue eyes, who looked right through me, but stared straight into your eyes!" she swallowed. "Or do you think we are both exhausted from our long day of traveling and with empty stomachs, so we just imagined those six kids beside the road?"

"Both of us, imagining the exact same thing and the same boy?" Victoria spotted a rock building with a sign out in front, reading: The Law Office of Vincent and Neuman. She pulled the car over and switched off the motor. They appeared to have the only car parked along the empty street. She turned to face her friend. "No Sam, we definitely saw something back there, and I hate to admit it, being a straight shooter for facts, but the only wise conclusion I can come up with is, those six children had to be ghost!"

CHAPTER 3

Victoria and her friend, Samantha, climbed out of the Honda Accord and studied the old town, stretching down the narrow tree lined street. On every block stood what looked like old-fashioned oil lanterns, dating back as old as the town. Looking closely, Victoria could not see any trace of wires converting the lamps over to electricity. The girls could make out the businesses closes to them. Across the street stood an old, worn brick establishment, which appeared to be one of the largest shops. Samantha read the old tin sign aloud.

"Lunsford General Store, owned and operated by the Lunsford family since 1773! If we don't have it, we can get it, if we cannot get it, it ain't worth having!" she gave a little chuckle. "It sounds like the Lunsford family has a funny bone."

"Either that, or they are covering their rear to satisfy the customer." Victoria looked at the stone building sitting next to the get anything store. "Aunt Berta's Café!" Vicky smiled over at her friend. "Let's hope Aunt Berta is open for supper."

"She seems to have several customers eating a late lunch. It is either great food or the only place to eat in this old town." Samantha squinted her eyes from the evening sunrays as she read the big letters over the long building next to the diner. "Holy moly! They still have an F.W. Woolworth five and dime! This old town is amazing! Can you make out the two, old brick buildings facing one another in the center of town?"

"The two whitewash buildings? The one with the gable roof is the town Hall and courthouse. The one with the pillared entrance is Castleton Museum." Victoria checked her watch and knew the meeting with Mr. Neuman was getting close. "I'd really like to check out that old museum. I bet it is packed with Revolutionary and Civil War memorabilia." She reached inside the rental car and gathered their handbags. "There could be a lot of history there on the Stanford Hall Plantation."

Samantha took her bag and followed her friend up the side

walk to the lawyer's office. Looking around, she noticed a church steeple at the edge of town. "At least there's a church at the edge of town. If we decide to stay, we'll have a church to attend on Sundays." Sam kicked at a rock she stumbled over. "I wonder what denomination it is? I'm guessing Baptist or Methodist."

"As long as the preaching is good and the love of fellowship lives there, does it really matter, Sam?" Victoria stopped before entering and smiled back at her friend. "We might not have any other choice, if I choose to except this old plantation. God knows it going to take a ton of work." Glancing down at her watch, Vicky knew the time to find out all the details had arrived.

The two friends walked inside the small but quaint outer office where a middle-aged woman peered over her wire rim glasses at the two strangers. The stout redhead gasped out a surprised breath, before she rose from her chair with a childish giggle.

"Mercy me, you about gave me a shock there, Miss Stanford." The friendly woman extended her hand for a handshake, as Victoria graciously excepted it with a firm grip. "There's no mistaking who you are, my dear. You are the spitting imagine of Madam Victoria Bell." The woman relaxed as she introduced herself. "My name is Flora McBride, Mr. Neuman's secretary."

"It is a pleasure to meet you, Flora. My name is Victoria Elizabeth Stanford, from Natchez, Mississippi." Vicky pulled her friend up beside her. "This is my best friend, Samantha Brandon, who made the trip with me."

"It's nice to make your acquaintance, ladies." Hearing a click on her desk, the secretary picked up a shorthand tablet and pencil and made her way to the lawyer's door. "I received Mr. Neuman's signal ladies. He is ready to see you now." Flora opened the office door and stood to one side as the two girls walked in and noticed a fairly handsome man standing behind an old oak desk.

"Welcome to Castleton, ladies. I hope you found your trip pleasant as you drove through the peaceful countryside."

"The countryside was indeed pleasant and peaceful, Mr. Neuman, but the trip was anything but uneventful."

"You don't say." Jefferson Neuman changed looks with his secretary. "I cannot imagine anything exciting happening on Carriage Wheel Road except perhaps a passing farmer going from one field to another. Well, if you wish to share your adventures with us, then you shall have plenty of time to tell us after I go over your Aunt Stanford's will." The lawyer picked up an old, yellowed sheet of paper, then turned to his secretary. "Flora, will you please serve our guest a glass of madeira and I will have one as well."

The secretary walked over and opened a small cabinet, containing old-looking bottles of wine, then poured four small glasses full and replaced the lid, closing the cabinet. Placing the rich sweet wine on a small tray, she passed it around.

"I hope you enjoy this rare wine, ladies." Mr. Neuman held up his glass. "It is the exact kind our first president enjoyed." He reached over to clink their glasses, then his secretary's.

"I couldn't help but noticed the wine bottles, Mr. Neuman. They look very old. Are you saying George Washington drank this exact year you are so generously sharing with Sam and I?" Victoria since there was more to this man's bragging and her detective skills were kicking in. "Could George Washington actually have passed through Castleton on his southern tour and drank some of your fine madeira?"

"My dear Miss Stanford, you really are good at what you do." Jefferson Neuman propped up on his elbows and looked at the young woman in admiration. "During his tour down south, George Washington did drop by our fair town and stayed at the plantation, with the first Victoria. Victoria Rose Stanford and her husband Nelson. My family ran the tavern back in 1773 and they began stocking up on madeira when rumors of war broke out. My brother still runs the tavern where he serves great brews and wine, but the cases of the old madeira is reserved for special occasions, such as this."

"Yes, I see Victoria Bell's will was written sometime back and it appears to be handwritten, even though the old manual typewriter was around in the 1930's" Victoria glanced over at the beautiful writing. "I can see she used an ink quill and inkwell."

"Once again the young sleuth is correct." The lawyer smiled and picked up the old will. "This will was hand written in 1939, the year that your aunt, three greats over, wrote it. She died shortly after at 100-years-old, still of sound mind and great determination. Even at this age, your outgoing aunt had all her faculties and a mind sharper than most people at forty. Always a high-spirited lady who had the gift of prophecy and knew things most people could never began to understand. You will hear in her demands, her steadfast love and devotion to her grand plantation, especially the manor house. The iron lady makes it painfully clear what she expects from the new heir, Miss Stanford, so the decision to except all of Miss Victoria Bell Stanford's request, is completely up to you, my dear." The lawyer looked up over his black rim glasses. "I will answer all your questions after I have read this will to you."

"Then, by all means Mr. Neuman, please read what my aunt had to say." Vicky leaned back in the chair, not knowing what demands this woman had for her. She would soon find out.

"If Mr. Neuman is reading this will to you, Victoria Elizabeth, then it is obvious the years have passed and it's now 2019." He paused so the heiress could catch her breath after hearing the first glimpse of her strange aunt's prophecy. "I did warn you about her gift." After receiving a nod from the beautiful woman in front of him to continue, he read on. "If you choose to except my gift to you, the sole owner of the Stanford Plantation, then I know your gift of solving mysteries will be rewarding when you find the secret to the past. My demands may sound a bit strong to a young girl of twenty, but once you have experienced the magic of Stanford Hall, you will understand why I insist that absolutely nothing can be changed, in the manor house, or on the grounds. Everything you see when you arrive at my home, and hopefully yours, sweet child, must remain the same. I insist that you stay in my rooms, because it is there you will learn the secret to the past. There is nothing to fear, sweet Victoria, for I will always be keeping watch over you as well as others you will meet in time. I have left you a personal letter, hidden away in a secret drawer and I know the detective inside you will find it quickly, but only if you choose to remain at Stanford Hall, forever. You may travel into the old town or even distant places when you've a mind. I know your parents in Natchez, Mississippi, will like a visit from their only child, but once you start to solve mysteries from the past, it will be hard for you to leave your new home. I have left a substantial amount of money to maintain the grand manor house and all the property. There will be plenty for you to retain your local workers, who have been taught by their parents to resume any position they had, such as a personal maid, a small staff for in home jobs, a butler, a cook, two local house maids, who both clean the house and take care of the soiled laundry. To your delight, I did furnish the big house and living quarters for staff, with electricity. Up until this date, there has been no need for this new luxury called air conditioner, but if you cannot get by with the big fans and open windows in the hot summer, by all means, insert one. Just be sure it is kept well-hidden as not to lose the ability to return to the past.

"Feel free to look over the property and if all my orders have been carried out, you should find Stanford Hall Plantation in great shape. I sincerely pray you will fall in love with Stanford Hall and desired to call it your home. Victoria Bell Stanford   My Last Wish Will   May 15, 1939."

"Well, there it is. Read for the first time since your aunt sealed it on May 15, 1939 at 100-years-old!" The middle-aged lawyer shook his head, somewhat in disbelief. "That well-educated lady sure has a way of making a soul feel strange. I'm only glad I never see her."

"Don't you mean, you are glad you have never seen her, Mr. Neuman?" Victoria caught him by surprise "You spoke of her as though she was still around. Is my aunt haunting the manor house sir?"

"A…I could not exactly say if her ghost is still there, Miss Stanford." Again Mr. Neuman exchanged glances with his secretary, who gave a little nervous cough. "Have you any questions regarding your aunt's will?"

"Yes, I do, Mr. Neuman. If it wasn't for the fact that my

Aunt Victoria seemed to know so much about me, way before I was born, I would come to the conclusion that she was an overly dramatic lady living in a dream world with a flare for a great story!" Victoria took another small sip of the surprisingly good wine. "Can you explain how a woman living years before me could possible know so much about my life, right down to the year her will would be read to me?"

"It's all a mystery to me, Miss Stanford." He picked up his glass and took a long sip. "You are the detective my dear, and I just bet if you stick around you can solve this very old mystery."

"You ask us about our trip into Castleton, Mr. Neuman. It would appear this old town is consumed in un-natural occurrences." Victoria noticed the eye connection between lawyer and secretary for a third time.

"Would you care to share what you saw, Miss Stanford. Perhaps we could shed some light on it." he casually, lend back in his chair and waited, a trickle of sweat running down his neck.

"Gladly! My friend saw six children walk out of a patch of woods and stopped to gaze at something on the other side of Carriage Wheel Road. Sam said they were dressed in early 1800's clothes, she guessed. When she waved at them, they seem to be looking straight through her."

"Children, you say?" Jefferson Neuman started tapping his pencil on the desk. "Did you see these children also, Miss Stanford?"

"Not at first, but I had slowed down for a herd of pigs crossing the road. Most unusual! They just seem to appear out of some tall grass." Victoria glanced over at Samantha who shook her head in agreement. "It was obvious those children were not looking at those pigs, sir!" Samantha recalled the unusual sighting. "Two older boys and four small girls, dressed like they were from Little House on the Prairie!"

"When I started to move again, I noticed Sam turning completely around in her seat, trying to see those children, so I glanced up in my rearview mirror and saw five of them slipping back into the trees. The oldest boy, around 12, looked directly at me, for what seem like a full minute, before I eased away, glancing back up, I seen him still staring after me, then he simply disappeared!"

"Can you describe the boy, Victoria?" Flora McBride asked wide-eyed.

"I can never forget that boy, Flora. A very handsome youth, with black hair and incredible blue eyes." Victoria gazed out the big window and gave a little shiver. "This may sound strange, but, I feel somehow connected to that boy."

Flora McBride leaned over toward her boss and spoke softly. "You don't suppose he was…Zechariah?"

"The description fits the Castleton boy when he was twelve, alright." Jefferson Neuman pushed his chair back and stood up. "Miss Stanford, the Castleton children have not been spotted for years. I had heard the tales about them appearing on Carriage Wheel Road all my life, but I was beginning to believe they were just a made-up legend. The last spotting was around the late 1800's."

"Are you saying those children really were ghost, Mr. Neuman?" Victoria could not explain her close feelings for a boy she had never seen and who obviously was deceased.

"The Castleton children belonged to Joshua and Isabell Castleton, the founder of our fair town in 1773. They built their four-store mansion just on the outskirts of town and opened the Castleton trading post, the biggest store in our town. The friendly couple welcome anyone who wished to start a business in Castleton, and by charging a small rent on the properties, made it easy to start one's own business. Within a year, the town was flourishing and people were moving into our town by the dozens."

"That doesn't explain why those children were so far from town with no adults to watch them." Samantha looked up, confused why rich kids would be wondering alone in the woods so far from home. "Surely they did not run away from home."

"They wouldn't have run away from such sweet parents, Sam. These children were privilege and for 1773, being wealthy was a rare thing for most families." Victoria joined the lawyer standing. "I think someone kidnapped those children

18

for a big ransom and somehow that got away from their abductor, took refuge in the woods until daytime, came out to see if the person or persons had left, and noticed they were still camping across the road, turned and went back into the woods." She walked to the window and gazed out, then closed her eyes and the incredible blue eyes came into her mind. "All but that boy you called, Zechariah. Was this the first time he had stopped and looked in another direction, right into the person watching, eyes!"

"The sightings recorded in the musicum stated the witnesses saw the Castleton children slipped out of the patch of woods that sit on the old mill property. A small clean creek runs just beyond those trees and it was thought those children had chosen that spot to spend the night, having fresh water to drink and being accustom to being clean, could wash themselves if they should get dirty." Jefferson Neuman joined the tall, beautiful woman at the window and pointed to a row of trees just beyond the town. "Those woods hide the same creek as the ones you and your friend Sam saw on Carriage Wheel Road. All but one witness stated in the report that the older brother, Zechariah, seem to be the one in charge and was very protected of his brother, James 10, and four sisters, Allana, 8, Barbara Anne, 6, Mary Jean, 4, and 2-year-old Rebecca." The lawyer gently tuned the young sleuth around to face him. "The witness who added almost the same statement you did, about the 12-year-old turning around to stare at you, was your great Aunt Victoria Bell Stanford. The only difference was she was returning from New Orleans and reported after she passed the ghostly group, she stopped her carriage for one last look. Her statement went,

"I watched the lost Castleton children slipped back into the forest, as if they were shadows, old illusions of the past reaching out as if to cry for help, yet looking right through me, until…the tall dark hair youth, so handsome and grown for his age, stopped following his family, turned around and stared directly into my eyes, as though he recognized me. His eyes were as blue as a male bluebird or a lovely cluster of violets. As quickly as he turned to look at me, he just as easily seemed to lose his interest as he faded away, leaving me to shiver from the unusual sight."

"It would appear there is one small difference in what occurred out there on that road, Mr. Neuman." Victoria walked back over to her chair and picked up her shoulder bag and hung it on her shoulder. "Zechariah did not seem to lose interest in me, get bored and turn away, only to disappear! Zechariah turned back around as though he recognized me, Mr. Neuman, Not the first Victoria Rose, nor the second Victoria Bell, but the Victoria standing directly in front of you, Victoria Elizabet Stanford!" Vicky could not explain her feelings, but she was determined to get to the bottom of this mystery.

CHAPTER 4

The lawyer filed away the will of Madam Victoria Bell Stanford, and walked with the two ladies toward the front door.

"It is far too late to drive out to the old plantation this evening, ladies. Although it is only ten miles from Castleton, there is far too much for us to cover in such a short time. The manor alone will take hours, and even then, I am sure we shall miss many of the rooms. Then I am sure you wish to check out the grounds and the outbuildings, barns, carriage house as well as the workman's quarters, very well built with a good four acres lot provided so the families can grow a nice healthy garden for themselves." Jefferson opened the door and squinted up at the late afternoon sun. "One thousand acres covers a lot of ground, so to see it all you would have to go out with your foreman, Reginald Myers, probably on horseback."

He chuckled. "I hope you know how to ride a horse, ladies. It really is the best way to see your property."

Flora McBride came from the old law building, swinging a single key, then handed it to Victoria. "We took the liberty to book you a room at the Castleton Hotel. A charming old place, kept restored to its original glory by the owners, Richard and Veronica Barrett. Veronica is a relative to the first owners, Carter and Margaret Stanford, also your distant relatives. Carter was next to the oldest son of Victoria Rose and Nelson Stanford, who, you may recall, built Stanford Hall Plantation in 1770. As was the custom in those days, the eldest child inherited the estate, so Victoria Bell's father, William, was sole heir to Stanford Hall. Carter, as well as the other two younger brothers, Edwin and Franklin, twins, received large sums of money and property. Enough to build any business of their choice and the kind of mansion they desired."

"So, Carter chose to build the finest hotel around." Samantha blushed as she grabbed her growling stomach, causing the well-dressed lawyer to chuckle softly. "I hope that café is still open down the street. My quick lunch at the airport ran out hours ago."

"Do you think we have time to grab something to eat before we check in the hotel. Mr. Neuman? I must admit I could use some nourishment about now." Vicky draped her arm round her friend's shoulder. "If it is still open, will it be alright to leave our car here and walk to the café?"

"Ladies, you may park here as long as you like." The generous man pulled out a twenty-dollar bill and three ones. "Please take this. Supper is on me and I won't take no for an answer. I feel responsible for holding up your meal." He gave them a genuine smile. "I keep forgetting the lack of eating places coming from the airport to our little out-of-the-way town, since I rarely get away from here."

"Then I'm glad you can keep so busy, Mr. Neuman, with what appears to be s quiet, laid-back town." Victoria returned his smile. "I take it by your generous offer to buy our meal, that the café is open and there is no rush to check in to the Castleton?"

"I do apologize for not answering your questions, my dear, but it has been a long day." He waved down the road. "After eating at the five A.M to seven P.M. café, just drive to the end of town. Castleton Hotel sits proudly at the end of town and there is a lovely courtyard for parking your car. Complimentary full breakfast is served in their morning room and if you prefer a more luxurious evening meal tomorrow night, the grand dining hall at Castleton is excellent. A great place to celebrate receiving such a splendid inheritance from your great aunt, Victoria Bell. If you say yes, Victoria, I will gladly buy the champagne, to toast your great fortune. The entire meal will be a gift to you, from your relative and owner of the hotel, Veronica Stanford Barrett."

"I am at a loss for words, Jefferson." Vicky knew from his bright smile, he approved her choice in saying his given name. "I shall simply say, thank you, for your kindness and we shall see what tomorrow will bring."

Even at four o'clock in the early afternoon, Aunt Berta's cafe was buzzing with chattering customers, eating and talking at the same time. When the two female strangers entered, everyone stopped eating and grew silent as they watched the beautiful girl with the raven black hair and alluring blue eyes move swiftly to the table in the corner. Stepping from her busy kitchen to investigate what made her chattering customers grow suddenly quiet, Berta Temple knew the instant she spotted the two young women waiting at the corner table.

Berta grabbed two menus after spotting her two waitresses frozen in the shoes and took them personally over to the corner table.

"Good afternoon ladies! Welcome to Aunt Berta's." the friendly owner glanced around to see the curios dinners still staring in a trance-like state. "Pardon me ladies while I straighten out my old customers. They think they are seeing a ghost, my dear." Her kind eyes fell on Victoria, then, placing her hand firmly on her hips, she faced the frozen crowd.

"My good friends and neighbors, you can all take a deep breath and relax. You are not seeing the ghost of Victoria Bell Stanford coming back down from heaven just to have a slice of Grandma Berta's apple pie!" Berta smiled broadly when the dinners relaxed and began chuckling softly at her wit. "I know you have all read in the Castleton Daily that the new heir, Victoria Elizabeth Stanford, would be arriving today to hear her aunt's will read. Now, I know what good, kindhearted people most of you are, except you, Luther Simmons, owner and editor of the Castleton Daily." That bought another chuckle from the crowd, knowing that Berta and Luther were sweet on one another and each one loved to pick.

"That's alright, Berta Temple! I may not be good or kindhearted, as you put it, but little darling you sure do love how I kiss you in my old Ford truck!" Luther Simmons brought more laughter when he winked at the heavy-set cook and she hit him playfully on his head with her order pad.

"I've got customers waiting, so everyone, just eat your food before it gets cold or pay up and go home!" Berta chuckled to herself when everyone resumed eating and talking. She gave Victoria and Samantha her winning smile as she lifted up her order pad.

"What will it be ladies? The scrimp and grits is a specialty of the café. An old family recipe past down for five generations." Her eyes twinkled as she added "Your Aunt Victoria made special trips into Castleton just to order those yummy grits and hickory smoked scrimp, with a secret sauce, responsible for the surprisingly great taste!"

"Sounds perfect! With a glass of your special iced tea!" Victoria handed her the tempting menu of homemade meals and dessert. "What for you Sam? Will that be enough to fill up your empty stomach?" she laughed when her friend punched her arm.

"If it's what your friend, Mr. Simmons is having, then it looks plenty big." Smiling, Sam returned the menu and added. "I'll have the tea as well and a slice of that apple pie, smothered in vanilla ice cream."

"I will bring two spoons for that big dessert, if you care to share some with your friend, and put a rush on your supper." Placing the pencil behind her ear she started for the kitchen calling out orders. "Two scrimp and grits specials, two tall glasses of iced tea and hold the dessert till they finish their meal."

After paying the bill for the delicious meal, the two friends left the friendly café, with the curious diners remaining at the café until they were leaving to apologize for staring and just as Berta said, the group proved to be good, kindhearted people, many of whom invited them to their church, The Church of the Christian Brethren. Which set next to the old hotel.

Finding the hotel was no problem, with only one street running the length of the town. The Castleton was everything Jefferson Neuman and Flora McBride said it was. Pulling into the courtyard, you could almost feel time being erased and visualize fancy carriages parked along the marked spaces. Removing their luggage from the trunk, they turned to see a footman, dressed in 1700's period clothes, pushing an old cart out to meet them. Bowing slightly, he spoke politely.

"May I take your bags, ladies, and usher you both to the hotel lobby? The owners await your arrival."

CHAPTER 5

"My stars, aren't you the spitting image of Aunt Victoria, old Uncle Williams only child!" Veronica walked around the huge walnut counter to welcome her distant relative. Giving the beautiful girl a big hug, she held her back at shoulders length, to check her out. "Never have I seen two people who look so much alike! Don't you agree Richard?" the tall slender man smiled from behind the counter as he shook his head in disbelief.

"It is very canny, I agree Veronica." He offered his hand and Victoria gracefully took it, just to watch him kiss it. "It is good to finally meet the heir to Stanford Hall. We couldn't be any prouder of Victoria Bell's choice."

"If I choose to except this fine gift, attached with many demands, I will look forward to living in such a friendly and loving community." Victoria's smile was filled with perfect love and sincerity as she looked around at the exquisite lobby with the high ceiling and matching crystal chandeliers, that had to cost a small fortune back in the 1700's. The walls were lined with period furniture and a large round coffee table made of fine wicker and topped with old glass, dominated the center of the grand room. "Your hotel is lovely, Veronica. It must be a pleasure for you and Richard to call this home and be the proud owners of such a magnificent hotel!"

"I am so glad you love it, as well as our friendly town." The owner of Castleton pulled a large brass key from her skirt pocket. "We sincerely hope, you choose to make Stanford Hall your home, Victoria. It would be nice to have another relative living there after so many years." Mrs. Barrett motioned for the footman, who had been waiting patiently after returning with the empty cart.

"Jamerson, has everything been stored away properly in Miss Stanford's rooms?"

"Yes madam. Clothes are folded in the clothes closet,

toiletries have been placed neatly away by the chamber maiden, and the complimentary bottle of champagne is chilling with two glasses." The footman bowed slightly. "Miss Gretchen awaits to assist the ladies with whatever they require, madam."

"Thank you Jamerson, that will be all. I will take my cousin up to her rooms myself. You may be excused."

Samantha was watching the proper footman walk away when she felt Vicky grab her hand and pulled her toward the wide staircase that rose to the second, then third floor. Reaching the top floor, Veronica made her way down the hall to the end doors and opened them up to a magnificent sitting room with high ceilings, another large crystal chandelier and a huge marble fireplace, crackling with a soft flame.

"This old hotel has a tendency to get drafts when the sun sets, so a nice warm fire helps ward off the chill." Victoria's distant cousin handed her the brass key. "Lock up, if it makes you girls feel safer, but I can assure you, nothing ever happens in our lovely old town. Gretchen will take care of any needs you might have before bedding down for the night. Do you have any questions for me before I return downstairs?"

"Yes, two actually." Vicky smiled as she took in the large spacious space. "What time is breakfast served and will you put Mr. Neuman's call in the room when he lets us know what time he will be leaving for the plantation?"

"A full, sit-down breakfast will began serving at 6:00a.m. and run until 10:00a.m. You will find there are no telephones in the bedchambers or adjacent guest rooms. Jefferson will inform the front desk and they shall pass the information along to you when you come down for breakfast." Veronica smiled politely and made her way to the entrance double doors. "We find ringing telephones are not suitable for this period hotel. We prefer to keep everything as close to the original 1773 area. That is what's needed and the hotel guest like it much better that way."

"I guess ringing phones would put a damper on the charm and excellent restoration you have achieved here." Vicky noticed the blonde chamber maid stepped from the back rooms and walked over to open the chilled champagne and continued to pour two crystal flutes almost full and replace the cork and a fancy stopper. The young detective turned her attention back on her distant cousin. "Thank you, Veronica, for your generosity and hospitality. May you have a good night and we look forward in seeing you soon."

"May both of your stay be a pleasant one. I come down around 9:00, so if you are still here, I shall see you then. Good night, ladies." Veronica slipped from the room as Gretchen handed each special guest her glass and walked toward the open hearth and chipped away at the blackened log before turning shyly to the two girls observing her.

"I have turned down your beds, Miss Stanford, Miss Brandon. You will find your bed clothes lying on the sheets and fresh soft robes lying next to your beds. I have laid out in each personal bath, the things you will need tonight and now, if it pleases my ladies, I will lay another log on the fire."

"That will not be necessary, Gretchen, we prefer to sleep in a cooler room." Victoria found the shy blonde's accent quiet charming as the chambermaid nodded her head.

"Whatever pleases you miss."

"Gretchen, that is such a beautiful name and your accent is lovely." Victoria slipped slowly from her thin glass. "My guess is Sweden, correct?"

"You have a good ear for dialect, Miss Stanford, and Gretchen is a very common name among our people." The maid seemed to relax, from the friendly manner of these guest, unlike all the others before that treated her like the help she was instead of a real person. "Will there be anything else, miss?"

"As a matter of fact, there is Gretchen." Victoria sensed her reluctance to feel like an equal to this special guest who had been rumored to be the new owner of the largest track of property in Stanford County. "First, please call us Vicky and Sam, short for Victoria and Samantha. All our family and friends call us by our nicknames and we would like to consider you a new friend, If that's alright with you?"

Tears filled her sky-blue eyes, finally feeling a part of someone's enter circle of friendship instead of just another employee, waiting to take orders, then fulfilling them from morning till night, seven days a week. Vicky and Sam were different, they had offered true friendship and there was no doubt Victoria Stanford meant every word. What could it hurt, she thought. Surely, she would not lose her much needed job by becoming their friend. Still nervous and unsure, Gretchen glanced over at the entrance door. The young sleuth caught on quickly.

"Gretchen, There's, no reason for you to be nervous or afraid of losing your job by becoming our friend. The truth is, friendship is based on liking someone and enjoying the time you spend with your friends, sharing happy stories or even sad stories." Vicky looked over at her long-time friend for a statement. "Wouldn't you agree, Sam?"

"Vicky is absolutely correct, Gretchen! What do you say, could you use some more friends? The more the merrier!" Samantha finished her champagne and gently set down the fragile glass.

"I had a lot of friends back in Sweden before we moved to the states. I was only twelve when my folks informed me they both had acquired a big position working in this luxury Hilton hotel in New York City and we were moving to the United States of America the first of the year." Just the reminder of leaving everything she had known and finding herself in one of the busiest cities in America, brought back all her worst memories. Sadness filling her pale blue eyes, the Swedish beauty walked over to the big window and gazed out into the growing darkness in the rose garden below.

"I never went out of the flat very often in the big city. City folks and all the many tourists kept the streets flooded in the daytime and all during the night." Gretchen turned her head to find both girls were seriously paying close attention to her bad memories. "Papa and Mama insisted that I attend the nearest school, in walking distanced so I managed to find one or two acquaints in the local high school." A genuine smile fell across her pink lips when she added "That is where I met Samuel Parker, about the cutest boy I've ever saw. Despite being the most unpopular girl in school, who spoke differently from everyone else, Samuel liked me and ask me out on a date, then to the junior and senior prom. We were to be married when Samuel graduated college but my opportunity arrived in the mail right after high school graduation. The old historic hotel in Castleton, Louisiana, was looking for a top, upstairs chambermaid who had a Swedish bloodline and they had done extensive research and found that my mother fit the position perfect. Mama called the number listed and persuaded the Barrett's to heir me instead. Convincing my lady that she had trained me in all her skills, which she had, all my life, mama got me the top paying job." Gretchen glanced nervously at the door when Victoria asked her to have a seat and relax for a while. After convincing the nervous maid that she would take full responsibility for having her sit down, Gretchen thankfully sat down, glad to finally be off her tired feet.

"What happened to Samuel and the two of you getting married? Surely he did not ask you to choose him or this great opportunity to get the perfect job your mama had trained you for all those years?" Samantha sat up, feeling anxious for her new friend's possible loss. "Do you keep in touch with Samuel or is he just another sad memory."

"It does my heart good to know your sincerely care, Sam." For the first time, Gretchen felt like laughing, knowing these two girls really wanted to be her friends. "Samuel and I keep very close contact, my friends! My wonderful Samuel skipped college, married me, got his own great job here at the hotel and we happily call Castleton Hotel our workplace and our beautiful old home!"

Sam blew out a relieved breath and leaned back again, feeling the long trip catching up to her. "That's a relief, Gretchen. Now, I can sleep like a baby tonight and hopefully not dream about the ghost on Carriage Wheel Road."

"Ghost?" If the Swedish chambermaid seemed to fear the word, it did not show as she smiled and stood up. "This old town has been known for ghost sightings all its existence. Even in this 1700's hotel! This very apartment of rooms." Gretchen noticed she had Victoria and Samantha's attention. "Oh, I wouldn't worry none. The ghost of Victoria Rose Stanford, the first owner of the Stanford Hall Plantation, hasn't been spotted here since the late 1800's, according to Ingra, the last Swedish chambermaid before me."

"Did this Ingra share any of the details with you, Gretchen? If it has to do with my distant relative, then I would love to hear what the witness saw."

"Vicky, can we just drop all this ghost talk right before going to bed?" Samantha skin felt like it was crawling at the thoughts of sleeping in a haunted room. "Much more ghost talk, I will be moving my pajamas to your bed!"

"Sam, you are always welcome to join me if you are that scared of ghost stories, but I would like to hear what was seen. It might help shed some light on my decision to remain here in Castleton."

After seeing Sam nod to continue, Gretchen tried to remember what the retiring maid had told her.

"Ingra had stayed on long enough to train me the ropes in doing my job here, so we had plenty of free time to talk. One evening, we were finishing preparing these rooms for the arriving guest and I noticed the 65-year-old maid staring down at the master bed, the very one you will be sleeping in, Vicky, and you too Sam, if you join her, although these old full-size beds aren't all that big. High, most certainly, but not as wide as today's generation is used to, the queens and king-size beds. I ask Ingra why she was so interested in this particular bed and what she told me gave me the willies!"

"What?" Sam sat up, interested now that it wasn't her bedroom that was the one haunted.

"One night, Miss Victoria Bell Stanford booked this room. No one ever knew the real reason for her insisting on staying just the one night and in this particular room, but Miss Victoria's personal maid, who was sleeping in the other room, your bedchamber, Sam, heard her mistress speaking to some gentleman in her bedchamber, at 12:00a.m. Slipping from her room, the maid could not make out the man's face or hear what they were saying, except, the man, whom she stated had long black hair and a tall, manly built, clearly said, "You are not the right one! I look for another!" then she said he simply disappeared, leaving Victoria weeping in her pillow."

"Gretchen, did anyone know why Victoria Rose was here in this room alone, without Nelson, her husband, in the 1770's." Victoria had the same funny feeling in the pit of her stomach when she described the man standing by her aunt's bed. "Do you recall anyone who had seen her ghost recall a man with the same description as the one with Victoria Bell, in 1800's?"

"As a matter of fact, Ingra told of several accounts, all dating back to the 1800's, regarding either hearing a man's voice speaking to Victoria Rose's spirit, or actually seeing the couple, hugging next to the window in the master bedchamber. As before most of the words could never be recognized, much like having a dream, only each witness swore they were wide awake when the apparitions appeared, always late at night. They describe the male ghost as tall, well-built with long dark hair and the lady, no mistaking as Victoria Rose Stanford." Gretchen shook involuntarily "The only words each witness could remember understanding was, "You are not the right one. I look for another." Then the male apparition would simply vanish out the window, leaving Victoria Rose weeping, until she finally disappeared, exactly at 12:00a.m. midnight."

"Darn! Who could that mysterious man be searching for?" Samantha stretched, then noticed Victoria had gone almost white. "Don't tell me you're scared now? You may sleep in my room with me if you like Vic."

"That won't be necessary, Sam. I will be fine when I sort things out!" Victoria stood up and handed Gretchen the wine cooler, containing the rest of the champagne. "The other thing I wanted from you, my new friend, is to give this to you to enjoy with Samuel when you get off tonight. If someone should ask you why you have it, send them to me in the morning." The beautiful detective gave the smiling maid a hug, then ushered her to the door. We will see you in the morning. Sleep well, Gretchen."

"Thank you so very much, Vicky." Gretchen would have hugged her gift if it weren't so cold. "It does a heart good to know there are good Christian people in the world." She thought it best to leave before she started to cry, so she gave a sweet smile and closed the door behind her.

Victoria quickly locked the door with the big brass key and turned to see her friend chuckling. "Sam, what is so funny? Did I just perform a comedy act without knowing it?"

"You locked the door!" Samantha stood up, still laughing. "Are you really afraid we might have a visit from the ghost of the first Victoria or perhaps, the mystery man, with the strange message?"

"First, you are completely mistaken as to why I locked this door. You might not be aware of the fact that a ghost does not need an unlocked door to enter a room, they just simply appear out of the blue! If I should have a choice as to which ghost might visit me, which is very doubtful, due to the fact that it has been many years since the last person witnessed seeing Victoria Rose and the mysterious stranger, except of course Aunt Victoria Bell. Her personal handmaiden saw her with the mysterious man and heard him give her the same message before vanishing." Victoria walked into her bedroom, removed her traveling clothes and slipped on her gown, as Samantha stood waiting for her to say which ghost she would like to see.

"Do you want to see your relative from the 1700's or the handsome, mysterious tall man with dark hair?"

"Sam, no one said he was handsome. They did not see his face, only his back to them, remember? Vicky laughed and sat down at the old vanity and began taking down her simple up-do. "I guess one might conclude the man was handsome after seeing him break the hearts of two beautiful women."

"And how can you be so sure that both of these Victoria's were beautiful?" Sam enjoyed turning the tables on her intelligent friend. "Yes, it's true that you are beautiful, but you would be the last one to judge them from your description, so what are you going on, other people's word? They did not live back in the 1700's or the 1800's! I say just past down gossip!"

"Sam, aren't you missing one great clue? The people's reaction when they saw me. They were all taken back to the last two owners of Stanford Hall. They thought they were witnessing one of the ghost return." Vicky stood up and patted her friend's drooping back. "Cheer up, you're tired. I am sure the musicum has copies of some original paintings of each Victoria. Not wanting anything changed, Victoria Bell is certain to have the originals in the manor house, hanging in the exact spot she placed them."

"Vic, You're just too sharp for me, pal. That's why you're the detective and I'm just the back-up."

"Sam, go to bed, you're tired. I locked the door because it's safe and the ghost I want, Mr. Mysterious!"

CHAPTER 6

Victoria was sleeping soundly when she was suddenly awakened by a male voice calling her name. She forced her tired eyes open in her drowsy state and noticed a tall man with long hair standing over her. Victoria blinked her eyes several times to be sure she wasn't dreaming, but the man was diffidently there. His face was barely visible in the dim light, but his voice was rich and clear and seemed very much alive.

"Victoria, my darling, you have come! I've been waiting so long, but now that you are here, the wait seems to have faded away with the past." He stretched out his hand for her. "Please arise my dearest, our time is limited in this place. I must hold you in my arms and kiss the lips I have long for. You are the right Victoria. I need not look for another any longer, for I have finally found you, my Victoria, my Vicky!"

"You know my nickname!" Victoria sat straight up in the canape covered old bed and looked down at his long tan fingers.

"I know everything I need to know about you, Vicky, my love." His voice came soft and his manners seemed to be very gentlemanly as he continued to hold out his steady hand. "Please darling, make into my arms with haste before my time runs out."

Vicky scrambled out from under the sheets, and forgetting the bed was much higher than her own at home, she stumbled and fell to the floor. She felt completely embarrassed as she forced herself to look up, only to find him leaning over to help her stand, his face covered with concern.

"Did you hurt yourself, my darling?'"

"Only my feelings! That is a bad way to meet for the first time." Victoria narrowed her eyes when he laughed softly. "Is my graceful dive from bed amusing, sir?"

"Sir? You know my name, Victoria, please repeat it." the apparition grew serious. "Past dreams you have had,

34

remember? Repeating dreams about a mysterious man dressed in 1700 fashion, with raven black hair, to match your own, and intense dreamy blue eyes." The handsome face looked down as he drew her to him closer. "And on the Carriage Wheel Road, the 12-year-old boy you could not stop thinking about." He swept his fingers gently over her blushing face. "Say my name, my love, for I have long to watch you say it, standing within inches from your beautiful sweet lips."

"Tell me first why you keep referring me to your love, your dearest or darling?" Vicky felt safe here in his strong arms and her mind was twirling with mixed emotions, she could not explain. "Perhaps you just mistake me for someone else."

"I could never mistake the woman I love most in the world, Victoria Stanford. I know you are living in another century from the one I left, but I have no doubt in my heart we are meant to be together! Someday soon you too will know this revelation, then we can start to sort out how we can be together, forever!" he looked into her blue eyes with desperation as he pleaded. "Please Vicky, say my name before I must go, time grows short!" he pointed to an hourglass sitting on the window seal. Victoria's eyes grew wide when she saw the sand was nearly at the bottom.

"Zechariah, please, you cannot just disappear without telling me if we shall ever meet again!"

"In the manor house on the Stanford Hall Plantation! There is a secret to the past that is hidden away inside your private rooms there. Your detective skills will help you find its hiding place, my love. I am waiting inside for you to find me." Zechariah moved her up closer, their lips almost touching, I love you, Vicky, with all my heart."

"Zechariah, I hardly know you, but yet, I feel somehow I do know you," her eyes fell on the glass, the last drops of sand were drifting through. "I...I..."

"Just say it Vicky."

"I love you, Zechariah." Their lips met in a burning kiss and when she opened her eyes, her mysterious love was gone.

Victoria looked over on the window seal, expecting to find an empty hourglass, but found the big window seal empty, and no sign of the old hourglass that took Zechariah away from her. Her shaking fingers gently touched her lips, as she recalled the passionate loving kiss that sent radiating sparks through her body. Never had her steady boyfriend back home made her feel anywhere close to the way she felt tonight with Zechariah. She had told him she loved him, a man she did not know anything about. A man who had been dead for years.

"The whole thing just doesn't make any sense!" Victoria grabbed a book off the booklined shelf and carried it over to the high bed. Before climbing up on it, Victoria switched on the bedside lamp, then she stuck her tongue out at the bed. "And you high and mighty old bed made a fool out of me in front of the man I just met tonight, who just laughed, although I guess I did look pretty ridicules!" Vicky mumbled as she climbed under the sheets to read, in hopes of getting sleepy again. "Mum! I'm just glad Zechariah wasn't here to witness that little act just now! Sticking my tongue out like a schoolgirl and talking to a stupid ancient bed that could care less if this modern girl fell off like a clumsy idiot!"

It did not take Vicky long to realize she couldn't concentrate on the book for reliving everything that had happened to her since she made this trip to Castleton to see her inheritance. If she chose to remain here and take up the responsibility of running a Plantation and a stately old manor house dating back to 1770, Vicky knew, without a doubt, what her first mystery would be. The mystery of Stanford Hall! She knew she would not get paid for this case, but after all, there's not too many cases that contain the same person for both detective and client. This case would be very personal to Victoria and there were many unanswered questions.

"What is this mysterious thing hidden inside that old house that is connected to the past? Surely not some kind of time machine. Those things where only found in fiction novels or movies that jump up to the future or back to the past. Whatever it is, the thing must exist, because Aunt Victoria mentioned it as well as Zechariah." Just saying his name aloud made her stomach flutter with butterflies. "What was I thinking when I thought of the remote possibility of maybe not choosing to remain here, even if it does mean taking on full responsibility of Stanford Hall? I'm a smart girl, ever bit as smart as Aunt Victoria. If she could run a big plantation, along with a large home, so could I! And I have the advantage over the 1800 century grand lady. I have a computer and a smart phone!" Vicky hit her head when she remembered just how far this old town and especially the plantation was, sitting a long distance from all the big towns, which had satellite services.

"I guess dear Aunt Victoria made it clear, if I chose to except my inheritance, I must live the exact lifestyle she did and make do with whatever gismos and trinkets she has left me to work with." Victoria reached over and cut out the light. "Well. Madam Victoria Bell Stanford, if you can manage all that work with no modern-day equipment, so can Miss Victoria Elizabeth Stanford! You have met your match and I shall make you proud you waited to choose me!" Vicky squeezed her eyes shut, and Zechariah's face came into her view, his blue, intense eyes looking down with longing, the same blue eyes that captivated her out on Carriage Wheel Road.

The two out-of-town friends had their choice of tables in the bright morning room, and chose one in the very back so they could talk freely about their day's exciting visit to the Stanford Plantation. After the waitress took their order, they waited for her to disappear behind the swinging door, they assumed led to the kitchen.

"How did you sleep last night, Vicky? You seem too relaxed to have been visited at midnight by a ghost." Samantha sipped on the hot coffee and found it completely perfect. "Mum, if the food here is as good as this coffee, my mouth will be happy!"

"It's probably slow brewed in a big coffee urn and you're right, it is terrific." Victoria watched an older couple come in for breakfast. They sat by one of the big windows which was flooded with sunlight. "As for my night, I slept like a baby for the first several hours. Around midnight, I was awakened by a male's voice, calling my name."

"Vicky! Are you sure you weren't just dreaming? This was

the last thing we talked about last night before turning in. Even I had a dream about those kids out on Carriage Wheel Road."

"Speaking about the kids we saw, on that road, do you remember the twelve-year-old boy that stopped to stare at me?" Victoria looked around the breakfast room and noticed several other diners had arrived. Most were looking over the menu sheet, but Vicky could see one man was more interested in the two girls sitting at the end table than he was about what to order. Samantha drew her attention back to their conversation.

"You mean the dark-haired boy with the alluring intense blue eyes?"

"The same! He was the tall handsome mysterious spirit that appeared last night, waking me up." Victoria smiled at her friend when she almost got strangled over her water by her friend's bold statement. "Only, he didn't appear to be just a spirit, Sam. He seemed as real and alive as you and I. I have never heard of a ghost that could give a great kiss the way he gave me."

"He…he kissed you?" Samantha's eyes grew wide with surprise. "You actually felt his kiss?"

"Sam, I not only felt it, it was the most romantic, passionate kiss I have ever received!" Victoria closed her eyes and remembered his head lowering to meet hers then he parted his lips over hers and she just knew this stranger was the man she loved.

"Gee whiz, Vic, what the heck else happened?" Samantha looked up at the waitress as she sat two filled plates with bacon, eggs, grits, and a basket of buttermilk biscuits. Homemade peach perseveres and real butter rounded off the first-class breakfast. After thanking the friendly waitress, Vicky told her friend what happened.

"His name is Zechariah, I guess named after the prophet in the bible, the same man seen with Victoria Rose, then by Victoria Bell's private maid, leaving both women weeping after telling them they were not the one, he was seeking another." As Victoria watched her friend absentmindedly buttering her biscuit while her full attention was on what was being said, Vicky hit her with the unbelieving truth. "Sam,

Zechariah told me I was the one, the woman he had been waiting for!"

Samantha dropped her knife, and it clanked loudly as it hit the marble floor. Before she could retrieve it, the gentleman watching, was out of his seat scooping the knife off the floor and replacing the soiled one with a clean shiny knife.

"Are you alright, young lady?" His face held sincerity as he gazed down at an embarrassed Samantha Brandon. "You seemed to grow pale as your friend regaled you with her obviously intriguing tale."

"It was very gallant of you to come to the lady's rescue, Mr. Vincent, but I can assure you both of these highly educated young women can take care of themselves." Jefferson Neuman had come into the sunny morning room just in time to witness Miss Brandon's actions over something she had just been told from her close friend.

"Ladies, may I introduce my associate, Mr. Anthony Vincent. He will be accompanying us today to Stanford Hall Plantation. Tony might pick up something I have missed, that might be of some interest to you." Jefferson patted his partners back. "Tony, let's have our breakfast over at your table so these girls can enjoy their breakfast and continue their chit-chat." The senior lawyer waved his hat in front of him in a formal manner as he added. "Ladies, take your time, we won't be leaving for another hour." With that, he ushered his partner away, speaking softly to him.

"Sam, I was just about to tell you the best part when you dropped your knife." Victoria did not have look toward the two lawyers to know they were looking their way, so she kept her voice low. "Zechariah told me he could not remain at this place for a long period, so he said I could find him at Stanford Hall, by finding the secret to the past."

"Same as your Aunt Victoria mention." Samantha ate excitedly. "This just might be the toughest mystery you have ever had to solve, Vic."

"That's why I have to except this gift from Aunt Victoria!" Samantha swallowed as she reached for the peach perseveres. "Just listen, I know we are being watched." Vicky smiled down

Joan Byrd

when her friend glanced over to the lawyers' table, only to watch them quickly look away. After Sam nodded she agreed,

Victoria continued. "I got to find Zechariah, Sam. I cannot leave him stuck in the past when he is relying on me to released him from the thing that holds the secret to the past. I cannot explain what happened next and why I said the thing I did, except, I said what was in my heart." Victoria leaned over toward her friend, knowing this move would probably bring both lawyers to attention, but what she had to say was very private and only for the ears of the only one she could trust. "Sam, Zechariah confessed his love for me."

"The handsome mysterious man told you he was in love with you?"

"That's not all. He pointed to this hourglass and said his time was almost out, so I grew desperate, seeing the last of the sand swift to the bottom. That's when I asked him if I'd ever see him again and he told me about searching for the thing that held the secret to the past. Zechariah told me that's where I'd find him, and since I was such a good detective I should find it quickly."

"He knew about you being a detective?" Sam almost jumped from her seat.

"Yes, and he knew I would be born in this century and the date I would arrive here to see my inheritance." Vicky took a bite of bacon, feeling too excited to eat the great food in front of her, then checked her watch. Thirty more minutes before Mr. Neuman would come over to see if they are almost finished. "Sam, the hourglass was almost empty when he asked me to say his name, then he added, just say it Vicky. He called me Vicky." The young sleuth noticed her friend grow pale so she reached over and took her friend's hand as her words came just above a whisper. "I said, Zechariah, I love you." Tears filled her eyes. "Then he simply disappeared."

"Excuse me, Victoria, if you wish to finish your breakfast, we can wait on you in the lobby." Jefferson Neuman smiled down at her half-eaten plate of food. "Sometimes too much excitement can rob a soul of their appetite." The lawyer chuckled and patted his bulging stomach. "I never seem to have that problem. The more excited I get, the more I eat." He smiled down at Samantha's empty plate. "Much like your friend here. I couldn't help but notice she was really caught up in your story."

"Vicky just knows how to tell any story with flare, Mr. Neuman." Sam smiled over at her longtime friend, knowing not to diverge their true conversation."

"I couldn't eat another bite, Jefferson." Victoria stood up after laying her napkin on the white linen tablecloth. "Give us ten minutes to refresh ourselves, then we shall meet you and Mr. Vincent in the lobby."

"Victoria, are you sure you weren't visited by a ghost last night?" If Jefferson Neuman were joking, Vicky could not tell as she managed a perfect smile.

"A ghost? I seriously doubt a ghost paid me a visit last night, Jefferson. I can assure you, if they did, I slept right through their haunting. I hope I did not hurt their feelings. Perhaps they'll try again tonight." Swinging her bag over her shoulder, Victoria and Samantha walked by all the staring dinners, then rushed quickly to their suite.

CHAPTER 7

As the two friends busied themselves with brushing their teeth and checking their hair and make-up, they discussed the case, so far as they knew it.

"Vic, how do you figure your aunt knowing so much about you, not to mention Zechariah." Sam couldn't tell her best friend's heart beat faster at the sound of the name of the man she loved and couldn't understand how or why.

"Sam, unless there really is a secret object somewhere inside that manor house, there has got to be a logical answer to this puzzle." Victoria sat down at the fancy mirror to comb her long black hair into a ponytail. "Just suppose, Aunt Victoria had someone working for her she trusted. And gave them the request to pass along to their children what she wanted. The next generation would be on the lookout for the next Stanford baby girl to be named Victoria. Then this person's sole job would be to follow this girl until she was grown up and when she reached the age of twenty, have her contacted about her inheritance."

"Do you think Mr. Neuman's grandfather was involved in her plain somehow." Samantha applied a rose colored lipstick on her lips before flopping down to wait on her best friend.

"I am sure my Aunt Victoria got Jefferson Neuman Senior to help her with the first will, although I cannot out rule the lawyer's involvement in her scream." Vicky looked through the mirror at her friend. "If he were part of her plan, he would have had to insist his son, Jefferson Neuman the 2nd would name his firstborn Jefferson Neuman the 3rd and leave him full instructions to seek me out until I reached twenty, then send me the telegram."

"Racing rats! Vic, if Mr. Neuman the 1st left these instructions for Mr. Neuman the 3rd, does that mean this lawyer who is showing us around, has been watching you all your life? Creepy!"

"Sam, the one thing that may rule out the Neuman's involvement, is the family seal on the yellowed paper. It had not been broken when he pulled it out. The excitement to finally know what it said was written on his face, unless our Mr. Neuman is a very good actor."

"Then if you noticed the will was written on old, yellowed paper and had the original family seal pressed into wax. How could anyone living today have written that will? It had to be Victoria Bell."

"Not necessarily Sam, if it was that friend or staff member I referred to earlier, their grandchildren could have done it." Victoria checked the time and saw their ten minutes were up, but men knew women usually took longer than they said, so she would use that tactic on the lawyers. She needed to finish her theory, so they both could be looking for clues. "Let's say, Victoria was very close to her personal maid and taught her how to write, exactly like her. Then trusting her loyal helper with her secret, she told her of the plan to teach her daughter the same writing script then her granddaughter and by leaving them a large sum of money, they could work secretly on her ideal."

"So, the granddaughter would be almost like a forger, using the same yellowed paper from the early 1900's then sealing the new will with the historic family S!" Samantha looked at her friend with admiration. "You are a genus, Vicky!" then a worried frown creased her brow. "But, how on earth did they switch the new will with the old will? It had to be inside a safe, locked away at the lawyer's office and it probably had an alarm for security."

"And you are probably correct about the safe and the alarm, but just suppose someone was paid off to break into Vincent and Neuman and knew how to disable an alarm and open a safe, make the switch and no one would ever suspect a dead woman successfully getting by with the plan hatched 80 years ago."

"Vic, that is the perfect answer to this mystery, if it wasn't for one little fact." Samantha caught her bag when her friend laughed and gave it a toss her way before grabbing her own.

"Yes, a very handsome fact! How does Zechariah Castleton

know everything there is to know about me and I know absolutely nothing about him?" Victoria sighed. "Except, for one thing, I love that man with all my heart."

"He must have made some impression with you, pal." Samantha followed Victoria out of their room and waited for her to lock the door and placed the old brass key inside her brown leather shoulder bag. "What was in that powerful kiss, Vic? Some secret potion from the past?"

"Trust me, pal, Zechariah did not need any secret potion!" The girls laughed joyfully as they walked briskly down the wide staircase to where the two lawyers stood waiting, admiring their innocent beauty.

The trip out of town was noneventful until they reached the dirt drive where Johnny Pennywise rode out in front of them on his bike. Mr. Neuman turned his station wagon in the road and dropped his speed to 15 miles-per-hour. The girl friends looked at each other and shrugged their shoulders, unsure of the reason for going to Pennywise' farm.

"Excuse me Jefferson, but isn't this the road the Pennywise family live on?"

"Why, yes Victoria. I never realized you knew Mable and Harvey Pennywise, my dear, they being field workers and all."

"I wouldn't know what they do for a living, Jefferson. I have never met Mable or Harvey before, but Sam and I did meet their little boy, Johnny, yesterday." Victoria caught his eye in the rearview mirror and noticed him shake his head.

"Was that boy out near the main road again? Sheriff Baker has warned the Pennywises to keep him close to home."

"Vicky just about ran over the cute kid when he drove out into Carriage Wheel Road to turn around, right in front of us!" Samantha chuckled, remembering the little fellow's southern slang and his choice of old timey words. "Johnny was a very polite little boy, even though he talked about seeing a deceased woman."

"Victoria Bell Stanford? He is most likely referring to her painting that hangs inside Stanford Hall Manor." The lawyer's eyes met Victoria's in the mirror. "I take it the child thought you were the late Victoria Bell Stanford."

"He was taken back only for a moment, Jefferson. He seemed to be very smart for someone who appeared to be from a poor family." Vicky's attention went to the landscape on either side of the spacious sand driveway. "Is this the drive to the plantation?"

"Yes, my dear. It is almost four miles long, so just sit back, relax and enjoy the scenery."

Samantha leaned over and whispered in Vicky's ear "If that little kid rode his bike all the way down this road and back home again, he must be in great shape!" she, lend away, eyes wide with wonder. "That is eight miles total."

"The young have more energy than most adults, Sam and riding on a bike that distance can't be much slower than Mr. Neuman is driving." Vicky noticed an old cabin in a small clearing and pointed it out to her friend. "It appears to be abandoned. I wonder how long it has been sitting way out here?"

"What? That old cabin back there in the forest?" Mr. Neuman once again peered up in the review mirror, obvious to the girls for ease dropping in on their private conversation. "That was where the old gypsy lived, after befriending Zechariah Castleton and Victoria Rose Stanford, or so goes the tale of Gypsy Delmarrio." Both lawyers glanced at one and gave a soft sarcastic snicker before Jefferson continued. "Just ask anyone working at the plantation about the legend of Gypsy Delmarrio, they will gladly share their version."

"I take it you or Mr. Vincent don't believe in this legend about the gypsy living out in those woods." Victoria was still trying to sort out the two lawyers, true motives for taking on this very unusual case. Where they, perhaps just ordinary lawyers who sought out common sense solutions when working with a client? Or were they in deeper than they appeared and chose to laugh off what they knew was real but wanted to keep the true facts from the new heir of Stanford Hall.

"I can only say, it is a very convincing legend, Victoria. One must hear it for themselves, then come to their own conclusion." Jefferson Neuman slowed the car to a stop, so the girls could take in the grand avenue of majestic live oaks, dating back to the 1700's. They stood like proud soldiers, flanking both sides of the white river sand drive, easily wide enough for two magnificent carriages pulled by a quartet of the finest steeds, money could buy. Neuman slowly moved forward and continued down the charming old southern plantation drive until they came to a stately rock entrance, connected to an elegant rock wall, covered with hanging moss and delicate lavender flowers. The huge wrought iron gate stood boldly closed to reveal the large oval gold emblem with the letters S.H.P, permanently engraved in rich dark black.

Samantha and Victoria stared up at the impotence of such a magnificent display of wealth.

"I am impressed, my friend!" Samantha looked with child-like fascination. "You will be the envy of every classmate we have back in Natchez! If this very impressive gate is any indication what the manor house will look like, I'll have to start calling you Princess Victoria."

"That would please mother." Vicky noticed both lawyers shaking their heads in a quick negative. "What's wrong fellows? You act as though we just fell off the circus train."

"Never, and I do mean, never, refer to yourself as either, Princess Victoria or Queen Victoria! If you wish to start out on the wrong foot with all your staff, it will be for showing favor to their enemy, anything British! This town still holds England in contempt for that war in the 1700's, not to mention killing many of our young men and boys, who were just fighting to become a free nation, clear from British rule."

"Then we shall avoid any thing British, Jefferson, except the visit from my beautiful British mother, Irene." Victoria sat back, already feeling the need to change a few personal ideals her staff still clung to, after over two-hundred years. "When my mother and father, who happens to be 100% southern, come to pay me a visit, my staff 'will' treat this proud, half- Brit, and her mother with respect, if they wish to keep their boss-lady happy! Do I make myself clear, Mr. Neuman?"

"Extremely clear, Victoria." He chuckled. I see you already

attain quite a bit of your Aunt Victoria Bell and your monarch ancestor who also ruled this plantation with an iron fist, Madam Victoria Rose Stanford. It was this first strong-willed lady that took charge of everything regarding the running of such a successful plantation, which is still in operation today, much like it was in the first Victoria's control. She passed down her expertise in how to manage such an enormous project without owning a single slave." Neuman smiled at his partner when the girls glanced at each other, looking confused.

"I know what you both are thinking. How can a plantation with one thousand acers, managed back in the 1700 and even 1800's without the help of slaves?"

"I know slavery was wrong, Jefferson, but I thought anyone rich enough to own a plantation such as Stanford Hall, could buy all the field hands they needed, as well as kitchen staff, and still treat them with dignity and respect." Victoria never did understand how any free American could approve of keeping another child of God in bondage, but living in Natchez, one of the oldest towns in the states, she saw signs of slavery all around her.

"Victoria, your family never believed in slavery either, same as you do, but knew they had to have help to get up their yield of crops each and every season, to keep the grand plantation self-efficient. Their wealth gave them the advantage over other plantations nearby. Knowing the black people were excellent workers, they made their trip to the slave market, bought the woman and men, along with their children, loaded them in clean, big wagons, drove on to the court house and purchased each soul on board those wagons, freedom, that very day, took them home to the plantation, and gave them all a new set of clothes. Two work shirts and strong pants for the men and their sons, bright checked dresses for the woman and little girls. All the happy servants received a Sunday dress or suit, each free person got two sets of shoes, one pair for every day, the other for Sunday morning worship and the day of rest, for all God's children." Stepping up to open the gate for the new owner of Stanford Hall, Reginald Myers had overheard the lawyer and the beautiful raven hair woman, speaking on the subject of slavery and he had grown up at the plantation, where his own father was foreman, just like he was now. Removing his big rim hat, he bowed slightly, as he swiped the hat gallantly in front of him.

"I never meant to startle you, Miss Stanford. I saw Jefferson drive up and came out to open the gate and welcome you to Stanford Hall." The blondish-grey hair appeared uncombed, most likely from wearing the hat all morning. Rather thin and slightly tall, the head of the grounds staff smiled, reflecting kindness and patience, both good qualities in a head boss. "Permit me to introduce myself, my name is Reginal Myers, your grounds foreman."

"It is very nice to meet you, Reginal. If I choose to except all my aunt's terms, I guess you and I will be working close together and I trust you to show me what it takes to run a plantation." Victoria already liked the foreman and estimated his age around forty. "Is there a Mrs. Myers, Reginal? I should like to meet her as well and any children you might have."

"Of course, Miss Stanford, Charlotte is looking forward to meeting you. She will be working close by you as well. Charlotte has been groomed to be your personal maid and she is truly a lovely person." Another bright smile graced his weathered beaten face. "Our son Jake is seventeen and in training for the next foreman, like I was with my father, and his father, my grandfather, and so on down the family tree, when the first Myers got the job after the plantation was purchased in the 1700's."

"You have quite the family history here at Stanford Hall, Reginal." Victoria smiled from the car window as she reached out to shake his hand. "It will be a pleasure working along someone who knows this plantation like the back of his hand."

"Yes Victoria, you cannot go wrong with Reginal guiding your way. He worked alongside his father for almost twenty years, starting at the age of ten in training. Poor old Walter died with pneumonia ten years ago at the age of seventy." Jefferson put the car in gear "At forty-years-old, you will be foreman for a long time, Reginal, as long as you keep Miss Stanford happy."

"Don't you worry none about that, Jefferson. I think me and Miss Stanford will hit it off real, good." The foreman stepped away from the entrance so the black station wagon could pass through.

"He seems real nice, Vicky. It helps to have someone who knows what to do around here without being told, since you have no clue what to ask them to do." Samantha made a face at her best friend with she chuckled at her remark, then froze in her seat when the enormous pillared manor house came into to view. "Jumping Jupiter! Take a look at your new house!"

"It's…absolutely breathtaking!" Victoria had put down her window to get the full effect of the grand house with stately round pillars that rose to the third floor, then wrapped around the white-washed brick. It was as if time had not set foot on Stanford Hall, for it appeared to be the same as it was the day it was built. "This place is remarkable, Sam! Nothing seems to have changed around here, as though time itself, has stopped!"

"You are exactly correct, Victoria! Not just beautiful but smart and clever." Anthony Vincent turned around in his seat, a smile stretched across his usually stern face. "It is quite alright to be dazed over the masterpiece before you. You are not the first to be taken back with one's first glimpse Stanford Hall and when they depart, it is not easily forgotten."

"So, Mr. Vincent, why does my amazement over seeing Stanford Hall for the first time, make me smart and clever?" The young detective turned her attention on Neuman's partner.

"For starters, my dear, please call me Anthony, or Tony if it pleases you. Since you refer to my partner as Jefferson, then it's only proper, don't you agree, Victoria?"

"Whatever you think, Tony." She forced a grin. "The smart and clever, remark, Tony?"

"Oh yes, smart, clever, and beautiful! Mustn't forget, beautiful!" the thin lawyer gave a little wink, causing Victoria to tense up. "You take after the first two Victoria's. They both were extremely smart, clever, and beautiful ladies." He wrinkled up his nose in a silly way before adding "Since they are not here to hear my next comment, just let me add, they might have been beautiful, but you, my dear, are far lovelier

49

than either of them, who lived here before you."

"I shall try hard not to share this opinion with either Victoria Rose or Victoria Bell if They appear to me in this house." Vicky tried hard not to laugh when Samantha laughed out and Jefferson cleared his throat.

CHAPTER 8

Jefferson Neuman and Anthony Vincent led Victoria an Samantha up on the wide wraparound porch, then stopped just outside the huge oak door.

"My dear, Victoria, please overlook the rambling of my partner back there in the car." Jefferson Neuman pulled nervously at his white stiff collar to let some air in. "He always gets a little nervous when the thought of going through this door gets the better of him."

"And I guess my comment referring to the appearance of both Victoria's ghost, didn't help matters." Vicky looked sincerely sorry for her clumsy joke. "Perhaps, Tony would feel better staying out here on the porch and wait for you to show me around."

"Your thoughtfulness is very kind, Victoria, but Tony needs to get over his fear of Stanford Hall." Jefferson patted his partner on the back, and Anthony nodded weakly. "And just so you'll know what Tony never got around to telling you in the car about clever and smart, this place looks this way because it was the determination of those two ladies to keep this place the same, always. That is why her will stated clearly, if you except to be the sole owner of Stanford Hall, you 'must' never change anything and what needs repairing, see that it does not alter the looks or the integrity of Stanford Hall."

"Even with Aunt Victoria gone since 1939, those workers left behind have followed her commands right down to the smallest nail." Victoria pointed to a small rusted nail in one of the floor length window frames. "I will bring that up with Reginal, when I see him."

"There now, see how you are already feeling the need to keep things restored." Mr. Neuman opened the heavy door and stepped aside. "Miss Stanford, please come in and see your new home."

Victoria and Samantha walked in and caught their breath at

the majesty that waited before them. The oval grand entrance hall was as big as Victoria's entire first floor at her home, Sunrise, in Natchez, Mississippi. Two white marble staircases descending from the third floor, met on the second landing becoming one wide and graceful open arms staircase. The rich red carpet danced up the center of the easy access risers.

It was obvious that Stanford Hall had been built by gifted artisans and like the grand mansions in Natchez, the builders chose only the finest accessories, such as the English sterling silver doorknobs with Sheffield hinges, decorative mantles of Italian Carrara marble, same as the staircase. French pier, over-mantle mirrors and great solid gold chandeliers, brought the already large rooms alive to reveal magnificent floor to ceiling windows, adorned with the finest material money could buy. Each matching parlor had exquisite furniture place graciously around the extraordinary interiors.

"This is totally cool, Jefferson!" Samantha stepped back out into the entrance hall. "I must admit growing up in Natchez, I have seen some really grand houses!" she looked over at her friend, who was trying to soak in as much on this first visit as possible. "Vicky Wouldn't you agree the inside of Stanford Hall looks a great deal like Stanton Hall, built in 1851? The outside has the charm of Dunleith, built in 1856. It is the only house in Mississippi with a colonnade that completely surrounds the house, just like Stanford Hall."

"You are right Sam, I can see a little of both houses in this elegant place." Victoria finally drew her attention away from the exciting tour and looked up at Mr. Neuman. "Jefferson, I know Stanford Hall was built in 1770 by Nelson and Victoria Rose Stanford. Would you mind sharing the final cost? I realize the sum might sound small to such a modern world but, living and growing up in this very environment, knowing the cost of each grand house when it was built in Natchez, teaches each citizen in town, the cost then would be equivalent to a very large sum today. Stanton Hall for instance, cost the incredible sum back in 1851, $83,300, probably in the high millions now, counting the interior collection of furniture and the many antiques, in today's market."

"Smart girl! As you know, Stanford Hall was built with 1700's prices and the Stanford's were extremely wealthy, so expense was not an issue. The loving couple wanted the finest home in the state of Louisiana and it still holds the record this day. Of course, the very largest house was built later in the state of North Carolina, just off the Blue Ridge Parkway, in Ashville. George W. Vanderbilt built his 250-room French Renaissance-style chateau and simply called it the Biltmore House, don't you get it? The catchy name?" Anthony Vincent chuckled at his own remark. "George Bilt-more house! You know, he built more house than anyone else!"

"Very amusing, Tony." Victoria faked a smile then stared over at his partner. "The cost, Jefferson, how much?" Vicky was slowly losing her patient because she desperately wanted to see her Aunt Victoria's suites.

"The final cost for the manor house alone was a whopping $100,000! An enormous sum for 1770." Jefferson Neuman waved his hand down the hall, so Victoria followed reluctantly, as her attention swept up the stairs where the bedchambers lay. "Ladies, I know the parlors seem hard to beat, but the room I am about to show you is the biggest, the grandness, and the most magnificent you have ever seen, even in your lovely town of Natchez." The cocky lawyer opened the heavy double doors back and gave a princely bow before announcing. "Miss Victoria Stanford, step into your very own Ballroom!"

The grandeur and wealth of the place was felt in this grand ballroom, as it danced slowly around its oval walls, covered with four French gold-leaf, floor length, mirrors, curved to fit the oval shape room. Floor to ceiling windows, becoming doors when needed to take the party of guest out on the colonnade, found their way gracefully around the huge ballroom. Individual rosewood chairs covered in rich plush red velvet, of the finest grade, were pushed up neatly against the soft white walls, leaving plenty of room on the dance floor for a party of 100 guests to waltz the night away to the orchestra played in the balcony box, placed specifically in the middle for the best acoustics. Oversize marble fireplaces with ornate Italian marble mantles, dominated both ends of the magnificent room.

"There are simply no words to describe this deluxe ballroom, Jefferson. The four crystal chandeliers hanging from the seventeen-foot-high ceiling must have been flowing down on the long dresses and sparkling gems that hung gracefully around each beautiful lady present." Victoria could visualize the scene, fancy dressed wealthy woman, shyly telling her beau, with southern charm, just how handsome and gallant he was as they waltz around under the flickering candlelight.

"I find it a little bit sad, Vicky." Samantha noticed everyone had turned to look at her, unsure over her unusual remark. "Well, what I mean is, at one time this place was the life of the house, so to speak. It was in this room where people could just have fun being together, to laugh, to talk, drink good wine or champagne, then dance the night away with the partner of their dreams." Sam took a long sigh. "Now, it just sits here, big, quiet, and alone, with nothing but happy memories of times gone by forever."

"Darn, that is depressing!" Anthony Vincent gave his own sad sigh. "It's downright sad how it just sits here, feeling left out and only has memories to keep it entertained."

Vincent's law partner rolled his eyes up in discuss, then cleared his throat. "Just calm down, Tony. I'm sure the new owner of Stanford Hall will once again bring this old ballroom back to life and throw at least one grand ball like her aunt did every year."

"A ball? You expect me to throw a big ball, right here in this room, with an orchestra playing waltz's from up there, in that balcony?" Victoria gave the lawyer a questioning frown. "Do people really expect me to continue such an old tradition?"

"Absolutely! It was always the gala of the year!" Mr. Neuman's eyes widen with excitement, hearing the oldest citizens in town recall the happy event. "All the ladies made sure they had the prettiest dresses to wear and the finest jewels money could buy. The gentlemen wore black silk tucks with stiff high shirt collars in brilliant white. Even on her 100th birthday, Victoria Bell threw one last spectacular ball for the community and it's still the talk of those who were alive at the time or old enough to remember."

"Then, if I choose to except the plantation, I will be seeking out one of these citizens that actually attended my aunt's ball and find out what is required from me." Victoria turned and walked back to the entrance hall and started up the steps, Jefferson Neuman and Anthony Vincent raced up the steps behind her as Samantha trailed behind, trying not to laugh at the two lawyers.

CHAPTER 9

When the young detective reached the second level, she glanced to the left staircase, then to the right and without hesitation, Victoria raced up the flight of steps to the third floor.

Both lawyers had to stop briefly to catch their breath when they reached the second floor, giving Samantha time to catch up with them. She stepped past both men and looked up to see her friend disappear down the hall.

"Mr. Neuman, what's up there on that third floor?"

"The entire west side of the third floor was both Victoria Rose and Victoria Bell's private quarters!" Neuman motioned the girl forward, as they all began the flight up. "Now, how did that girl know that? No one ever told her!"

"Vicky is a great detective and she has a special gift for feeling things that most of us cannot." Samantha slowed down when she heard the lawyers breathing heavy as they walked slowly up the risers.

Vicky had reached the third-floor landing and noticed just down the hallway was white double doors trimmed in gold leaf. Praying the solid gold lock was open, she slowly turned the knob and smiled when it turned smoothly under her fingers. When she opened the door, she had the uncanny feeling she had seen this parlor before and she knew exactly which way the bedchamber was. Vicky made her way across the room and entered into the bedchamber, located at the right end of the private rooms of the late owners of Stanford Hall.

A canopied four-poster bed stood proudly against the center wall, decked out with pure white laced bedcoverings and most of the furniture dated back from antebellum times. The only piece of furniture that seemed out of place was a very old black vanity with an arched mirror, plain by all the other furnishings in the house, but the glass looked as new as the day it was built. Vicky could not stop staring at the old vanity's mirror and jumped when Samantha called out for her.

"I'm in Aunt Victoria's bedchamber, Sam. Come on in and see how beautiful it is." Vicky smiled at her friend when she walked over and looked around. "What do you think, pal. Think this place looks like me?"

Samantha started to make a joke until she caught sight of the painting over the fireplace mantle. "I...I'm not sure this place looks like you, Vic, but Victoria Bell could be your twin!"

"What?" Vicky laughed, then noticed her friend was looking at something across the room, so she turned to see a big oil painting of her aunt, dating back to the 1800's. "Yes, I see what you mean. How did I miss that?"

"Maybe it's because your attention was strictly on that old black vanity." Mr. Neuman had walked in behind Victoria's friend and noticed her staring at the old mirror. "If you want me to have that eyesore removed from the house, I will be more than glad to get rid of it for you."

"I rather like this old vanity, Jefferson. It is the only thing that is different in this big house." She gave him a quick smile. "The vanity stays, along with the wonderful old mirror."

"Old mirror?" Samantha walked up and bent over to check it out closely. "The vanity may be old as the hills, even the mirror's frame, but the actual looking glass has to be brand new, right?"

"Not necessarily, Sam." Victoria had an unusual feeling about that mirror and for the moment she did not wish to discuss it in front of these two men. To lead their thoughts away from the special mirror, she simply said "Well, whether it's an old mirror or a new replacement glass, it makes no difference to me, it stays, or I go!"

"No, no, my dear, the mirror stays right here if that's your wish, but please give us your answer tomorrow." Mr. Neuman gestured toward the door. "I'm afraid the day has slipped away and I did want you to meet some of the staff before we head back to town."

Reluctantly Victoria agreed and followed the group back to the main floor where ten people stood waiting in a line. The tall man on the end, dressed in a black butler's uniform, stepped forward and took a polite bow.

"Welcome to Stanford Hall Manor, Miss Stanford. I am Thornton Hancock, your butler and captain over the entire staff on the plantation. My job is to keep everything moving in a smooth orderly direction and your fine, loyal staff is both friendly and efficient." The well groom man tilted his head slightly. "If it pleases my lady, you many call me Thornton."

"That would please me greatly sir, but only if you call me, Victoria, or Vicky if you like." Vicky noticed a friendly smile grace his serious face.

"I think it more appropriate, what with my being your butler and all, that I called you, Miss Victoria. I wish not to offend you, so, I will order my staff as well to refer to you as, Miss Victoria." Mr. Hancock stepped from the line and started at the end. "This is Edward and Odessa Brown and along with their cute twenty-two-year-old daughter, Imogene. They take residence in the largest cottage on Staff Row." The butler waved the seven-foot, muscular black man to step up.

"You may call me, Big Ed, Miss Victoria. I am the captain of the stables with a very spry young fellow working as my helper, that would be my stable hand, Frankie Horn. We dropped the original title for his job way back in 1770, so goes the talk from all the older folk who lived on the plantation."

"What name was that, Big Ed?" Vicky knew she already loved this lovely family, whose happiness reflected from each smiling face. "Did the original name describing the stable hands job sound unusual?"

"It was offensive Miss Victoria, that's what it was." True kindness showed on Big Ed's face as he reflected back on the offensive name. "You know most my kinfolk came to this land as slaves and to belittle the poor souls, those white men referred to my black brothers as 'boy'! House boy, stable boy, lazy boy or just plain poor boy!" Mr. Brown gave a toothy grin. "Why, that Madam Victoria Rose Stanford, said she would have no part in that slave business. Being a good Christian woman, she announced that every soul born was a child of the Almighty, and needing good help to run a plantation, she would buy as many slaves as she could use, and that saintly woman did just that."

"But…didn't you just say that good Christian woman first declare she wouldn't buy slaves, then turned right around and bought some." Samantha had got caught up it the big man's story when Victoria lightly punched her arm.

"Sam, don't you remember being told how Victoria Rose took a long wagon down to the market and bought several slaves, mostly families, drove straight to the courthouse and bought their freedom so they could work for wages, have a plot of ground, and build a house?"

"Oh Yeh, now I remember." Samantha blushed. "So, Victoria Rose refused to call the stable hand, boy, not wanting to belittle him."

"Excuse me Miss, but is your given name really, Sam, like a boy?" Imogene had never heard of females using male's names. "You are far too pretty for a tomboy, miss."

"Permit me to explain why I call my friend Sam, Imogene." Vicky draped her arm around her best friend. "Her given name is Samantha Braddon. We both grew up in the town of Natchez, went into the first grade together, then twelve years later, both of us graduated. We were always inseparable, except for my two years in college." Vicky laughed remembering the other children mocking her after she lost her two front teeth and tried to say her friend's name. "The other thing we shared was losing our two front teeth at the same time and neither one of us could pronounce the other one's name correctly. We discovered what we could say was Sam and Vic, so it stuck, even after we grew our permanent front teeth."

"What a cute story!" The five-foot-four, heavy set black lady chuckled. "My name is Odessa Brown, Miss Victoria, Big Ed's better half and Imogene's terrific mother, and your dream cook! The kitchen is my domain and my baby girl, is mama's helper."

"You are truly a lovely family and if I chose to stay here, I look forward to seeing you every day." Vicky noticed the worried brow form on the cook's face. "Did I say something to offend you, Odessa?"

"Oh, no ma'am, you are a lovely person and it will be a delight working for you, miss." The heavy woman rung her hands nervously. "It's just what you said about if you chose to stay, Miss Victoria. That just got me fretting over the ideal of you saying no, to Miss Victoria Bell's gift."

"Oh miss, you just got to stay! Don't let the size of this house scare you done, you don't need to be worrying yourself about that." Imogene Brown's eyes had grown wide with excitement. "We can take care of everything there is to do, Miss Victoria. It's our job and we love doing it!"

Charlotte Myers, a petite blonde stepped out and gave a curtsey. "Miss Victoria, I was looking forward in becoming your personal maid. Imogene is right, ma'am, we do need you to take over this plantation! All our lives depend upon your decision!"

"Charlotte, we cannot pressure this lovely young woman to except the total ownership of Stanford Hall Plantation based on what would become of everyone living and working here." Reginald Myers took his wife's hand and pulled her back beside him. "This is all new to Miss Stanford, my friends. We must respect her decision and give her the time to make it without making her feel she will be hurting all of us."

"We know you're right, Reginald, but this is the only home we have ever known." Marvin Ward, the head footman, glanced over at the new owner. "Madam, if you choose to except this most gracious gift, I will be honored to see that you and any guest you might have, are served with great care. There are three footmen to attend your meals, and I am Marvin Ward, the head footman, along with John Phillips and Jeremy Taylor. My wife, Roberta, serves as the head maid for a staff of five maids, two on the first floor, two on the second floor and your personal maid, Charlotte, in the west wing."

"The east wing of the upper floor contains the living quarters for the staff." The butler stepped forward and motioned for the staff to reform the line. "Pearl Jones and Aubrey Phillips, work on the second floor, Theda Taylor and Earline Porter are on the main floor, along with Roberta Ward. You can meet your entire staff when you return, that is, if you make the decision we are all praying you will make."

"Miss Stanford, my name is Chaplain Joshua Whittington.

I have been obtained to serve as the minister of the small chapel that sits just beyond this lovely house. When it was built back in 1772, to take care of the black servant's Christian needs, the Stanford family simply called it, the Chapel. Later on, after Mr. Stanford passed away, Victoria Rose and the other white servants started attending the Chapel, along with seventeen-year-old Zechariah Castleton, who helped out at the stables, as well as other small jobs the lady of the plantation found for him to do." The minister couldn't help but notice the young woman blushing when he mentioned Zechariah's name.

"Chaplain Whittington, how do you come by all that information dating back to the 1770's?" Victoria needed to know so she could see these old records or diaries for herself. "History has always intrigued me, living in a historic town all my life."

"Yes, Natchez, I'm told. A lovely old town with lovely old mansions and plantations, spread out across the countryside." He noticed his statement about her hometown was approved by her smile and positive nod. "The ministers before me kept great journals and some of the other staff living in the big house had their own diaries, recording history for future owners. I've been told by a very reliable source, both Victoria Rose and Victoria Bell, kept a day-to-day diary, although no one has seen either leather bound book since they were hidden away in some secret compartment."

"That sounds like a good job for a detective, don't you agree, Victoria?" Jefferson had checked his watch and knew they needed to be heading to town. His late breakfast had run out and time did not allow for lunch, although the friendly cook and footman had offered it when they arrived.

"A detective would be right at home here, Jefferson." Victoria could tell the lawyer was getting anxious to leave. "I do believe Mr. Neuman has to return to Castleton." She addressed the staff. "Maybe this will ease your worried minds, dear friends. As of this very moment, I am leaning toward keeping this beautiful gift, my gracious aunt gave me. I never knew she existed until I received Mr. Neuman's message in the mail, asking me to come to Castleton, Louisiana. Victoria Bell has put in my trust something that obviously meant the world to her and with all the mysteries she has planted inside me, it would be almost impossible for me to say no." Victoria was glad to see all the relieved faces in front of her. "In respect to my parents, I must speak to them first before I give my final answer. I have never lived away from our family home except for the two years I attended law school to attain my private detective degree."

"Just two years, Miss Victoria?" Roberta Ward looked confused. "My cousin took four years to finish regular college, then another four to get her degree!"

"Vicky is a gifted student, Roberta. She graduated high school at fifteen, won a full scholarship to Wake Forest, and walked up for her degree at seventeen years old." Samantha bragged, always amazed at her friend's intelligence.

"Excuse me, Miss Samantha, but I know I remember hearing Miss Victoria say you both started the first grade together and twelve years later, walked up for your diplomas. Correct?" Anthony Vincent had been keeping a watch for any sign of growing darkness and wasn't paying much attention until this small-town girl started bragging about her friend's intelligence. "That would have made Victoria three-years-old when she started school to have graduated at fifteen."

"I am sorry to bust your theory, Tony, but you have it all wrong." Vicky laughed at his clumsy attempt at detective work. "What I said was, we both grew up in the town of Natchez, went into the first grade together, then twelve-years later, both of us graduated." She laughed when he arched his eyebrow. "What I did not say was, when Sam was graduating at Natchez High, I was getting my second diploma at Wake Forest University in North Carolina."

"It will be rather nice having a real-full-fledge detective living here, Miss Victoria!" Thornton Hancock walked the four visitors to the front door. "There are quite a few unsolved mysteries floating around this big plantation and not the usual kind. Some dating back as far as the planation itself."

"That sounds very intriguing Thornton. If I'm the owner of Stanford Hall, I just might have to hire myself to solve all these mysteries. Would you be the one to talk to about them, Thornton?"

"Not I, I'm afraid to admit. I just know bits and pieces, but there is one resident on the plantation who knows a great deal about all of them and how you might seek them out." The butler caught the lawyer's eye and noticed him pointing at his watch. "I must not hold you up, madam, but I'll tell you this much, the old woman stays manly to herself, coming out only to gather vegetables from the garden or attend both chapel services, one on Wednesday, the other one on Sunday morning. She knows secrets she will only share with the lady Victoria's of Stanford Hall. I think she is staying alive just for you, Miss Victoria."

"Where does this strange, mysterious lady live? In one of the staff cottages?" Vicky followed the lawyers to the porch and noticed how jittery both men seem. "Jefferson, I promise, this is my last two questions, but I need to know where that old woman lives on the plantation."

"Just tell her what she needs to know, Mr. Handcock! We haven't got all day and she will learn about that woman sooner or later." Mr. Neuman paced around nervously, as he waited.

"Jefferson, you make it sound incredibly mysterious." Vicky looked seriously at the butler. "When you were telling about the staff, Thornton, you failed to mention Johnny Pennywise and his parents."

"Oh yes, Mable and Harvey Pennywise, strange little couple, showed up asking for work, said they would do almost anything for a roof over their head and food on the table. You would never know that poor, thin woman gave birth to that six-year-old rounder who can find his way over every inch of this house or the entire plantation." The butler tried not to chuckle at the nervous lawyers when they walked toward their car, stating, "We will wait for you ladies out here, so please make it brief, Handcock!"

"Forgive me for laughing, ladies, but those two grown men are afraid of their own shadows." The butler shook his head to clear away the chuckles. "Mable and Harvey Pennywise do odd jobs until the crops are ready for harvesting. They are mainly field workers and to be honest, very reliable. The old woman lives in the old cabin you probably saw coming in."

"Is she a relative of the old gypsy named Delmarrio, who lived there in the 1770's?" Vicky knew Zechariah had befriended the old gypsy for some reason and must have convinced Victoria Rose to give him a place to live, but why?"

"The old lady was not blood kin to the old man, she claims to have been a runaway girl he took in and gave her a place to live, then treated her like his own daughter."

"Thornton, that cannot possibly be true. That would mean this girl was born in the late 1770's, around 1777. That would make her 240, Thornton, so unless she is a ghost, this poor old soul has lost her mind."

"I'll say, Vic! A real, nut case!" Samantha grabbed her hand "You might want to leave that one alone, pal, and if we don't get in that car, I think those two clowns might leave us here."

"I'm coming." Victoria reached for the butler's hand. "I can see there's a lot of mysteries to be solved, that woman is just one of them. By the way, what is her name?"

"Her name is Grace, that all anyone knows." Victoria thanked him and started to leave when he took her arm gently and whispered. "The chaplain failed to tell you what Victoria Rose changed the chapel's name to."

"What is it called now?" Vicky knew she must know this one last thing before leaving or she would wonder why he even brought it up.

"Victoria Rose renamed it, Grace Chapel, after the gypsy's stepdaughter, Grace."

CHAPTER 10

"Yes Mom, Dad, it is in perfect condition and the most beautiful house I have ever seen!" Victoria had called her parents as soon as she returned to the hotel. "I didn't have a chance to see much of the plantation, but I did get to see the rooms I wanted to see the most."

"Which rooms were those dear, the magnificent parlors? Were they as grand as the ones in Stanton Hall?" Irene felt relieved to finally hear from their only child. "They could not possibly be as grand as Stanton Hall."

"Perhaps not grander, mom, but just as grand and the massive ballroom was the largest of any I recall seeing in my lifetime." Vicky laughed softly "Perhaps the grand dining hall in the Biltmore house is equal in size to Stanford Hall's grand ballroom, right Sam?"

Samantha smiled up from glancing at the Castleton daily and said loudly enough for the Stanfords to hear.

"Plenty of room for a huge party of dancers, Irene! You'll be blown away when you come to visit!"

"Sounds like you've already made up your mind, darling." Steven Stanford had been listening on the other line, in his office. "It won't be the same without you here, baby girl."

"It would appear our baby girl has grown into a big girl now, Steve." Victoria thought she heard her mother sniffing back tears. "Didn't you say, the will stated if you excepted all Victoria Bells demands, to remain there as sole owner for life and keep things the way they have always been, you may have the plantation?"

"I know it sounds like an impossible demand, mom, but you cannot help but fall in love with the place once you see it." Vicky knew being so far from her parents would not be easy, especially for them, but she needed to get out on her own and Stanford Hall already felt like home. Zechariah was there and she needed to find him. Victoria decided she would wait to share that bit of information with her mother and father for now, at least until she understood herself why she loved a complete stranger who lived in the 1770's.

"Vicky, didn't you hear your father, dear? Are you losing your cell in that far away town?" Irene had hoped they hadn't lost connection with their only child after waiting so long to hear her voice.

"No mom, I'm here, I guess I let my mind wonder. What was it you ask dad?"

"If you choose to except this amazing gift, can you ever come for a visit occasionally?" Steven had his fingers crossed for the right answer.

"Nothing will keep me away from coming back to Natchez to see you dad. I will visit you and Mama as often as I can and I hope to see both of you frequently at Stanford Hall. I never got to check out the guest rooms, but I am sure they are beautiful and situated on the second floor." Vicky checked her watch when she heard Sam's stomach growl. "I guess I have to move this call along before poor old Sam dies from hunger. We skipped lunch and the fancy restaurant opens in fifteen minutes."

"I bet my girl is getting hungry as well." Steve smiled, just happy to know he would be seeing his daughter on visits. "What about all your things, darling? Would you like us to send them to you?"

"What I would really like dad, is for you and mama to bring them to the plantation for a nice long visit. I'm dying to show you what I've just inherited from Aunt Victoria Bell!" Now it was Victoria who had her fingers crossed. "Can you both arrange a trip down in the near future? I can manage for a while with what I brought."

"Vicky darling, dad and I will make it work!" Irene looked hopeful at her husband who gave her his approval in a wink. "Dad's on board, sweetheart! Will you be able to get calls out on the plantation?"

"Golly mom, I wouldn't know! I never tried and I'm not sure there's even a phone way out there!" Vicky bit her lip as she thought. "Don't worry mom, if I cannot call from the plantation, I'll make a trip to town and call you!"

"Will you miss all your detective work running a plantation, sweetheart?" Steve hated for the call to end, so he knew how hard she worked to become a detective. "There cannot be much happening in that little town. So, what about your lifelong dream of becoming a detective?"

"That's the best part, Dad, the plantation is packed with mysteries to solve. They won't be like any other mystery I've ever solved!" the excitement rose in the young sleuth's voice. "Mysteries dating back as far as 1770!"

"Mysteries from the past?" Steve sat up, new interest building. "How will you even begin to find clues after so many years?"

"Diaries and records, kept every day since the plantation existed! I'm just busting with excitement to get started, first, by finding the hidden diaries written by Victoria Rose Stanford and Victoria Bell Stanford! The chaplain's records are somewhere in the small chapel behind the manor house, of which I've yet to see."

"This place is right up your alley, Vicky, but darling, how can you busy yourself with all these mysteries and keep your plantation running?" Irene had to be the sensible one in the group after hearing local plantation owners tell how hard it was to keep up a plantation in the modern world. "Won't this grand plantation take up all of your time, dear?"

"Not in the least, mom. The thought had accrued to me also at first, when I heard about the size of the plantation, but after meeting the friendly staff, I was put at ease in that department." Vicky smiled when her friend gave her a thumb up, her way of saying, I agree. "It appears everyone loves their jobs and the plantation. It has been their home for their entire life, except for the chaplain."

"Then our young sleuth has plenty of time to solve all these historic unsolved mysteries surrounding Stanford Hall!" Steven was proud of his daughter's achievements in discovering and bringing to light facts in hard to solve mysteries. "I only wished I lived closer to help you read and decipher the meaning of some of these 1700-1800, words.

Being, a history teacher all these years has taught me a lot about the different language people used, like phrases, even spelling the way they pronounced their words if they weren't highly educated."

"I will put you to good use when you come for a visit, dad. You always helped me a lot decipher bad handwriting and if I need some help when you're not here, I'll fax you a copy to study, my second assistance, with Sam being my first, like Mr. Watson was to the legend Sherlock Holmes." Vicky laughed.

"Yes, your hero, I remember your sweet young voice declaring, move over Holmes! A little detective from the start!" Steven knew their fifteen had past and the girls had to eat, so he graciously said. "As much as I hate to say goodbye, Vicky, your mother and I want you and Sam, to get something to eat before they fill up their tables. We will see when we can come down for a visit and bring your things. You had better call us back in a few days, just in case we cannot get through, and we should be able to give you a date."

"Vicky darling, if your things arrive a little bit damp, it's because your father and I got emotional while packing your things." Irene gave her husband a weak smile, mixed emotions running through her mind about her little girl moving out. "What about Samantha's things, want us to bring them as well?"

"That would be great mom! Sam called her parents right before I called you and Anna was going to call you about her bringing Sam's things over. I've invited Thomas and Anna for a visit when they are free and can get away for a vacation, but they just couldn't come for a while."

"We would love to bring Samantha's things with us, darling. After all, she is almost family." Irene felt tears filling her eyes as she managed "I love you, Vicky. Take good care of yourself and don't take any unnecessary chances trying to solve these mysteries, especially if they are dangerous."

"I wouldn't worry about danger mom. We are talking about dead people, ghost or spirits, maybe, but I'm pretty sure I won't need to wear my crucifix twenty-four-seven!" the young detective laughed. "These, ghost seem very friendly, mom, very!"

"Ghost? You have seen a ghost?" Irene's eyes grew wide with concern. "Are you saying, Stanford Hall Manor is haunted?"

"I'm almost certain of it mom, at least, I hope so. I met my vision right here in my hotel bedroom!"

CHAPTER 11

The night went by without another visit from Zechariah, leaving Victoria a little disappointed. She had lots of questions for the handsome ghost, but they would have to wait until she found the secret to the past and find him.

The friends had a busy day planned, so they arose early, had breakfast, then called to be sure the Castleton Museum would be open. Mary Francis Wagstaff had agreed to meet them there at ten sharp and give them a private tour, since there weren't any more visitors in Castleton at the moment. The petite 4ft-8 clerk, greeted them at the entrance door, a warm smile on her elderly face.

"Do come in Miss Stanford, Miss Brandon. It will be my pleasure showing you around this very old museum with its original artifacts."

As they followed politely behind the spry woman, they noticed the musty smell from years of ageing things, such as fringe covered carriages, cannons, old muskets, from both the Revolutionary War and the Civil War. There were well preserved uniforms from both American wars and dated women's long expensive dresses, displayed beautifully on life-like manikins who looked as though they could come to life.

The tiny clerk was describing all the old relics when Victoria saw a wall filled with large oil paintings. As Mary Francis had her friend Sam interested in some of the costly jewelry ladies in the 1700's wore, Vicky slipped into the art gallery to examine the faces on the canvas. She suddenly found the Castleton family portrait dated 1773 and noticed just two children in the picture, two boys, and even though Zechariah couldn't be more then three in the painting, she knew from his hair and eyes it was the soul she was in love with. Vicky wasn't aware that the clerk had found her missing and caught sight of her in the gallery, and arrived behind her just in time to hear Vicky whisper

"Zechariah."

"You are exactly correct, my dear. That is young Zechariah Castleton with his brother James and mother and father, Joshua and Isabell Castleton!" Mrs. Wagstaff shook her head in dismay. "How on earth did you know who that boy was?"

"I saw him twice since I've come to Castleton, Mrs. Wagstaff. Once on Carriage Wheel Road when he was twelve and two nights ago in my hotel room, a grown man." Vicky steadied the shaken woman when she turned white and almost lost her balance. "It was really alright, Mrs. Wagstaff, he was very polite."

"Extremely polite, is more like it, Mary Francis." Samantha was checking out another painting of the entire Castleton family, recognizing all the children's faces. "Dang Vic, it was those Castleton kids we saw out there on that road!"

Vicky walked over to checked out the group and her attention fell once again on the handsome twelve-year-old.

"That's them alright and I would guess the exact same day we saw them."

"Wow! That is simply amazing, Miss Stanford!" Mary Francis swallowed the nervous lump in her throat. "The family had a traveling artist paint that portrait in front of their massive fireplace in the Castleton mansion. It took the moody stranger almost a week to finish the painting, so the family grew friendly with him, or so the story goes. On the evening he completed this masterpiece, Mr. Castleton paid him, shook hands, and watched the artist drive away on a black carriage. Joshua and Isabell had been invited out to a friend's home for a relaxing dinner, with wine flowing. The children's nanny was to see that the six children were fed and sent to bed by nine p.m. Around nine p.m., the nanny got a message from one of the staff members, asking her to take a package to the Smithers house, where they were dinning and to leave as soon as the children went off to bed. They had sent their carriage back for her and the driver would be waiting just outside."

"What was in the package that made it so important and urgent for them to want it, ASAP?" Vicky knew what was going to happen next, through deduction. "This distraction gave that artist time to double back and kidnap those children, then somewhere on Carriage Wheel Road, the kidnapper or his group stopped to camp! Somehow the children got away from them and took refuge in the woods across the road. They couldn't run back home to town because it had grown dark, so the forest was their safest place to hide until morning."

"Then they slipped back out of the woods the next morning to see if their kidnapper had left, but must have found him or them still there, looking for the runaways!" Samantha added, as the clerk looked from one girl to the other, mouth wide with shock for knowing so much. "Could the motive for the kidnapping be to demand a ransom?"

"I doubt that, since the children just disappeared and did not return until five years later." Mary Francis suddenly got drawn into the conversation. "There was never a note sent for a ransom to be paid to have the six children returned."

"I'm thinking it had something to do with that old gypsy man that showed up at the plantation with Zechariah asking for refuge and a safe place to stay, protected from the law." Vicky just had a hunch this entire mystery over the missing Castleton children, had something to do with Demarrio and the moody artist that painted the family portrait, then drove away in a black carriage, the choice color for a band of gypsies, known for kidnapping children to claim as their own.

"My question would be, why after five years, would this old gypsy bring those children back, knowing he could get caught and be sent to jail or even hanged, by 1700's law." Victoria felt there was another reason Zechariah felt close enough to the old gypsy, that he would sneak him to the plantation and ask Victoria Rose to hide him. "Did Zechariah return home to his parents after he had his friend settled down at Stanford Hall?"

"The records show, the four girls and the younger son, James, showed up on Easter morning, dressed neatly and clean." The small clerk scratched her head, trying to remember the old, yellowed report, dated 1787. "I recall it stated, Isabell Castleton fainted when she opened the front door after a knock was heard and recognized her children, even after five years missing. Zechariah Castleton showed up two days later."

"What kind of reason did the young people have to share with their shocked parents?" Samantha couldn't imagine having small children disappear, not heard of in five years, then suddenly show up, alive and obviously healthy and well taken care of."

"They just said a kind old gentleman found them and brought them home." Mary Francis pointed to adjacent room with big oak cabinets lined with drawers. "All our old history records are kept inside those drawers. Each wide drawer is dated, staring with the year, 1700, way before this town was built or even the old plantation, which is now the oldest landmark around." The petite woman smiled with admiration at the beautiful young sleuth. "It does my heart good to know someone as bright and creative as you, Victoria Elizabeth, will be taking over that grand old treasure from the last Victoria. It will certainly keep the path open to the reflections of the past mysteries, that have gone unsolved for centuries. It would have been a shame if you had turned down this unusual inheritance and that wealthy developer would have bought it and turned it into a suburban housing development with over two-hundred pricey homes, fancy condos, a swanky club house and a top of the line golf course designed after the famous golf course in Augusta, Georgia!"

"It will be a cold day in Death Valley, mid-summer, before I let that fancy-pants touch Stanford Hall Plantation!" If Victoria Elizabeth Stanford had any doubts about staying and accepting this inheritance, this revelation washed it away! This was her home now and she would see to it, that everything remained exactly the way it had always been. If she had to go out in the fields with the field workers to help bring the crops in, she would! All the unsolved mysteries were just waiting on her to solve and it had something to do with the old black vanity with the perfectly clear mirror. But the main reason Vicky chose to remain and make Stanford Hall her home forever, was the fact that Zechariah was waiting there, someplace, and she knew in her heart, it had something to do with the reflection in the old mirror!

"By that remark about it will be a cold day in Death Valley, mid-summer, before you let that fancy-pants touch Stanford Hall Plantation, I assume you have excepted your aunt's generous gift?" Jefferson Neuman had been standing in the open door listening to the conversation between the young detective, her friend, Samantha, and the museum clerk. "This calls for the big celebration I mentioned the day you arrived. A reception dinner in the grand dining room of the Castleton Hotel, complete with champagne, to toast the new owner of Stanford Hall!"

"Too bad my supportive staff cannot be on hand for such a gala celebration, Jefferson." Victoria secret inward thoughts were even more doubtful, as her eyes met those piercing blue eyes in the family portrait and she thought "My welcome celebration would be complete if you were here, Zechariah, my heart's desire."

"This place can certainly retrace the past, my dear." Jefferson lifted his elbow, a jesture for her to be escorted back to the hotel and prepare for the evening activities. "Perhaps you might return to look up the old records when you start all those investigations. As for your devoted staff, I am quite certain they are planning their own welcome celebration for you when you arrive to start your life at Stanford Hall. They are overjoyed that you spared not only their jobs, but their homes from Mr. Maxwell's racking ball."

"Maxwell? Mr. Fancy-pants hawk!" Vicky lifted her eyebrow, a sign of discuss. "Does this overbearing jackleg live around the area or hopefully, far-far away!"

"Mr. overbearing Marshall Maxwell lives in the Castleton mansion ever since he swept the 78-year-old maid, Delores Castleton, off her feet and propose marriage." Jefferson made a distasteful face, remembering how the well-dressed playboy started showing the older woman his gallantry and southern charm. "The gigolo knew all the right moves to fool this lonely wealthy woman to sign over everything she owned to him. In return, Marshall Maxwell promised to be a devoted, loving husband until one of them past away."

"So naturally, poor old lonely Delores believed this cagey

slick fox to guard her henhouse and married the man she thought would be true to her and they would live happily ever after!" Victoria had dealt with similar cases and because of her excellent detective skills, righted the wrong before the con artist could rob her client blind. "I can guess the outcome. Poor trusting Delores didn't see her 80th birthday and the grieving widower laughed all the way to the will reading! Too bad I had not got here in time to catch that jerk in action and throw his sorry rear in the slammer!"

"You don't suspect foul play in her untimely death, do you Miss Stanford?" Mary Francis Wagstaff had always felt there was something fishy with a woman as healthy as her friend, Delores Castleton, to up and get deathly ill after only two years of marriage. "Before Delores got infatuated over this younger man, she and I would hang out together a lot. We went for long walks almost every day, except for Holy Sabbath, an occasional luncheon with a group of ladies our age, all volunteers here at the Castleton Museum, we enjoyed playing bridge every Tuesdays and Thursdays, and when he showed up, everything just stopped."

"Was an autopsy perform on Mrs. Maxwell after her untimely death?" Victoria guessed the answer would be no, so Marshall Maxwell got away with his plan. "Let me guess and tell me if I'm wrong. The closes of kin would have to request and sign for an autopsy unless the police had evidence that foul play was involved. Mr. Maxwell, being the great con-artist and actor that he is, appeared to the entire town to be the grieving widower, thus fooling the authorities and medical examiner."

"You are very good, Miss Stanford!" the friendly clerk walked them to the front door. "It will be good for our small town to have such a sharp detective living here. You have probably already been informed about all the unsolved mysteries surrounding our small community, so feel free to visit the museum anytime." She passed the young sleuth her card. "Give me a call, day or night. I will open up for you!"

CHAPTER 12

Richard and Veronica Barrett, owners of the grand Castleton Hotel and descendance of Victoria Rose and Nelson Stanford, had invited all the important citizens of Castleton to the acceptance celebration, to meet and greet the new heir of Stanford Hall Plantation. The hotel's grand dining room was arrayed in white roses, both Victoria Rose and Victoria Bell's favorite flower. White lace tablecloths covered the big round tables, with sterling silver dinning ware spaced equally apart, partnering with English China and Tiffany crystal glass ware, sparkling under four great bronze chandeliers, lavished with fifty white candles each, flickering with glowing lights.

Victoria, her friend Samantha, and both Jefferson Neuman and Anthony Vincent, had been seated at the center front table, along with Richard and Veronica Barrett, the town mayor, George Underwood and his wife, Estell. Other distinguish guest included, Sheriff Harold Baker and his wife Pansy, Luther Simmons, editor and chief of the town's only newspaper, the Castleton daily, escorting his date, Bertha Temple, owner of Aunt Berta's Café. The town's two medical doctors, Doctor Ross Evans, a handsome bachelor, sought after by many of the eligible ladies in town, and Doctor Allen Houck and his wife Opal, a friendly outgoing family man in his mid-forties with a long list of satisfied patients. Allen & Ross Medical Center is located just before the dead-end of Carriage Wheel Street, just before the old hotel consumes the entire end. The Dentist, Ward and Paula Townsend, arrived with their famous son, actor Cole Townsend, handsome and unattached.

Most of Castleton's store owners were in attendance, along with the Castleton Ladies Club, responsible for looking after the old musicum, attending the gardens in the town park and flower boxes that line the carriage wheel cobblestone street. Mary Francis Wagstaff caught the attention of the beautifully dressed Victoria Elizabeth Stanford, and gave her a friendly little wave, proud as punch that she already had met the new owner of the great plantation the town's people felt so strongly about.

The mayor rose from the very head of the front center table and motioned for silence.

"Ladies and gentlemen" his eyes fell on the beautiful dark hair, blue eyed heir and smiled broadly. "and our most distinguish guest and new owner of the beautiful, majestic Stanford Hall Plantations, I have the honor of passing on the long-awaited key to Stanford Hall Manor, to Victoria Elizabeth Stanford on this 4th of May, 2019! Congratulations, Miss Stanford! On behalf of the town of Castleton, I am proud to welcome you into our small but loving community and to let you know how very glad we are that you chose to accept this one of the kind gift."

Mayor Underwood offered his hand for her to join him and receive the old, large gold key and the deed to the entire Plantation, hers for as long as she lives. The applause broke out as the well-dressed people rose to their feet and continued clapping until they heard one voice in the crown speak up, still seated and observing the townspeople overwhelming support of this stranger named Victoria Stanford. Giving the young woman one last smile, the group sit back down and turned to stare at the tall, dark man at the corner table, surrounded with men in identical uniforms. The mayor's eyebrow flew up, unaware that this citizen had accepted the last-minute invitation to this special celebration.

"Mr. Maxwell, we were under the assumption you would not be in attendance this evening." Not smiling, the mayor continued. "Do you wish to make a comment of your own in welcoming the new heir of Stanford Hall, sir?"

The new owner of Castleton Mansion stood up slowly, eyes fixed on Victoria Stanford as a clever smile formed on his lips. His steps to the front were deliberately slow, drawing the attention of everyone in the room, especially the ladies, who secretly swooned over his good looks and muscular physic. A true southern gentleman as he stopped in front of the only young woman in the room who was not impressed or fooled by his charming manners, and swept his arm out gracefully, then bowed.

As though the dark, moody man could read her thoughts, his smile grew even bigger, almost mocking the opposite serious look on her beautiful face, one of total mistrust.

"At last we meet, fair Victoria Elizabeth. May I say, seeing your beautiful face in person is even more breathtaking than it is in the large oil painting that hangs at this moment in my bedroom."

"I beg your pardon sir, you must be mistaking me for either my Aunt Victoria Bell or the first owner of Stanford Hall, Victoria Rose." Vicky managed to give the handsome man a smile. "It is probably the later, since the original owners of Castleton Mansion, Joshua and Isabell Castleton, built their home just a few years after Stanford Hall Manor was built."

"You seem to be familiar with the first Castleton family, Miss Stanford." A dark cloud appeared over his eyes when he stated, "Perhaps you know their eldest son, Zechariah." Another knowing smile fell on his face when he noticed her become rigid and focused on what he had just said. His next words came so softly, she felt they were meant just for her ears. "Yes, I thought as much. The painting belonged to Zechariah and it was his most cherished possession. Delores, my dear departed wife, told me all about young Zechariah's delirious obsession over the woman in that painting." Marshall Maxwell smiled, knowing he had won Victoria Elizabeth's full attention and could tell she wanted to hear more. "Perhaps, you might come have dinner with me next week, say Friday evening, around seven. I can send my car after you and make it easier to get through my guards at the gate."

"What makes you think I would want to come to your house for dinner, Mr. Maxwell, so soon after my arrival?" Victoria could not be fooled by this man's southern charm, but the need to know more about Zechariah, and if indeed, somehow, he had seen her in the future and commissioned a painting to be done, she would want to know. He was the eldest son, after all, and the mansion and grounds would be his at the death of his parents or if they just wished to hand it over to him, then remain there until their death. On the other hand, she did not wish to appear too anxious for information, so despite the need to hear more about the man she loved, she would push the temptation away until a future date and show restraint and control.

"Perhaps I can except your gracious invitation at a future date, Mr. Maxwell. Anything to do with the history of my new town is intriguing to me and you have been thoughtful in wanting to share what you know." Victoria put out her hand, intended for a friendly shake, but the gentleman smiled as he lifted her offered hand to his lips and gave it a kiss. "I trust you understanding, Mr. Maxwell."

"Marshall, my new friend, and I hope I may call you, Victoria." His smile seemed real. "I totally understand the sheer activity that one must do when you make a move and your move will be exceptionally larger than most people's, what with the size of Stanford Hall Manor, then there's all the buildings and fields, horses, sheep, and cattle, not to mention the large staff you must grow accustom to giving orders to."

"Marshall, I can assure you, I will not be giving my staff orders, for they already know far more than I how to run the house, the grounds, take care of the livestock, and see that the crops are harvested on time to sale at the market, wherever that place is." Vicky smiled when the crowd listening seemed pleased with her answer. "Just give me a little time to settle in, learn my way around a plantation way of life, then do what I do best."

"And what would that be, my dear Victoria?" Maxwell observed her closely and admired her strong will and determination.

"Start searching for clues, Marshall, facts that I can piece together, much like putting a jigsaw puzzle together, one clue at a time until I discover the right piece that sets off that spark inside my head and the unsolved mystery is finally brought to light, even after years of hiding in the darkness!"

"Vicky, you really put that handsome jerk in his place!" Samantha had climbed in her bed and called from the fancy hotel room. "I know you are dying to see that painting he claims is you, hanging in his bedroom, especially after what he said about Zechariah being obsess with it."

"It wasn't easy to turn down his dinner invitation after hearing that part." Victoria had filled her friend in on what this mysterious Maxwell whispered for her ears only, then she had spoke up so the people could hear their conversation.

"Vicky, if you're serious about accepting his dinner invitation, then I insist on tagging along. There is something about Marshall Maxwell I don't trust, and even though I know you feel the exact way as I do, and I can trust you to be sure he doesn't try to seduce you into believing he is falling in love with you, although that wouldn't be hard for any red-blooded American man to do. I would still feel better if I were there by your side." Samantha heard her best friend chuckle. "Go ahead and laugh, pal. I know what you're thinking, Vicky Stanford! I've known you far too many years not to see what's on that sharp mind of yours."

"Alright genus, tell me what you think I have in mind to do, concerning Casanova." Vicky fluffed up her pillow and glanced out at the darkness that had fallen over Castleton.

"You're thinking if Mr. Maxwell were to try something with me there with you, it would be you helping me out of trouble instead of the other way around, right?" Samantha twisted her mouth, a bad habit when she nervously waited a reply she didn't exactly wish to hear."

"Well friend, it does seem like I am always coming to your rescue where a good-looking man is involved." Vicky laughed softly when she heard her friend grumble gibberish. "Admit it pal, if Marshall Maxwell started hitting on you to distract you while at the same time the slick flirt was charming me, you would be the one falling into his net, not I. Does that sound about right, Sam?"

"So, I'm an easy target when it comes to a great looking man falling all over me." Samantha finally joined in laughing "But I think I can control my emotions when it comes to this gigolo, besides, I'm not the one who just inherited a billion-dollar plantation!"

"And I am, so you want to tag along when I go to Castleton

Mansion and save me from getting engaged to this black widower." Vicky had her own reasons for her friend coming with her. "You know, it might not be such a bad ideal for you to come with me when he gives me the dinner invitation. I'll just make up some good excuse for wanting you to come, while all along, I can use you as a decoy while I search out Zechariah's old room and see what clues, if any, he left behind for me to find."

"Then you think the painting could be of you? But, golly-gee, Vic, he lived way back in the 1700's! How could Zachariah have known about you so far ahead in the future, much less know enough about what you looked like to have your portrait painted?" Samantha had climbed from her bed and stood in Victoria's bedroom, totally perplexed. "Who could have painted such a perfect likeness of you, Vic? Marshall Maxwell seemed convinced it was you instead of the other Victoria's?"

"Don't think me crazy, Sam, but I believe Zechariah got the same mysterious painter who had painted that family portrait when Zechariah was twelve." Vicky took a sip of the cool spring water by her bedside. "And somehow, that old gypsy, Delmarrio, had something to do with Zechariah finding out about me, the woman he was destined to love for all eternity."

"That's almost creepy, finding out a man dead for over two-hundred-years was waiting for you, so you could unite and 'live' happily every after." Sam shivered, remembering how the ghost came to her friend in this very room the first night they were here. "Has Zechariah appeared to you anymore?"

"I'm afraid not." Vicky took a long breath and noticed the embers from the fire in the fireplace had drifted its smell into her room. "Maybe I will dream about him and hopefully find the secret of how to reach him from the past."

"The entire thing sounds like a science fiction movie, pal." Samantha waved sleepily, yawned and wondered back to her bedroom, mumbling before shutting the door that separated the two rooms. "Call me 'doubting Thomas' if you like, but I must see a ghost before I can truly believe in one."

"Sam, just go to bed!" Vicky laughed, then switched off the

bedside lamp, calling with her own yawn, "Good night, friend."

At twelve sharp, Victoria awoke to a rustling sound. She sat up and felt a rush of wind on her face, then the smell of flowers. To be exact, Vicky's favorite flower. Her mind was whirling around as she wondered, Am I only dreaming? Then why does it feel so real." The breeze gently blew across her face, bringing out the sweet aroma of the flowers. Being careful not to knock over the glass of spring water, the young detective reached over and switched on the lamp next to her. Victoria let out a gasp when she noticed the delicate white flowers surrounding her bed. She might have wondered who had placed so many flowers around her without once hearing them, but she need not guess who, for her heart already knew.

"Zechariah! I know you are here, darling. How…how did you know?"

"That Gardenias are your favorite flower!" The tall handsome man appeared beside her and reached for her hand. "Vicky, my dearest love, did I not tell you I know all that there is to know about you?"

"Yes, you did tell me that, Zechariah." She couldn't pull away from his incredible alluring blue eyes. "I only wished I knew as much about you, dear Zechariah. Like how you can appear for just a short time, then leave me desiring more of your time, or how you could so quickly replace the stale wood smoke from the fireplace with the smell of Gardenias, and so many at that? How you knew my face well enough to have a portrait done of me, back in the 1700's?"

"My beautiful Vicky is filled with questions, the perfect little detective!" Zechariah smiled for the first time, revealing perfect white teeth and a most handsome smile that would melt any heart. "Then let me answer your questions as briefly as possible, for my time in this place is limited." Once again, the mysterious handsome man nodded to the hourglass, sand sifting quickly away, causing Victoria to leap from the bed, quickly pulling her gown down over herself.

"Then, by all means, make it fast!" she noticed he had

extended his hand to her, so she gently laid hers in his strong one.

"I can only appear in this hotel room for one hour or less, due to the limited outside magic." Noticing her uncertain look, he smiled. "There's time later to explain everything in detail, just not here, my darling. Second, I opened the windows to release the stale smoky air, thus the cool breeze you felt, to make your gift of Gardenias more pleasant to your lovely senses. The amount, of Gardenias I brought was easy for a person of spirit. I merely wish them there and they appear. As for my very favorite possession, next to you of course, is the painting of you, my love. How, you must wait and learn. It is at the Stanford Hall Manor you will find all your answers, answers to many mysteries, unsolved for centuries, wondering spirits longing for closure."

"And is that what you wish from me, Zechariah, closure?" Victoria didn't want to find this man she loved only to lose him to Heaven. Yet, Victoria did not wish to be the one to hold back the one man she would always love and let him risk missing his only hope going home, never to wonder anymore. "Are you not tired of wondering around in this spirit world when you might be complete again in Heaven's Glory?"

"My dearest Vicky, the one thing that will make me complete again is having you! Holding you in my arms at last, kissing you as often as I desire to, giving you myself when God wills it for us! I love you, Vicky! I need you!" his eyes held hers. "Tell me Vicky, would you have me go to Heaven and never see me again until your death? Or, would you rather find me, become mine, so I can finally live again, like Grace!"

"Grace? The old woman who lives in the cabin where your friend, the gypsy, Delmarrio lived?" Vicky saw him look at the hourglass, then back down sadly. "You…you have to go now?"

"Vicky, just listen, hear me out before I vanish! The secret to the past is in your room at Stanford Hall. There you will see me again and learn how to use the magic it possesses within. Do not trust Maxwell! He is a thief as well as a murderer! You are far more beautiful than this evil man had imagined and he will long to have you, but you must not go dine with him until

I am released! I can protect you better then, my love! I must get possession of my home back from his dirty hands and reclaim your portrait and have it brought to Stanford Hall where it will be safe! There is a portrait of myself that used to hang next to yours, he has hidden it in the old attic, above my bedchamber. This too must be retrieved so we can once again unite the portraits." Zechariah pulled her into his arms and lowered his head for a kiss "I leave you, my dearest love, with a kiss! You will find me, I have faith in you, my darling!" He vanished.

CHAPTER 13

Victoria drove her rented Honda Accord through the tall gates of Stanford Hall, then up the tree lined driveway to the grand manor house. Instantly, she and her friend, Samantha noticed the welcoming line of workers, smiles on every face as she stepped from the car. Thornton Hancock stepped out from the end and gave the girls a gentlemen's bow before greeting them.

"Welcome home, Miss Victoria, Miss Samantha. The entire staff has come out to greet you and welcome you as well." He gave them his friendly smile. "The staff has put forth an extra attempt at sprucing up the old place. And you can be sure, it is a work of love and devotion, in appreciation for you excepting the last occupant's strict demands."

Victoria looked around at all the smiling faces, and saw trust and respect in each and every one watching her closely.

"I have had the privilege in meeting some of you already and look forward to knowing the names of those I haven't met yet." Vicky started at the end closest to her, Samantha following close behind. "Big Ed and Odessa, how good to see you both looking so fresh and young."

"Young at heart, Miss Victoria, that is the way we feel, ma'am, knowing we have a place to call home, thanks to you." Big Ed gave her a toothy grin while his heavy, cheerful wife stepped forward, smiling from ear to ear.

"Miss Victoria, it will be a delight to cook for the likes of a good Christian woman like you, just like my grandma did when she cooked for Victoria Rose." She chuckled. "Why, I could just give you a big hug for what you up and done for all of us!"

"That won't be necessary Odessa! I think Miss Victoria knows your deep affection for her." The butler tried to laugh. "You mustn't mess up her pretty clean blouse after sweating away in the hot kitchen."

"Nonsense Thornton!" Victoria smiled down at the

blushing woman. "I would like nothing more than a loving hug from such a dear devoted friend." She held out her arms to the smiling black woman, who in return, pulled her into her motherly embrace with one of the best hugs Vicky had ever received.

"Thank you, Miss Victoria! God bless you child!" The cook chuckled. "If ever Odessa can do anything for you, feel free to ask, anytime, anywhere!"

"I shall remember that, Odessa, and the same goes here, whenever you need me, just let me know." Vicky looked around at the tear-filled eyes. "That goes for all of you. We are family now. You need me and God knows, I need you." She smiled down at Imogene when she stepped up, tears in her big brown eyes.

"Miss Victoria, you made my mama feel special, you know, like a real friend. You are a stranger to us, yet, we already fall in love with you and your loving kindness. You do as the Lord says, you don't see black or white, you see us as a brother or a sister, like an equal, not servants."

"Imogene is right, Miss Victoria, you show us more love than even Victoria Rose or Victoria Bell showed their servants. They did not mind giving them orders and expecting them to carry them out or else, they would get punished in some small way, never whipped mind you." Charlotte Myers recalled stories passed down from her grandmother and grandfather.

"Victoria Rose ran Stanford Hall with an iron fist, but as you remember, this dear lady was against slavery and refused to put another soul in bondage. What she did believe in was hard work and she expected her paid servants to fulfill their commitment they had sworn when she bought their freedom, gave them work and a home, with plenty of food on their tables." Reginal Myers lifted her hand to kiss. "My wife, Charlotte and I are honored to carry on the Stanford tradition and do the best we can at our jobs."

"Thank you, Reginal, Charlotte." Vicky already felt a sense of belonging and knew, even though she would miss Natchez and her parents, dreadfully, she would feel at home here among these loving caring people, who already called Stanford Hall, home.

After meeting the rest of the staff, Thornton dismissed them to return to their duties, and had two of the footman to retrieve the girl's luggage and carry it up to their rooms, Samantha on the second floor, west wing suite, and Victoria on the third floor, in Victoria's Bell's rooms. Vicky waited until Jeremy Taylor and John Phillips removed the luggage and walked inside before she turned to the butler.

"Thornton, did you arrange for this rental to be driven back to New Orleans or must I take it back. That is a hundred miles away from Castleton, then another hundred back." Vicky looked over at her friend who had said her name.

"Vic, you did mention the need to buy a new car. I didn't see a car dealer in Castleton, so I guess New Orleans is probably your best bet."

"Yes, I know you're right, Sam. I cannot walk into town every time I need to go and I can't see riding a horse to town." Vicky laughed. "Maybe little Johnny Pennywise will loan me his bike."

"Yes ma'am, if'in you be needing it!" Vicky looked down to see the freckle face boy smiling up, revealing his missing front teeth.

"Johnny Pennywise, I was wondering where you were." Vicky laughed and rubbed a hand through his blonde curls. "Where have you been hiding?"

"I ain't been hiding none, Miss Victoria. I've been upstairs talking to Miss Victoria Bell about you coming here and my meeting up with you and Sam, over yonder!" His eyes grew big as he added. "She seemed real interested in what I was telling her. She even gave me this hard stick of peppermint, like the young'uns use to eat as a special treat for being good, she said."

"Boy, how many times have I told you to stop playing in the house, especially Miss Victoria's rooms!" The butler turned the boy around to face him. "Up until now, you have only been pretending to speak to that Painting and declare it speaks back, but now, you say she gave you that candy! It is obvious Johnny, you stole that piece of candy from that room, so just admit it!"

"I cannot admit to stealing something I did not take, Mr. Thornton! I told the God's honest truth, ma'am!" the young boy pulled at Victoria's arm. "Miss Victoria Bell has been asking lots of questions about you! Wanting to know if'in you gonna abide by her demands! She is worried about your liking the place for greedy reasons, miss. I up and told her, what a great lady you are and that you love everyone here just like we're all kin!"

"Johnny, how did Victoria Bell give you that peppermint stick?" Vicky could tell the boy was telling the truth, even if the proper butler couldn't tell.

"She used her magic, Miss Victoria. She said I had been a good boy and deserved a sweet treat, then she held out her hand. First, I swear there was nothing there, just an empty hand, then she smiled and the candy just appeared, like magic!"

"Like magic?" Vicky knew the butler wouldn't believe the boy and continue to scold him, when he yanked him back around.

"Johnny, enough with the lies! I am asking you right now to tell the truth!" The butler faced Victoria when she said his name.

"Thornton, he is only a child. To be perfectly honest, I believe him." Vicky could see his shock. "Please, go up and check on our luggage, let me handle this. Come back when you're finished."

"Very well, Miss Victoria, whatever you think is best." The butler frowned at the smiling boy, whose attention was back on the pretty young woman.

"Vic, do you really believe Johnny talked to Victoria Bell's ghost?" Samantha watched the irate butler walk away.

"Sam, do you remember what I told you this morning at breakfast, about Zechariah coming again last night, this time bringing me Gardenias?" Vicky waited for her friend to shake her head, then continued. "I ask him how he managed to get so many flowers in my room and he said, that was very easy for a spirit, they would just think it and whatever they wanted appeared, like magic!"

Sam stared at the small boy, then at her friend. "Then he is telling the truth."

"I knew you believed in ghost and spirits, Miss Victoria."

The small boy glanced over at Samantha. "You too Miss Sam, cause, I saw you both looking at those children's spirit, only they were still alive when they went missing. We were looking at holograms of the past, at least that's what they were until the day you stopped to watched them."

"What do you mean, Johnny? Why was it different from all the other times you slipped away to watch them?" Vicky smiled when he looked surprised for her knowing about him slipping away to watch the ghostly vision of the children.

"Miss Victoria, my mama would have my hide if'in she knew I rode my bike down Carriage Wheel Road, but honest Ab, there ain't hardly ever a single vehicle on that road!" The young rascal stared helplessly at the two grown women, eyes round as saucers. "Please ma'am, you won't be telling her, will you?"

"Johnny, if you can promise to stop riding your bicycle on that highway, busy or not, it's no place for a little boy, especially out there alone." She gave him a wink. "If I ever have the time to return and witness that hologram again, I'll take you with me. Is that a deal?"

"That's mighty kind and thoughtful, Miss Victoria, but we would just be wasting our time. Them young'uns just up and stop coming, after master Zechariah stopped and stared at you! They stopped appearing after the day you came and that's because things turned out different."

"What was different that time, Johnny?" Samantha looked over at her friend and raised her shoulders in confusion. "How could a hologram suddenly change, causing the kids to just vanish."

"The same way they just vanished back in 1782, the year they went missing. They didn't return until Easter morning, 1787." Vicky was impressed with the six-year-olds quick memory of events and dates, so she had a hunch he would know how they disappeared, since he knew they stopped coming out of the forest and going back in, on the day her and Sam had arrived to Castleton.

"Johnny, what did you see different on the day Sam and I drove down Carriage Wheel Road, slowed down for a herd of pigs, then saw the six children coming from the woods to our right."

"They would come out and look across the road, dirt back in their day. I wasn't sure what they were looking at for the longest time, cause, I couldn't see the hidden black carriage camped in a grove of trees." Johnny noticed the two girls look knowingly at one another, never knowing they were assuming it was the mysterious artist that painted the family portrait. "Before, Zechariah, the oldest, would usher the other kids back quietly into the cover of the woods, but this time, he stopped and saw you! Yes ma'am, that boy's spirit was smitten with you, Miss Victoria, I could see it in his eyes. He watched you for the longest time, and you seem to be staring back at those serious eyes of his. The youngest girl peeked out to find her big brother and he turned to see her, then went to her and disappeared." Johnny knew the girls remembered everything, up to that point, but it was what happened after they left. "You sat there for a while, as though you were deep in thought, maybe trying to figure out how you knew that twelve-year-old boy, then you saw him simply disappear, causing more confusion. Right?"

"Yes Johnny, I was very perplexed." Vicky wanted to finish this conversation before the butler returned, so she took a seat on the wide step and motioned for Johnny to sit. "What happen after we drove away, Johnny?"

"Zechariah re-appeared and watched until you drove out of sight. He was so transfixed on you, he never saw the man in black slipped up behind him, then gripped his shoulder." Johnny shook his head. "This is the puzzling thing, Miss Victoria, Zechariah didn't try to run or get away, he acted like he like the man as he talked, pointing occasionally toward the woods. The man in black shook his head in agreement, walked back across the road as Zechariah brought his brother and sisters out, and took them across the road. That's when I saw the big black carriage with red drapes hanging down the back, pull out on the road and drive away, until it faded and disappeared!"

Vicky glanced back at the door to make sure Thornton

hadn't returned and was waiting on her. "Johnny, how, do you get Victoria Bell to come to you? Does she just appear on her own?"

"Oh, no ma'am! I know the secret to the past!" the boy smiled from ear to ear. "I've seen Victoria Rose and Nelson, her book-worm husband. I've even seen Zechariah, all grown up, dressed in black nickers and a buffy sleeve white shirt. He had on a shiny pair of boots that went clear up to his knees and talked to me about all his adventures, what with fighting and chich! I reckon he's my biggest hero!"

"Johnny, can you tell me where I can find the secret of the past? It can be our very own secret, yours, Sam's and mine!" Vicky smiled hopefully. "What do you say friend?"

"Oh, gosh, Miss Victoria, I'd like nothing more than to tell you how you can find them spirts, but they done up and made me promise I wouldn't tell a living soul!" his sad eyes relayed he was telling the truth. "But the spirits really won't you to find the secret, Miss Victoria, but they said you had to find it own your own, same as Madam Victoria Rose and Miss Victoria Bell! They say you being knowledgeable about solving mysteries is the blessing they have been longing for, waiting for!" Johnny moved up as close as he could, then whispered. "I can tell you this much, Miss Victoria, the secret to the past is in your bedchamber. It sorta stands out!" About that time the third-floor window flew open in Victoria's bedchamber, causing the white curtains to float out and get caught up in a billowy motion. "Whoops, I guess I said too much, Miss Victoria! Victoria Bell just took away my peppermint stick!"

Vicky stood up to stare at the open window, then noticed movement. Charlotte Myers poked her head out and waved.

"I hope I didn't startle you ma'am. I thought the room could use a bit of airing out since it hasn't been occupied for quite a while."

"We're find, Charlotte, I'll be up soon." Vicky glanced down at the relieved boy, whose attention was still on the window. His eyes grew big and he hopped up.

"I best be going home now, Miss Victoria. Miss Victoria Bell was just giving me the evil eye right up there in that window. She probably willed Miss Charlotte to open it, knowing the curtains would billow out and draw my attention."

Vicky looked in his hand and saw the candy was indeed missing, then casually looked up, hoping to catch a glimpse of the ghost and saw nothing.

"We wouldn't want your mama to wonder where you are, little friend. Run along home then and I will see that you get that candy stick back, since it was me you were helping when my aunt grew upset. Is that a deal, Johnny?"

His eyes lit up. "Yes ma'am! Thank you!" he started walking down the path as Victoria and Samantha stood up and started up the steps, only to stop at the sound of Johnny calling Vicky's name. She turned to see him running back, glancing up at the empty window.

"Did you forget something, Johnny?" Vicky could tell there was still something on the young boy's mind.

"I just wanted to tell you how pretty your long black hair is hanging down your back. The other Victoria's always wear their hair up in a baseball." Vicky and Sam tried not to laugh as Vicky thanked him. "I bet you like to brush your beautiful hair, Miss Victoria. That old black vanity has a really swell mirror. You can see really good in it! Why its so clear, I can count every single one of my freckles when I look in there!"

"Can you?" Vicky reached down at patted the blonde curls. "Thank you, Johnny, I shall brush my hair out there tonight."

Johnny gave her a big smile, then race off down the path, as Samantha scratched her head.

"Vic, what the heck just happened there? Did I miss something?"

"Our little friend just gave me a clue that will help me find the secret of the past!" Victoria walked up the steps smiling "I will know tonight when I brush my hair."

"When you brush...your hair?" Sam looked as though a light bulb just flashed off in her mind as she pulled her friend around. "The old vanity mirror! Somehow, the secret lies inside that very clear old mirror, but how?"

"I shall soon find out, pal, even if I have to stay up the entire night!"

CHAPTER 14

"You may go now Charlotte. I've got everything I need." Vicky smiled as she took a seat at the old mirror. "Tell Reginald I would like to check out the property tomorrow morning, right after breakfast."

"Yes, Miss Victoria. Enjoy your first night in your new home. I hope you like peace and quiet. Once everyone turns in for the night, you hardly hear a squeak, except maybe the old rafters moaning and groaning if the winds decides to blow." Charlotte walked over and opened the door. "If you ever change your mind and need me to sleep in the maid's quarters, adjacent to yours, just let me know."

"I'm a big girl, Charlotte and I think your husband would prefer your staying with him." Vicky smiled, hoping the personal maid would leave so she could start investigating the old mirror. "Thank you for your sweet offer and have a goodnight."

"Very well, Miss Victoria, but if you have a change of mind, Reginal will understand." she smiled. "After all, it is my position and I really enjoy being the one to personally look after you. Goodnight." Charlotte closed the door behind her as Victoria slipped off the stool and walked over to check down the hall. She smiled when she found everything quiet and the hallway empty. Vicky silently closed the door and locked it, just in case her personal maid was sent back up, by the very proper butler, Mr. Hancock.

"There! Now hopefully they will respect my privacy, should they have another key." Victoria walked back to the old vanity and sat down slowly, her eyes scanning the circumference of the mirror's frame. "Now to find the secret." Sliding her fingers slowly around the frame, she found the wood smooth, no hidden buttons or secret opening. Propping up on her elbows, she stared at her reflection. "Think Vicky! You're the clever detective! If little Johnny can find the secret, this should be a cinch for detective Stanford.

Her attention wondered to the room's refection behind her. The mirror took in the marble fireplace with the ornate mantle. An old crystal vase displayed a dozen fresh white roses, Victoria Rose and Victoria Bell's favorite flower. Victoria smiled, as she remembered all the sweet-smelling Gardenia's in the hotel room and Zechariah smiling down at her.

"Oh, I have just got to find the secret to the past! Zechariah is there and he is waiting for me to bring him out!" her eyes went up to the reflection of the giant portrait of Victoria Bell, wearing a beautiful dress with a matching emerald green neckless and earrings. Her face was somber, yet very attractive and she looked as though she was focused on something, or someone, when the artist was painting her portrait.

"Aunt Victoria, it appears your mind was on someone across the room from you while the artist's brushes captured your likeness." Victoria smiled, as she pictured a handsome suitor keeping her occupied. "Who was your handsome beau, Victoria Bell Stanford?"

"Zechariah Castleton, at least I had hoped to be his Victoria!" the voice caused Victoria to twirled around, thinking Samantha had slipped in her room and was playing a joke on her.

"Sam, just come out from hiding! That was not funny!"

"Your friend Samantha is down in her guest room, reading a book in bed." The vision became clear and Vicky knew she was looking at her distance Aunt Victoria. "This place, it has already made its way into your heart, hasn't it, my child?"

"Yes, Aunt Victoria. I already feel like I belong here." Vicky couldn't get over how alive the spirit appeared. "It truly feels like home."

"The painting of me, you could see I was looking at someone, someone I loved?" Victoria Bell kept a serious face, and Vicky suddenly wondered if her Aunt really brought her here to harass her because Zechariah was in love with her instead of Aunt Victoria, herself. "Child, do not fret, thinking I have brought you here to torment for stealing away my dearest love."

"You think I stole Zechariah from you, dear aunt?" Vicky stood up. "How could I? I only met him four nights ago, where he appeared declaring his love for me."

"Yet, you confessed your love to him, barely knowing him for more than fifty-eight minutes, did you not?"

"You seem to know a lot about our meeting, Aunt Victoria, not to mention knowing my friend, Sam was in her second-floor bedroom, reading a book. The fact is, you also knew what I was thinking about the possibility of you bringing me here because of your jealousy with Zechariah loving me. Then you reassured me you did not give me Stanford Hall just to haunt me, but because of my detective skills." Vicky knew she had uncovered another truth when the well-dressed ghost shook her head in wonder.

"I am very impressed with your gift for learning the truth and not completely in the same way as most detectives. Not only can you smoke out clues and piece them together, but you have a special gift of vision, an understanding of things that cannot be explained." Victoria Bell gave the young woman a beautiful smile. "First, I will tell you about a spirit's gifts. With practice, we can read thoughts, conjure up items, such as the peppermint stick candy, or beautiful flowers." The elegant lady gave her niece a wink. Our invisible spirit can roam quickly from room to room, so it was easy to check in on your friend when you thought I was her, then return back here in a moment's thought."

"That answers those questions, so I will answer yours. I do love Zechariah, with all my heart, Aunt Victoria, but I cannot explain why! Why I fell so deeply in love with a man I hardly know anything about! A man who has been dead for over two-hundred-years!" Vicky reached out and touched the magic mirror. "Zechariah is in that mirror. Somewhere in the past and he expects me to find the secret and bring him back!"

"Dearest child, you have already found the secret to bring his spirit back, same as you did mine, just now."

"I brought you back? I just assumed you always hung around your home, loving it so much, you never wanted to go with the light when it was ready to take you to heaven."

Joan Byrd

Victoria Bell laughed. "You assumed I was a permanent resident ghost, that haunts the halls of the old manor, scaring anyone who dares to visit. I stayed my dear to help Zechariah find you and to share what knowledge I can, with you, in finding the channel of life, the most sacred passage for a spirit to pass through. The secret lies within the mirror and has been only found one time. The old gypsy has giving Zechariah the first stage, the passage to go inside the channel, but only his true love, you, my dear, can get him through." Vicky thought she noticed the spirit tremble with uncertain fear. "Once Zechariah enters the channel of life, he can never escape and he will be trapped inside for all eternity if you cannot find the secret of life!"

"Dear Aunt, that is a heavy burden to lay upon me!" Vicky nervously sat back down. "I would die if I could not find the secret and rescue my dearest Zechariah from certain wondering!" she looked at her reflection and saw she had gone white with anxiety and fear. "Victoria Bell, you said I found the secret to get your spirit here. Did I return to the 1800's or early 1900's?"

"Victoria Elizabeth, take another look around this room and tell me what has changed. Is everything the same way you found it when you arrive in your room today?" Vicky's aunt smiled as her niece stood up and looked around

"Of course, I remember now, there were two flower vases on the mantel before with red roses. Now there is one large crystal vase with one dozen white roses. The lamps are no longer electric, they are burning with oil and the family photo of me, with my parents, is no longer sitting up there either." Vicky walked over to her bedside table and picked up the hardcover book, then glanced up at her aunt. "Romeo and Juliet, by William Shakespeare! A lovely story, but I never liked the ending, letting that beautiful young couple die as soon as they found each other." She picked up an amber trinket box and smiled. "The 1800's would not have an alarm clock or a paper back novel by my favorite author, Joan Byrd. I hope my copy of The Good Seed-The Bad Seed reappears so I can finish reading it!" Vicky smiled, happy to know she had actually

96

found her aunt and turned back the time. "Did I guess it, 1800's?"

"Now that you have discovered that fact, child, what does your detective skills tell you was the solution to finding me?" The spirit rested her hand on the mantel and breathed in the fragrance of the sweet smelling roses.

"The secret to finding the past is to look into the magic mirror at the images behind you, then speak the person's full name and if you're wise to the truth, you will soon notice the reflections of the past appear in the mirror. The one that you have summons will become visible!"

"Victoria Elizabeth, it does my heart good, to see everything I have heard and witness for myself, is true. Your quick detective skills are second to none!" Victoria Bell laughed cheerfully, then reached out, in an attempt to give her niece a hug, only to have her arms pass right through her. "I keep forgetting I cannot touch a person and actually feel them, I seem so alive when I am called. I can conjure up material things, but a spirit can't make contact with a living person, only another dead soul."

"Then, how can Zechariah make contact with a living person, Aunt Victoria. I know I was not dreaming of those strong arms wrapped around me or his kisses, burning on my lips."

"He kissed you?" Victoria Bell's thoughts drifted back to the night she stayed in the same hotel room as her niece and felt Zechariah kiss her goodbye after telling her she wasn't the one he had been searching for. Longing to feel his kiss one more time, the ghostly spirit touched her lips and closed her eyes.

"Sweet child, Zechariah is different. Like I told you, he has been touched by the magic of Delmarrio, the gypsy, who loved that boy like his own. You must ask Zechariah why he is different than most all spirits. This is a thing that can only be discussed between two lovers, you and Zechariah."

"Lovers?" Vicky felt sorrowful for her dear aunt's heartache and yet the gracious lady accepted the fact that her niece was Zechariah's chosen love. "You speak the word as though we have been intimate, with this new-found love. I can assure you, Aunt Victoria, we have gone no future than hugs and kisses!

"Relax yourself, sweet innocent girl, I am aware of your purity, almost unheard of in this modern world you live in. It was our custom to speak the word, lovers, far different than this risqué generation you live in, where to be lovers you bed one another, married or not. In our day, the word meant two people, madly in love, longing to be together throughout eternity. The great play writer, William Shakespeare, said it best when he called two people so deeply in love they would risk everything just to be together. Star-cross lovers, much like you and Zechariah, born under the same stars but decades apart."

"Aunt Victoria, the fact is, we were born decades apart and yet both you and Zechariah know everything about me?" Vicky looked at her reflection in the mirror, and noticed she still wore her white gown and not a Victorian gown from the 1800's. The spirit smiled, reading her thoughts.

"You wear your same gown because you did not choose to personally go back to the past. To look like I dress, you must first request it."

"Mum! From the mirror!" Vicky smiled at her aunt as she thought. "Perhaps, I could try a rhyme, like the wicked queen in Snow White!"

"What is a snow white and why would a nice girl like you wish to summon a request like an evil queen?" Victoria Bell was perplexed over her niece's unusual words."

"It's your time to relax, dear aunt, I speak about a make-believe queen, written in a children's book about a young woman named Snow White. The old queen would stand in front of her mirror and repeat the same words to her magic mirror and she would be please with its answer, until the beautiful innocent Snow White came along and the mirror chose her as the fairest one of all."

"You're the detective, Victoria. Are you willing to take a chance and see if it works?" Victoria Bell chuckled from the very ideal of saying a rhyme."

"Then I shall see what will happen if I'm clever enough to

give the mirror the right words." Vicky faced the old mirror and said clearly "Mirror, mirror, sweet and clear, help me appear just like the year!" in an instant, Vicky's gown was changed to a high-neck lace long white gown. She twirled around laughing along with her Aunt Victoria.

"You did it! The rhyme worked and now to get you back to 2019, unless you intend to call up Zechariah tonight." Victoria Bell checked the old clock. It was almost twelve. "It grows late, perhaps tomorrow night. We need to get you back to your time, so you can rest. Mirror, reverse the time back!" Victoria Bell blew Vicky a kiss, then disappeared.

"I know you were just thinking about my beauty sleep, Aunt Victoria, but I need to see Zechariah now. I have waited far too long. I need to make sure he is alright."

Vicky looked into the mirror and noticed the reflection had gone back to 2019. She took a deep breath before speaking.

"Magic mirror from which I see, bring the past back to me. Zechariah Castleton." Victoria held her breath, hoping that was enough of his name. She did not know his middle name, so she kept her fingers crossed in her lap.

A minute past by and nothing seemed to change. Tears began to fill her blue eyes, then through the misty haze, she saw a different portrait hanging over the mantle. The portrait of another woman, obviously wealthy by the red velvet dress lined with several diamonds, matching the very large diamond choker that hung gracefully around her neck. The same portrait that now hung in one of the parlors.

Victoria knew it was the first owner of Stanford Hall, Victoria Rose, but she dared not say her name, not tonight. It was Zechariah she wanted to see. Zechariah, she had waited up to kiss. Would the mirror respond once again to her clever words?"

"Magic mirror, wise and true, bring the one I love dearly through." Victoria had been searching the reflection behind her and jumped when she felt a hand touch her shoulder.

"My darling, the magic mirror finds you very charming and says you remind him of the lad that found him, lying in a London dump many years ago, gathered him up, wrapped him inside a worn blanket, carried the dirty mirror home, then using

99

his gift of carpentry, built him this beautiful vanity to attach it to, then painted it a rich black." Victoria looked up into Zechariah's alluring blue eyes and smiled.

"The mirror told you all this?" she gave him an unsure look, wondering if he were joking with her because of her corny rhymes.

"On the contrary, fair Victoria. Your choice of words in rhyme, have greatly please the old mirror and he is very delighted that you know about the Snow White legend." Once again Zechariah knew he had surprised her by his knowledge of her words to her aunt, only moments before. "Dearest darling, this is no ordinary mirror, as you might have guessed by now. It not only goes back to the past, as it has now, but it can also go up, to the future, were my friend, Delmarrio introduced me to the woman I was destined to love and marry, one day. You my adorable Victoria Elizabeth."

"So, this is how you and Aunt Victoria knew so much about me." Vicky stood up and walked over to the mantle, smiling to herself when Zechariah followed close behind. "It appears you still know far more about me than I do about your past life."

"Vicky, there will be plenty of time for learning about me. Mostly through old diaries, hidden here and at Castleton Mansion. But for the moments we spend together, are precious and should not be wasted on old history. We must speak of marriage and a life together, my deepest love."

"Marriage and a life together sound like a beautiful dream, my dearest Zechariah, but must we just forget that you are a spirit?" Victoria knew her heart belonged to Zechariah, but he had been dead for over two-hundred-years. How could one living, really marry a ghost? It sounded more like a movie to Victoria than reality.

"Darling, what exactly is a movie? Some new title for a person who transfers one's possessions from one place to another?" Zechariah looked so innocent with his statement, Victoria laughed brightly "What, pray tell, is so funny, my love? Did I just ask a fool's question?"

Victoria took around the man she loved more than life and gave him a reassuring hug.

"Zechariah, you had no way of knowing what a movie is, since they weren't around in the 1700's or the 1800's, for that matter. They were long after the first photograph." Once again, she saw confusion fill his handsome face. "Woops! No cameras in your lifetime either. Just an artist, an easel, paints, and brushes, to create a portrait."

"So, if movies aren't movers, then what are they?" Zechariah held her lovingly in his arms, enjoying the lessons of the future she was teaching him.

"Well, it started with a camera which takes a picture of a person, first on a special photo plate then transferred to paper, creating a perfect image of the one sitting for the picture. After years of improving the camera, someone had the incredible ideal to connect a group of photos together, making small movements in their arms and hands, or even their legs, to give the effect of dancing when the strip of pictures rotated quickly around." Vicky smiled when the handsome man, moved his head in a positive motion., thrust out his hand and moved his finger slowly up, counting one, two, three, four five and six.

"So, it looked something like that? Six different photos which appeared to move! Movies!"

Victoria laughed happily, glad he caught on so quickly. "Exactly! Over the years they kept improving on their technique and the stereo phonograph was invented to play music and the silent movies, called films, went high tech to speaking, singing, you name it! Now with surround sound, action movies come to life almost, as canons fire off in the war for independence are shown, or soldiers, marching across battle fields, guns loudly firing, fake bullets, of course, loud blast from enemy canon fire, airplanes and battleships, loudly firing from other wars and even fake battles like in Star Wars!"

"I can see I've got a lot to learn, Vicky." Zechariah crinkled his forehead. "I think I was pretty blessed to have been born in the 1700's instead of the 1900's! Life seems so much simpler then, than those things you have been describing. My poor baby. Maybe, you had rather go back to my era to live a life with me. Things were never always perfect, but it would be different with you in my life."

"Go back and have you die so soon, leaving me mourning in a strange place, with strangers I do not know?" Vicky shook her head. "My life is now, Zechariah! The people I love and know live in this era. I could never leave my parents or Sam in the twenty-first century! The only thing missing is you, my darling Zechariah! Those things I spoke of do not concern my life and I find things pretty peaceful most of the time!" Victoria noticed a slight smile fall on his handsome face. "Besides, I'm pretty close to living in your era now, Zechariah. Never having the chance to change Stanford Hall from the past, I am, pretty much there now!"

"Sweet Victoria, you brighten my world, dearest one." Zechariah grabbed her in a warm embrace. "I would never ask you to give up all you know to come back to a time of candles and wood stoves, bitter feuds over the rights for freedom from England's King William and those whose sympathies lay with the homeland. Those of us who fault for liberty were traitors to his royal majesty and although I was quite small during the great battle, my father and uncles fought and served in Independence Hall and helped sign the Declaration of Independence in Boston, where we lived before moving to what is now Louisiana, purchased by Thomas Jefferson from the French."

"So, your family lived in Boston before moving here in 1773, when you were three and at age six, the war was won and this became a new nation, the United States of America, replacing the American Colonies." Victoria always enjoyed learning History and now that she knew someone who actually lived this History, she was intrigued and wanted to know more about the man she loved. "I haven't had time yet to search out the diaries of both Victoria's, but I hear they are loaded with great clues to past mysteries and now, I find out by you, my darling, that they tell of your life as well. It is a must that I find these tell-all books, well-hidden over these many years. But, I am a good detective, sir, and I will find them! It's just a matter of deduction and a little investigating, both of which I'm great at!"

"I have no doubt, dearest one." Zechariah kissed her

tenderly, then smiled. "I would wager my girl will seek out and discover said writings before the morrow is out!" he noticed Victoria's eyes growing weary, then heard the old mantle clock gonged one a.m. "My girl is tired after her long day. I confess I forget sometimes a live soul can grow tired and sleepy, as I once did when I roamed these forest and valleys." Zechariah kissed her one lengthy time, then helped her to bed. "Permit me to return to the mirror."

"You are saying goodbye, Zechariah? I do not wish for you to leave my side." Vicky clutched his hand tightly. "Could not you stay with me, now that you are out and free."

"This is but temporary, dearest Vicky. Soon I will be alive with you forever." With that, she fell asleep.

CHAPTER 15

Odessa had prepared a big breakfast of country ham and scrambled eggs for Victoria and Samantha, to start their day on the plantation. Sending word down with Charlotte that she would be eating an early breakfast before exploring the grounds with Reginald Myers around nine, the cheerful cook had everything prepared and the table set in the bright breakfast room for the two friends when they came down.

"Mum, Odessa, this smells wonderful!" Samantha licked her lips when she sampled the fresh squeeze orange juice before taking her seat.

"My cooking taste pretty wonderful too, Miss Samantha!" the friendly black woman gave a happy chuckle. "I learned from my mama how to cook country ham tender. Most people fry it a little tough, but not Odessa, no ma'am." She gave Victoria a toothy grin. "Enjoy your hearty breakfast, Miss Victoria, cause, you ladies got your day cut out for you, what with riding all around these grounds in Mr. Myers' carriage." She started for the kitchen and called back. "You best be taking soft pillows to sit on, to help cushion them bumps! Yes ma'am, nice big pillows!"

The friends watched the cheerful cook disappear through the big door, then looked at each other and laughed.

"What a delightful person!" Victoria wiped her watery eyes and took a bite of the extra tender ham. "And a wonderful cook to boot!"

"I take it that you are pleased with your cook, Miss Victoria?" Mr. Hancock stepped into the bright room and gave a polite bow. "I hope you find all your staff to your liking. We want your life here to be a pleasant one." His attention went to Samantha, eating her breakfast hungrily while listening to the butler. "And you, Miss Samantha, do you intend to remain here at Stanford Hall indefinitely, or will you be returning to Natchez, Mississippi in the near future?"

"Thornton, Samantha is more than just a friend to me. She is truly my heart sister as well as my girl Friday." Vicky didn't care for this man's attitude toward her best friend and the last thing she wanted was to hurt Sam's feelings or to lose her helper. Sherlock had his Watson and she had her Brandon. "To be perfectly frank with you, Thornton, we have not discussed her wishes for staying or going back home. As for my wishes, I would like nothing more than have my friend remain right here with me forever. As far as I'm concern, this home is plenty big enough for all my family and friends, if they choose to move here. But, for now, if she wants to stay indefinitely, my home is her home. Are we clear on that, Thornton?"

"I beg your pardon ma'am, I never meant to insinuate your friend was not welcome at Stanford Hall. I was merely inquiring about the girls plans for remaining or going." The butler forced a smile. "I was simply asking so we would know whether to keep her in the guest room or have her move into a more suitable permanent suite, much larger, with a sitting room, private bath, and a much larger wardrobe to store her clothing."

"What will it be, Sam? Do you wish to remain my guest or be a part of this big family, retaining your position as my assistant?" Vicky drank down the great fresh brewed coffee, only to have her cup refilled by Imogene Brown, Odessa's daughter and helper. Noticing she had used cream before, the cheerful servant held up the silver creamer.

"More cream, miss?"

"Yes, thank you, Imogene." Vicky waited for her to pour a small amount into her coffee, then added. "Tell you mama the breakfast was excellent as was her beautiful daughter's gracious service."

"Why, thank you Miss Victoria! It's going to be a pleasure serving you, ma'am." She heard the butler grunt and turned and raced off to the kitchen.

"My apologies for the interruption, Miss Samantha, but what will it be, guest room, or a permanent suite of rooms?" the butler noticed the groundskeeper stepped inside the entrance hall, to wait for his tour of the plantation grounds.

"Would you care for more time to decide, my dear? I'm sure this is a big decision to make, to pull up your roots, leave everything you know behind and move to an unfamiliar place with a lot of strangers."

"Poppycock! Hardly strangers now, Thornton, old fellow!" Sam laughed. "Vicky is here, so this is where I wish to be as well! You cannot expect me to walk away and leave my very best friend! Besides, she needs me as much as I need her! Have you ever heard of a great detective without their sidekick, their goffer, their righthand girl Friday!" Samantha heard her friend start laughing when the stiff butler raised his eyebrows in sequence with his shoulders.

"Relax Thornton, Sam just said she was staying on permanently, so you may have her things moved to her new rooms just as soon as she goes after her pillow."

"Her…pillow, miss?" Thornton looked confused.

"Just a little advice taken when riding around on a carriage for an extended period, Thornton." Victoria stood up and walked through the entrance hall and smiled at Reginal, standing, hat in hand and a big smile spread on his face.

"Reginal, I have been told, a soft pillow was something I might need to bring along for the outing."

"That won't be necessary Miss Victoria. I have seen that a carriage pillow has been installed for you ladies. So, if you're ready to start, we have a lot of ground to cover."

"Very well, Reginal. Sam, forget the pillow. It appears the carriage has been equipped with one already." Vicky noticed her friend moving nervously and knew what that meant, so she patted the patient man's shoulder. "Just permit us to attend to one little necessity before departing. One tall glass of fresh squeeze orange juice and two hefty cups of great coffee can get troubling for a lady when there are no restrooms available on the tour."

The head groundskeeper chuckled loudly and tilted his hat, like a true gentleman. "Please, by all means ladies. Be excused and take all the time necessary. I'll be waiting just outside the front door by the horses and carriage." He started to walk away, then turned with his own suggestion. "A bonnet is advisable though, for getting off and walking around when needed."

"We're fresh out of bonnets, Reginal, but we both have caps for walking." Vicky smiled at his blushing. "It shall not take long and thanks for the tip."

The butler and groundskeeper exchanged serious faces before the later made his way out the door without a single word spoken. Thornton Hancock walked over to the closed door to wait for the new owner to come down, making a low grunt.

"That pompous, overrated groundskeeper! You would think he has the highest-ranking job on this plantation!" the butler fumed. "My position is ten times higher than that sniffling little dirt mouse!"

"Dear Thornton, just who are you referring to as a stifling little dirty mouse?" Vicky tried to keep a straight face as she and Sam walked down the stairs. Her friend was trying to cover up her giggles listening to this grown man carrying on about another one of the staff leaders. "Would there be some kind of feud between you and Mr. Myers?"

"The Myer's family have always been a contrary lot! Always thinking they outwork, outrank, outsmart, everyone else around here." He lifted his eyebrow in discuss. "They're nothing but a bunch of over-reaching, bragging thieves, and that's a fact!"

"Thornton, surely you are not saying Mr. Myers is a thief? Being of the male persuasion, his big ego could in no doubt attempt to brag on his top position, same, as perhaps, he sees in your attempts to prove you have the greater position." Vicky patted the perplexed man's back. "Let me give a woman's point of view on this matter, Thornton, I find you both capable in the position you each hold and feel, as your employer and friend, that if each of you find equal ground over the jobs you hold, you, a reliable, excellent butler who keeps his staff in total control and Reginal, also reliable and excellent in the field of keeping this very large plantation, so…'grand'!" Victoria looked into the very large oval mirror in the entrance hall and placed the cap securely on her head, pulling her long ponytail through the back.

"Thornton, if the two of you cannot get along, just stay out of each other's way as much as you can, at least until you can learn to get along in a brotherly manner. We are one big family living on this very large old plantation, and personally Thornton, I think everyone one of you are special and I love you all. Now, take a deep breath, and go do what makes you happy. We should be back in a few hours."

"You are a lovely, warm hearted young woman, Victoria Stanford. I am truly grateful you came into our lives." The butler finally released all his built-up anger and gave her a genuine smile. Things might still be a long way from healing between him and his ex-friend, but Thornton knew he would strive to make amends for the resentment he had been living with ever since he lost his betroth to the one guy he always looked up to and trusted. There was something different about this Victoria, something fresh and exciting, clever and an excellent detective, with skills that went far beyond all other detectives. Her greatest gift was the gift of reaching into someone's heart and finding what had been hidden there for ages, like some cancer, eating away at its victim's happiness until it finally destroys every real feeling the person processed. Thornton Hancock knew it was only a matter of time, this caring detective would search out his secret and help him to once again unite with his best friend, his heart brother. Yes, Victoria Elizabeth Stanford was truly a blessing to all those tortured souls, wandering lost for hundreds of years and those living right now at Stanford Hall Plantation, drowning in their own problems. Yes, Miss Victoria's good heart had been seen by everyone at the old plantation, and the light that radiated from within her reflected from the Light of the world!

"Reginal, this place is very well spaced." Victoria had been surprised to find everything spread out, far away from the main house. The great barns and stables down a charming, tree-lined road, of crushed river stone. "These old barns look as though they were just built yesterday and never have I seen such a clean carriage house, and with so many carriages, of various sizes, and believe me, I have seen my share, living in historic

Natchez all my life." Victoria smiled over at her best friend taking in the expansive horse stables, her eyes wide with entrance. "Wouldn't you agree, Sam?"

"Huh? Oh, you are referring to these well-kept buildings, first class carriages and the stables can house at least fifteen grand horses." Samantha glanced over at the groundskeeper, eyes full of questions. "There seems to be an absence of horses though, Reginal. Have they been put out to the pasture?"

"Big Ed, along with his stable hand, put the horses out in the large pasture this morning, so they could feed on fresh grass and get their exercise in, galloping around the large enclosure." Mr. Myers turned the two black stallions onto another road that ran through a beautiful forest until it came to what resembled a little English village. The road became its main street, lined with Chestnut trees and gas lanterns, high on wrought iron polls. There were neatly spaced cottages on a large track of land. Each with its own single stable-carriage house, like most people today might have a garage for their car.

"Reginal, this living community is so warm and charming. It's like stepping back in time." Vicky knew why the working staff loved this place and were so relieved when she chose to accept the plantation gift. "Does each family have a horse to deliver them back and forth?"

"They have two, actually, Miss Victoria. It has been that way ever since the first Stanford's built this plantation. Mrs. Victoria Rose declared, treat a person with dignity and respect, and they will be excellent workers, give a soul a place to call home and food for their empty stomach, they will cherish the ground they are attending!" Reginal laughed. "That dear lady was strict when it came to performance and working hard for a day's pay, but deep down, she had a heart of gold. That lovely couple dressed up like Santa and Mrs. Clause every Christmas Eve and had a big Christmas party! Food galore, gifts and a bonus' for all the adults—and, Lordy, me—they spoil all the children with whatever the small tots ask old Santa to bring them. They made special memories for so many children, not just here on the plantation, mind you, the whole town of Castleton was invited and no one left without a gift from the merry couple!" Tears filled the man's eyes as he recalled the last Christmas they spent with the town. "Then came the sadness Christmas for the entire town and plantation family."

"What happen that last Christmas? Bad year for crops and no money for the many gifts?" Sam asked.

"Far from that, Miss Samantha, it was recorded to be the best year ever in crop sales." The usually calm man, took out his handkerchief and blew his nose.

"Then what happen on that sad Christmas so long ago it still touches your heart with so much emotion, dear friend?" Victoria reached over to take his trembling hand. "Someone died, didn't they?"

"Why, yes, Miss Victoria," he looked at her with wonder. "Someone everyone loved and respected. Everyone had escaped the dreaded yellow-jack, as they called it, that had spread throughout the states, Louisiana included. The citizens of Castleton had felt blessed by God for not having one case of the deadly disease until December rolled around and young Zechariah Castleton returned from paying his old friend a visit. He had brought the old gypsy here to Stanford Hall for safe keeping and the good heart of Victoria Rose took him in and gave him the track of land you saw coming in with an old cabin on it, sort of hidden in the woods. Things were different then, it was springtime and blossoms were blooming as everyone prepared for Easter service in the chapel." Reginal stared out as though he could see the day's events unfolding. "The Castleton children had been missing for five years when Delmarrio brought them home. Zechariah had grown into a handsome seventeen-year-old man and he had a close bond with this gypsy, whose band had been known for stealing children, to sale or keep as their own. No one really knew what made the old gypsy decide to bring the children back, breaking the gypsy code of brotherhood. Many thought he was hiding as much from his own people as he was the law, but this remained a secret between him and young Zechariah. There was something unusual between Victoria Rose and the young man, and the staff swore that was the reason for the lady moving into her own rooms, but never voice their opinions openly, in fear of hurting Nelson."

"They just assume Victoria Rose and Zechariah were having an affair!" Victoria knew for a fact, this had been bad judgement on the worker's part. "It was a good thing they kept silent over their suspicions, Reginal, for they were wrong! Zechariah was never in love with Victoria Rose, and being the gentleman, he is, he would never take advantage of a woman who might have had special feelings for him." Vicky could tell the groundskeeper was confused as to how she could possibly know all this. "I learned in the hotel by one of the maids, that Victoria Rose's ghost has been seen with Zechariah Castleton and in the very bedroom I slept in. The one lucky enough to see the spirits reported, the young man told her 'You are not the right one, I look for another'. They saw him kiss her goodbye, leaving her weeping!"

"Alright, that makes sense, Miss Victoria." He took a deep breath. "Then perhaps you can in light us as to what happen when Zechariah showed up in December, bringing with him the dangerous virus germs?"

"You said he had just come from his old friend, Delmarrio, the gypsy." Now it was Vicky gazing out into the unknown. "I believe the gypsy had gotten sick with Yellow-jack from a long, forgotten germ that had been living inside his body ever since it wiped out his entire band of brothers and sisters, and their children. By some miracle, the Castleton children escape the deadly decease, until…" Vicky felt sick, suddenly knowing what had taken her beloved's life on this earth. "Until Zechariah contracted the germ, which was now growing inside of him, to rob him of his life one day." Vicky couldn't control her own tears now as she continued. "The people were sad on Christmas day because they had a double funeral in the Stanford Hall cemetery, Victoria Rose and Nelson Stanford both attracted the Yellow Fever and died on Christmas Eve."

"The legend past down stated, as the service was coming to a close, a group of eight reindeer appeared, walked up to the graves, looked down, then raised their heads as though someone held them with reins and they gracefully ran off into the forest, side by side." Mr. Myers had been amazed that this young sleuth had everything exact and he knew the things they had been told about her brilliant detective skills was right on.

"Enough sad stories, shall we move on, ladies." He checked his watch. "There is just enough time to check out the east field. It is a golden harvest of wheat and a pure example of all the fields on our property."

"Sounds beautiful Reginal!" Vicky sat back, ready to move on. She was anxious to get back, have a quick lunch, then head up to her rooms to search for the missing diaries

Reaching the east field took a good fifteen minutes but the massive field of flowing wheat, turned a golden brown, was a first-place, blue ribbon picture. It length seem to stretch completely out of sight. A field of wonder and beauty, ready for harvest.

"Reginal, are all the fields this large?" Victoria started to worry about having enough workers to gather the harvest if all the tools were from the 1700's. "I haven't had time to read Nelson's reports on the fields and how many servants he had working them, but just by looking at the size, I'd estimate close to five-hundred workers."

"The fields are all large. As for Nelson and Victoria Rose, they bought 600 slaves, freed them, hired them and gave them a home with land, for growing their own food, and paid them a decent wage. They gladly worked from sunup to sundown, Monday through Saturday, and rested on the Sabbath day, to attend chapel services and spend the day with their friends and families.

"I guess that was pretty generous back in those days when most people worked seven days a week!" Samantha stared out at the giant field and thought of all those poor souls toiling in the hot Louisiana sun all day. "Working from sun to sun, sure does sound like too much work to me! Please tell me those poor people had a lunch break or had some time off to go to town for a doctor's appointment or something."

"Sam, for starters, nobody, rich or poor, made appointments to go to the doctor's office in the 1700's" Vicky laughed. "Back then, if someone got sick, you would send for the doctor to come to you and knowing Victoria Rose's compassion, she would send for him no matter who got sick on the plantation."

"And as always Miss Victoria, you are correct. If one of the servants got sick or pregnant, Victoria Rose did not hesitate to send a horseman with a message for the town doctor." Reginal Pointed back to the road they had come in on.

"We do not need six-hundred workers anymore to bring in the wheat, corn, and cotton, ladies. We have three state-of-the-art tractors and all necessary attachments. All our laborers come from local people, both from town and surrounding farms, and they are paid $15.00 an hour." The groundskeeper winked at Samantha who had been taking in his words. "And as for the 1700's workers going from sun to sun, Miss Samantha, by the love and kindness if the Stanford's, they got thirty minutes rest and water break at 10:00 a.m., an hour break for a prepared and served lunch by house staff at 12 noon, another break at three and quick working at 6:00 p.m."

"Wow! These days if you have an hour for lunch, you either have to buy it or bring it from home!" Sam shook her head at the ideal. "What about here, now in 2019? Does the kitchen staff still cook and serve the field workers?"

"Just on the last day of harvest, Miss Samantha. You're right, my dear. Times have changed, but our change took place under Victoria Bell. Even though the money situation was really good and Miss Stanford was a wealthy available lady, she was very conservative with her spending. By cutting down the huge staff and retaining just what was needed, this effected other areas and traditions that called for heavy spending, such as supplying workers with lunch, served by house staff every day." Reginal recalled his grandparents telling him about the Harvest Feast.

"To show her gratitude to all those workers who had help bring the years crops in for sale, she threw a grand celebration! A new tradition, she called it, The Harvest Feast and set forth to make it another talk of the town, next to the seasons grand ball. A very long harvest table was sat up on the huge lawn. White tablecloths lined it from end to end. In the center there was a spectacular fall arrangement of big and small pumpkins, cobbs of Indian corn, fall fruits and nuts, surrounded by an assortment of autumn leaves of every color imaginal "

"Let me guess! Fried chicken, piled high, bowls of potato

salad, chicken pies, meat pies, sweet baked yams, pots of beans and blackeye peas, corn on the cobb, stacks of fresh baked wheat bread and hoe cakes. All sorts of cakes and pies for dessert, with fresh brewed coffee and sweet ice tea or lemon aid!"

Vicky winked at her friend when Mr. Myers looked speechless. "What, did I leave out something, Reginal?"

"Not a single item, Miss Victoria! Amazing, simply amazing!" he still could not believe she knew every single dish served so long ago. "Tell me your secret, my dear, just how do you know so much?"

"It's simple, really. I read it off Odessa's order sheet!" Vicky chuckled when the groundskeeper blew out and sit back, laughing himself. "I guess our clever cook is already preparing for the big event, that is, if we still have the Harvest Feast for all those hard workers."

"Yes ma'am, we do, unless you chose otherwise. After all, you are the new owner of Stanford Hall Plantation, Miss Stanford." He picked up the reins and titled his head, waiting for her reply.

"Not have the Harvest Feast and be known as the Stanford Hall Scrooge?" Victoria shook her head. "Never! The feast will go on as planned and by hiring some extra kitchen staff to assist Odessa and Imogene with all the preparations for the many special occasions at Stanford Hall, it will be even more spectacular, Reginal. Don't you think?"

"Absolutely, Miss Victoria!" he cheered. "Is there anywhere else you would like to see before going back for your lunch?"

"Is the cemetery close by? I think I might like to see how it is kept up." Vicky really needed to know if her dear Zechariah had been buried there since he seemed so close to the late Victoria Rose.

"The cemetery is just a stone's throw from the Grace Chapel and that's on our way back, another lovely landmark I'm sure you would like to see and check out inside sometime soon." The driver clicked the stallions into motion and they continued down the road, which whined back around to continue toward the manor.

CHAPTER 16

Reginal turned the carriage down a narrow old brick drive that led to an open lawn and a lovely white chapel, that sat right in the center, flanked by old cedar trees. He pulled the horses to a stop where the old road ended in a large circle, leaving plenty of room for several carriages, coming in for worship services. Getting off the carriage, the groundskeeper tied the reins to a hitching post, then smiled up at his riders.

"There's a path just behind the chapel that leads to the plantation cemetery. You might be surprised by its size, ladies, and how well kept it is. Everyone living on the plantation takes pride in maintaining the cemetery since all the residents here have loved ones buried here, with a few exceptions of those graves belonging to very close friends of the first owners of Stanford all." The polite man helped both girls down from the high carriage and led then around to the back, still talking. "Of course, Nelson and Victoria Rose Stanford, as well as their children, Nelson junior, his wife, Ester, along with their children, Rose, who never got married, and Albert, along with his wife, Louise, and their only child, Victoria Bell."

Reginal unlatched the brass bracket that held the white gate shut then stepped to one side so they could enter the massive cemetery. The girls knew at first glance the groundskeeper had not exaggerated over the enormous size. It was obvious which graves belonged to the Stanford family. Not only were the large gravestones bigger and fancier than all the rest, they dominated the flowing hill in the front center. A twenty-foot statue of Jesus stood peacefully in the very middle of their small family.

"This place is amazing, Reginal! For tombstones this old to be so readable is practically unheard of." Vicky moved her fingers reverently over Victoria Rose and Nelson Stanford's names. "What's your secret to keep them all so perfect? They're outside in the elements year-round, just like all the others you can either barely read or not at all."

"Our secret? Simple, our resident stone carver, Mr. Crews. He keeps all the tombs carved, including the two inside the black wrought iron fence. Actually, Alan Crews is the only man around here brave enough to venture inside."

"Why is everyone afraid of those two graves, Reginal?" Victoria had noticed the grass had overtaken the enclosed area and the only thing visible was the head stones, where Mr. Crews had been good enough to keep cleaned off.

"The people are afraid of the un-natural occurrences that went on between those wondering souls. There are a few who swore they have seen their ghost rise up at midnight and commune with one another."

Mr. Myer's words had given Vicky a bad feeling, for she knew who was buried in the unkept graves. It had to be her beloved Zechariah and his old gypsy friend, Demarrio.

"Reginal, Zechariah and his friend, Demarrio, were not evil men. A little different maybe and that's because Gypsies believe in magic and the supernatural. Their women read fortunes and a few of them possess old items that contain unseen mysteries and for the right person, perform unthinkable things. Not necessarily bad, even sometimes very helpful and lifesaving." Vicky noticed the groundskeeper had gone white, eyes wide with uncertain feelings over her strange words.

"Reginal, I understand this all sounds strange to normal, everyday people, like us, but these gypsies were from a different culture than we are and its sad they have completely disappeared. Being a Christian, my Lord, has ask me to love everyone, regardless to the race or nationality. So, if someone needs my help, then I will be there for them and never judge another living soul "

"But Miss Victoria, how do you help dead men?" Reginal had calmed down by her reassuring words, but he still couldn't wrap his head around how this loving girl could help men who had been dead for over two-hundred-years.

"First by cleaning up their resting place. If everyone else is too afraid to do so, then I will lovingly make it beautiful myself."

"Count me in pal!" Samantha smiled over at her best friend.

"Never let it be said that Samantha Brandon is afraid of ghost, especially handsome ghost like Zechariah Castleton."

"Excuse me, Miss Samantha, how would you be knowing that Zechariah Castleton was handsome?" The groundskeeper laughed. "Unless you've already seen his ghost!"

"Not as a grown man, Mr. Myers, but I did see his spirit at age twelve the day we arrive in Castleton. Just down Carriage Wheel Road, near a bunch of trees." Sam draped her arm over her friend's shoulders. "Now Vicky here, did not only see the very tall, dark and handsome Zechariah, fully grown, but received a kiss from him as well. Right pal?"

"I must admit I did have the extreme pleasure of meeting Zechariah Castleton and the kiss was extra special, I might add!" Vicky and Sam grabbed Reginal before his buckling knees caused him to fall to the ground. "Do relax, Reginal, it's not too hard to entertain a ghost whose as much a gentleman as Zechariah was in the hotel."

"Oh, the hotel? Not here?" He blew out a relief breath. "I thought you might have saw him here, in the manor house. That's a relief."

"And, if I should see him in the manor house or perhaps here, in the cemetery, while cleaning his neglected grave site, would you rather me keep it to myself?" Vicky patted her friend's back. "Except for Sam, of course. I tell her almost everything."

"Hey? Just almost?" Sam asked, wide-eyed.

"Well Sam, Somethings should remain private." Victoria smiled over at her friend's squinting eyes, then turn to the man taking in all their words so she chose to change the subject.

"Reginal, perhaps you can shed some light on why there seems to be not quite enough graves here for the six-hundred servants the first Stanford's bought and freed." Vicky's quick deduction showed her there were more people than there were grave sites. "I know those good owners would not have a separate graveyard for the black people."

"And you would be correct about that. Mrs. Victoria Rose saw everyone as family, black or white, even what few Indians she welcomed on the plantation. Everyone is buried right here, even though you see fewer graves. If you checked way down in the far east corner, you will notice a very large tombstone that makes a circle around an open clearing. Buried under that clearing are 450 jugs, containing the ashes of the 450 black servants that died from Yellow Fever. Half of them when the Stanford's died with the deadly virus, then the other 225, in 1800, when the deadly yellow jack fever struck Stanford Hall Plantation a second time." Reginal though back to the sad events that took place in the year of 1800. He walked up next to the wrought iron fence and stared down at the graves.

"Zechariah Castleton contracted the Yellow Fever, from events that accrued on December 24, 1800. It had been many years since his friend, the gypsy died with Yellow Fever and left him carrying the deadly germ inside his very healthy body. He had made friends with Nelson junior and his wife, Ester. They permitted Zechariah to stay in Victoria Rose's old rooms, where he requested to stay whenever he came for a visit. There was something special about the old mirror he and the gypsy had giving Victoria Rose, so many thought this was why he desired that set of rooms." Reginal squatted down for a better view of Zechariah's grave. "It was said, that was the reason why the upset couple came to Zechariah in the middle of the night, just before twelve, Christmas Eve, and ask for his help in finding their missing little girl, five-year-old Rose."

"They were aware of the mirror's powers and knew Zechariah was the only one there who knew its secret." Vicky tried to imagine the young couple, stricken in terror over finding their small daughter missing from her room and was nowhere in the house. "Zechariah ask the mirror to show him where Rose was. Since it was wintertime, it must have been freezing outside that time of night."

"What could have made such a small girl run away in the dark of night, and on Christmas Eve, at that?" Samantha couldn't picture the small child slipping from the big house and out the door, unseen."

"My guess would be sleepwalking. I imagine she was lying in her warm bed dreaming about Santa, heard the bells on the reindeer someplace outside, so in her realistic dream, she got up, slipped outside and maybe saw the sleigh disappear in the forest leaving her a magical trail to follow. Much like Dorothy in the Wizard of Oz, the sleeping angel continued living her dream." Vicky received a positive nod from her friend, but noticed Reginal was staring at her with complete fascination.

"Miss Victoria, no wonder you get such high praise for your great detective work! In the doctor's report that night, he stated the five-year-old had wondered off while sleepwalking, most likely living out her childhood dream." Reginald's attention went back to Zechariah's grave.

"It was not only bitter cold that Christmas Eve, a freezing rain had been falling all day, so at midnight, Zechariah led the search party into the forest, then split them up in twos, telling them to follow the river bank and look for the girl hanging on to a falling tree lying in the cold river. Edging their way slowly down the frozen bank, the party of ten men spit up in twos. They had been warned by their leader to be on the lookout for three perfect cedar trees, clustered together. The child would be found just beyond them, crying in the river."

"It was Zechariah that spotted the three cedar trees, wasn't it? I can see him climbing swiftly off his horse and racing down the sloping riverbank, grabbing on to tree branches to keep him from falling in the icy water." Vicky couldn't control her tears as she could see everything unfolding in front of her, like watching a movie. "He heard her crying and followed the sound until he spotted the almost frozen Rose. Lifting her to safety, he could feel her uncontrollable shaking. Zechariah raced back up to the three cedars and laid her down under their sheltering branches while he removed his heavy winter coat and wrapped her up inside it. Shivering now himself, the very thoughtful man placed her up on his horse, then climbed up behind her in only his undershirt and pants, now soaked through with frozen ice." Victoria opened the gate and walked in to touch his headstone, tears falling in droplets over its hard service.

"Zechariah, my darling, you gave your life so that child could live. Blessed is the man who lays down his life for another." Vicky fell to her knees and slowly traced his name and dates with her finger. "Here lies Zechariah Castleton, a dear friend and a little girl's hero. Born: December 24, 1770— Died: December 26, 1800, at 30 years old."

"I never meant to upset you, my dear." The groundskeeper stood up and wiped the dried grass off his pants. "It might make you feel better to know just how much everyone rallied around the young man for his unselfish act of bravery. He was deeply admired by the entire town of Castleton as well and never has there been so many mourners in the cemetery than was at that young man's funeral. I do believe the record stated, every single soul within miles came out on December 26, 1800, to give their last respects." Reginald choked up. "He was truly a hero to everyone around."

"I wonder what might have happened if one of the other nine found the child, instead of Zechariah?" Vicky ran her hand lovingly over the smooth stone. "

"They all were heard talking one night in a pub after the burial and said it was lucky for that girl when good hearted Zechariah had found her instead of them, or it might have been that poor child's funeral instead of celebrating Christmas with her family." Reginald heard Samantha grunted beside him and turned to see her frowning up at him. "Look, kid, they said it, not me."

"So, I suppose you would have saved her and wrapped the shivering girl in your coat, knowing you would probably freeze to death!"

"One never knows what they might do unless they are face with that hard decision, Miss Samantha." He stuttered. "But the fact was, Zechariah did not die from freezing, he came down with the dreaded Yellow Fever, remember? "

"The fact that Zechariah came down with that deadly Yellow Fever was because he died for the least of God's children. He chose to save little Rose, even if it meant losing his own life." Vicky could not take her eyes off the overgrown grassy spot where they laid the man she was in love with.

Mr. Myers passed her his handkerchief through the link fence as he spoke. "Yes ma'am, Zechariah was the local hero, there's no doubting that, but the sad part was because of saving the life of one child, the deadly epidemic spread throughout the plantation and wiped out 225 black hired servants. You will find all 500 names listed on the circler stone, with the date of each soul's death."

"And this is why you have found their hero's grave so neatly kept, Victoria." Vicky looked over to find out who had placed his arm around her and saw the young chaplain squatting down next to her. "Young Zechariah gave his life for one child, but in return, took 225 lives with him when he died. The people chant his praises, then turn right around and curse him! This is a strange lot you are living with, as are the old fashion people living in that very old town." He stood up and offered his hand, to assist her in standing.

"Thank you, Reverend Whittington. I suppose when you have been brought up with certain stories and traditions all your life, you adapt to a certain way of living and doing things as its always been done." Vicky smiled over at the groundskeeper. "Dear Reginald is one such person. The plantation way of life was passed down from generation to generation, and as this lovely man and his charming Charlotte, start their family, their children will learn their way around the plantation lifestyle."

"That pretty much sums it up, Miss Victoria." Reginald looked over at the preacher and nodded. "We were just about to return for lunch, Reverend."

"Reginald, if I could have a few minutes more. There is something I would like to ask you, Reverend Whittington, that is, if you're familiar with the chapel documents, regarding past events." Vicky did not wish to leave Zechariah's grave so soon and she did have questions for the chaplain.

"I have studied most of the records kept here, Victoria. You have something on your mind about when this brave man died?" The chaplain could not take his eyes off the beautiful woman in front of him and he was secretly glad she wasn't ready to return to the manor house just yet.

"I was wondering if anyone was sitting with Zechariah when he was sick and dying?" Vicky could not picture her beloved being by himself in his final hours on earth and wished she could have been with him.

Joan Byrd

"Yes, my dear, there was one brave soul who sat with him. I regret to say, it wasn't the chaplain. The bishop had ordered all clergymen to stay away from anyone with the fever and pray for them inside the safety of their church's." the chaplain dropped his eyes in shame as he continued. "The young girl who lived in the gypsy's cabin, she stayed with Zechariah Castleton from the moment they brought him inside his room, half frozen and burning up with a very high fever. Everyone being afraid of catching the deadly virus themselves, left her alone, to tend to his frost bite and high fever. The brave girl never left his side."

"It was Grace, wasn't it?" Victoria knew Delmarrio had saved her and now she was surely paying the gypsy back by helping his beloved friend, who had stayed with him when he was dying with the same virus. "Grace, the girl living in the cabin?"

"Oh, no my dear, Grace had run away when she heard of Zechariah catching the Yellow Fever." The chaplain took her hands. "The brave girl who would not leave Zechariah's side just appeared on that Christmas Eve and was found coming from the cabin in the woods. Her name was recorded because of the strange way she just appeared, stayed until the young man died, then disappeared just as mysterious. "

Vicky suddenly had a very unusual feeling, remembering a dream she had had when she was sixteen. She found herself in this strange cabin in the woods and heard horses galloping by, so she ran out to see what was going on. Vicky remembered counting ten horsemen, and the one in front was carrying something wrapped up in what must have been his coat, for he wore nothing but an undershirt and pants. Vicky remembered getting eye contact with the handsome stranger and knew she had to help him.

"Vic, didn't you hear what Reverend Whittington just said?" Samantha had grown white when Vicky glanced up at her friend, and tried to shake the dream out of her mind. "You looked as though you were a thousand miles away! You must hear this Vic, I simply cannot believe my ears!"

"I'm truly sorry, Reverend, I was recalling a dream I had at
122

sixteen resembling this very thing. Who did you say this girl was?"

"Her name was, Victoria Elizabeth Stanford!" the chaplain and groundskeeper both grabbed for the swaying girl, as Vicky fainted in their arms.

CHAPTER 17

Victoria opened her eyes and noticed the three worried faces standing over her. Looking around, she realized she was inside the chapel, lying on the back pew. Then she realized why she was here; she had fainted when Reverend Joshua Whittington had refilled the stranger who had suddenly appeared to stay with Zechariah while he lay sick and dying. It was too much for just a coincidence It had to be the magic mirror, reaching out to her two-hundred-years in the future. She relaxed and smiled up at her worried friend, knowing she would know the answer that night when she summoned Zechariah to come.

"Vic! Thank God you're alright!" Samantha knelt down and took her friend's hand. "You don't suppose there just happened to be another girl named Victoria Elizabeth Stanford, do you?"

"Of course, it had to be another person Miss Samantha. Probably someone who had heard the very handsome available Zechariah Castleton speak that name with pure love dripping off his tongue and sought to win his heart, even if it meant the possibility of catching the yellow jack." The young chaplain helped Victoria to sat up and held out a glass of water. "I'm truly sorry to have blurted out your name my dear, but to be honest, until Samantha told me Elizabeth was your middle name, I had no knowledge of it.

"You could not have known my middle name, Reverend Whittington, and there are quite a few of Victoria's flowing about." Vicky thanked him for the cool water and passed back the empty glass. "But it does appear you do have knowledge about Zechariah's devotion and love for me, since you know how he spoke my name, it would appear, on many occasions."

"Yes, my dear, I have read all about the young man's infatuation with Victoria Elizabeth Stanford. He was quite taken with her and for her to just show up when he needed someone the most, it was quite the miracle." The young chaplain shook his head, unable to make sense out of the whole story.

"Reverend Whittington, did it mention how the girl was dressed?" Vicky knew she would certainly recognize a description of one of her dresses or nightgowns.

"As a matter of fact, it did describe her attire, as well as the color of her eyes and hair." The chaplain gave her a big smile as he added "And please Victoria, call me Joshua, Reverend Whittington sounds too much like my father, who was also a chaplain for over sixty-years." He walked over and opened a lock cabinet and pulled out one of the diaries inside. Joshua quickly found the page and started reading it. "It was obvious to everyone the girl showed up with one set of clothes, for she never changed, nor returned to the cabin to retrieve any luggage when she just vanished. We assumed she had been attending some sort of ball or party, for she had on an incredible royal blue gown to match her alluring blue eyes. Her coal black hair had been braided with a blue and yellow ribbon and it appeared slightly ruffled, as though she had napped from exhaustion." Joshua glanced up at the girl standing in front of him and stared at her coal black hair, none up in a ponytail and her alluring blue eyes, then gave his head a shake, as though he tried to shake off the close identity between the girl from 1800 and the one standing so close. "Shucks, you could have been twins, if she was alive today instead of two-hundred-years ago!"

"Whittington, if you had lived here at Stanford Hall for as many years as my family, you might believe the Victoria Elizabeth standing right here today and the Victoria Elizabeth from 1800 could very well be one in the same!" Reginald Myers stared at the lock on the cabinet while the chaplain was staring at him, in disbelief. "Why have you locked that cabinet anyway? I would guess most residents have already read those records by now if they were curious. I know I did as well as the entire house staff."

"Then I'm keeping them safe from some thief stealing them!" the young chaplain turned to the beautiful woman. "You're the great detective, Victoria, what do you make of this mysterious woman who looked exactly like you and with the exact name?"

"On my sixteenth birthday, I had the honor of attending a grand Christmas Eve ball at the Stanton Hall mansion in Natchez, Mississippi. Everyone was to dress in 1800 period clothes, to celebrate their 158th Stanton Hall Christmas. The party lasted far up into the night and I was so exhausted when my parents and I returned home, I fell across my bed and went straight to sleep." Victoria looked at the two men, listening with excited curiosity. "Gentlemen, if I tell you what happened, you must promise to never say a word of it to anyone. This is part of the mystery I'm working on and if it falls to the wrong ears, it could ruin everything. I know I can depend on my friend, Sam, to keep it to herself. Can I trust you to keep it quiet?"

"Not even Charlotte, Miss Victoria?" Reginald looked sincere enough, but the fewer that knew her facts, the better to solve the mystery without mishap. "She will know I'm keeping something from her. I just don't want her to get the wrong ideals for my not telling her."

"If Charlotte grows suspicious, have her ask me to explain." Vicky knew some women could grow suspicious over the possibility of another woman. "Let me handle it, Reginald, but you must not tell her, at least not until I have closed this case. Well, what will it be, a secret kept or we go back right this minute?"

"Come on man, keep the lady's secret!" the preacher was dying to hear the rest of her story, and this man's married life was standing in his way. "Just tell the little woman you made a promise to Miss Victoria and to break it could prove dangerous to her. If she doesn't buy that truth, then send her to Victoria, just like she asked you to do!"

"I take it you are saying yes, to keeping it a secret, Joshua?" Vicky smiled at his anxious need to know what happen.

"Mum is the word, Victoria. I can keep a secret, even to the grave, if need be and you have my word on it!" The preacher slapped the groundskeeper on the back. "What do you say Reginald? It will make your boss lady happy and I won't

126

embarrass you Sunday when you fall asleep as usual during my sermon."

"I would not fall asleep if your sermons, wasn't so long, Whittington." The groundskeeper grunted as he turned to his beautiful boss lady. "Very well, Miss Victoria, I will keep this thing you are about to tell us a secret and should my Charlotte get upset with me, I will send her to you for an explanation."

"Very well, Reginald, I shall take you and Joshua at your words and I will know who to hold accountable should this thing I will be sharing among the three of you, get out and the gossiping begins." Victoria looked both men in the eyes. "I may seem meek and mild gentlemen, but go against my trust and you will learn I have enough of my Aunt Victoria Bell's gumption to take immediate action for betrayal."

"My word is honorable, Miss Victoria and once given, I'll uphold it until my dying day, if that is your desire." Reginald tilted his hat.

"Being a man of God, I would never break a sacred promise to a friend, Victoria. You have my promise, as God is my witness." The preacher smiled over at the groundskeeper. "And, neither do I have a spoiled little wife to pout about keeping this secret from her."

Noticing Reginald's bawled up fist, Victoria stepped up between them, pulling her friend Samantha up next to her.

"I trust you both, so there no need to get upset with one another." Vicky placed a hand on each man's hands. "We are all family here, gentlemen, so please shake and make up, then I will tell you about my very real dream when I fell asleep exhausted after that ball."

After the men gave in and smiled at each other as they shook hands, Victoria asked the group of three to have a seat on the pew, then she sat in a chair in front of them and began.

"I started dreaming about walking through a rainbow cloud, then I stepped out of a looking glass and found myself in an old cabin. I could see it was dark outside and I could hear ice hitting the tin roof. Noticing the fire glowing in the rock fireplace, I walked over to warn myself and that's when I heard horses outside, galloping toward the cabin. It wasn't but a few steps to the door, so I walked over and peeked outside. I counted ten horses and the one in the lead was ridden by a very handsome man who wore only his under shirt and pants, which looked soaked through. Looking closer, I noticed why he did not wear a coat. He held a small girl in his arms, wrapped up in a man's heavy winter coat. The strange thing was, he stopped suddenly and looked directly into my eyes, as though he was expecting me to be waiting there for him.

I followed them on a horse I found waiting outside the cabin and the next thing I remember, I was inside the same bedroom I stay in at the manor house. Two men dressed with protective mask and gloves carried the soaked man inside and laid him on the bed. I remember them telling me to leave if I did not wish to catch the fever. I don't think I spoke to them, I only remember shaking my head, no. They left and shut the door and never came back." Tears filled Victoria's eyes. "Those men left this man to die alone and I knew I would stay with him and do whatever I could to ease his suffering. I walked over and looked down into his incredible blue eyes and even suffering, he smiled up at me and said my name. He called me, Vicky, not Victoria.

"I didn't know then how he knew me, nor did I know his name until the day of the funeral Since I've arrive here at Castleton and Stanford Hall Plantation, I've found out why Zechariah knew my name two-hundred-years ago. I remained by side the entire time he lay there, holding my hand and telling me how much he loved me and that we would be together someday. Zechariah told me we would meet again in the far future and I recall his beautiful laugh when he said, "My darling Vicky, this sounds even strange to me when I say. You, my darling will be born in 1999, and we will meet twenty-years later."

"Zechariah has come to me three times since I've been here and I, like Sam, saw what little Johnny Pennywise called a hologram of Zechariah when he was twelve, out on the Carriage Wheel Road with his brother and four sisters." Victoria gave Reginald an I'm sorry smile when she added. "That was twice in the hotel and once, in my room at the manor house."

Reflections of the Past

"Vic, you mentioned hearing his name at the funeral, so this is probably why his name and face was so familiar to you when you saw his picture, the boy, and especially Zechariah, the man." Samantha recalled her friend having the feeling of knowing him.

"That's right Sam, and I had forgotten about that dream until I saw Zechariah's grave and heard Joshua read my name in records from 1800." Vicky hadn't noticed how quiet the two men had become or how they were staring at her, completely perplexed. "Sam, that dream wasn't a dream at all! Somehow, it was real and…" Vicky whispered in her friend's ear. "it had to be the magic mirror! It can travel to the future as well as the past! That is how Victoria Bell knew so much about me!" Vicky laughed, glad to have some clues coming to light. "I did walk through the looking glass, remember?"

"Exactly! Things are finally making sense and a few more unanswered questions from Zechariah and the Victoria's, you will have this impossible case solved!" Samantha smiled broadly and looked over at the ghost white faces of the chaplain and the groundskeeper. "Hey Vic, what's up with these two? They look like they just saw a ghost!"

"Too much information, gentlemen? I might understand why Joshua is shocked by my revelation, but you, Reginald? Did you or did you not just tell the chaplain if he had lived here on this plantation as long as your family, you very well might believe the 1800 Victoria Elizabeth Stanford and I are the same person?" Vicky noticed the groundskeeper blushing, as he gave her a shaky smile.

"Yes ma'am, I did say those very words. I guess I thought perhaps I could have been wrong, or a least, hoped I were."

"Gentlemen, let me warn you now, Zechariah is only the first of a long line of wondering spirits on this plantation as well as in the town of Castleton who will seek me out to uncover their long-hidden mystery. It appears, Victoria Bell and Victoria Rose, have been waiting for me as well, knowing my skills as a detective, so you might as well get used to ghost stories." Vicky stood up and gazed at them seriously. "If you think you cannot handle all these strange happenings, then I suggest you pack your things and go someplace far away from Stanford Hall Plantation and Castleton, because this is what they've all been waiting for and believe me gentlemen, they won't stop coming until the last spirit's case is solved."

"Victoria, forgive my sudden panic, but I must confess, I wasn't prepared for such a story, but now that I know the facts, I can assure you, I will be here for you and anytime you wish to see the church's records, feel free to come over." Joshua Whittington smiled and stood up. "I will also do what I can to help send these poor souls to heaven after their case is solved."

"Sounds like you're trying to make sure those, poor ghost, go far away so you won't get spooked anymore!" Reginald laughed "I've grown accustomed to bumps in the night or floating candlesticks. Going up the stairs. You are just weak in the knees to want to send all our ghost away!" He continued to laugh.

"Then why act so scared about this handsome ghost all the females seem to think is God's gift to women, Myers!" the young chaplain snapped angrily, referring to his being weak in the knees. "If truth be known sir, I am probably the bravest man on this haunted plantation, where two dead men rise from their graves to chat and beautiful modern young ladies can walk through a looking glass like Alice in Wonderland and find themselves back in the beginning of the 1800's!"

"Gentlemen, I would not worry about a shortage of ghost, even after a case is solved and that spirit is sent to their final resting place, and let's hope, for their sakes, it will be heaven, for the other place would be far worse than having an unsolved mystery hanging over your soul. "

"Could we discuss this later, Vic?" Samantha rubbed her growling stomach. "I am beyond hungry and I recall we have some investigating to do!"

"I could use some lunch myself, Sam." Vicky nodded to the chaplain. "We shall return tomorrow morning to clean up Zechariah and Delmarrio's gravesite."

"My apartment is just behind the church. When you arrive, just give me a knock and I will help you girls spruce up that sad site." Joshua glanced over at the groundskeeper and faked a smile. "I've offered to clean it up myself, out of respect for the dead, but Mr. Myers and his workers refused my help."

"The grounds are my department, Whittington. I just didn't want an amateur messing up my grounds!" Reginald grunted. "Maybe I should preach your sermon one Sunday and see how you like it!"

"Reginald, just stay out of my pulpit! It takes a God given gift to preach, but anyone can pull weeds!" "Fellows, you have got to start getting along! How are small children supposed to learn to behave when two grown men keep going after each other!" Victoria walked outside the church with Samantha, followed by both men, scrambling to get out the door first. Victoria and Samantha tried hard not to laugh when they got stuck, side-by-side for a few moments, before the chaplain broke free and practically fell out.

"Joshua, I will take you up on your offer to help us and Reginald, since you are over the grounds, you may come along to give us a hand, share what tools we might need and show us how to bring that gravesite around to your high standards as the head groundskeeper!" Vicky looked from one man to the other and noticed they were still acting hostel. "Boys, maybe working side-by-side pulling weeds and sowing new grass seed, might give you a new appreciation for each other. Reginald, you can give us your expert advice while maintaining a friendly approach, instead of snapping out orders, especially to Joshua."

"That sounds fair to me." The chaplain smiled broadly at the groundskeeper.

"Joshua, Sunday morning, try to keep your sermon on one subject, perhaps on, love thy neighbor as thyself or do unto others as you would have others do unto you!" Vicky smiled. "A short sermon on brotherly love. Would this keep you awake Reginald?"

"That sounds like an all-around great sermon for me!" Reginald held out his hand to shake with the chaplain, who was shaking his head in admiration toward the beautiful peace maker and laughing softly he shook hands with Reginald. "I will have the girls here by 9:00 a.m. with gardening tools, grass

Joan Byrd

seed, and flowers, not to mention a can of black paint, with a paintbrush to spruce up the faded wroth iron fence and gate."

"I'll be waiting!" the young chaplain lifted Victoria's hand to his lips and gave it a kiss. "Thank you, my dear, for setting two grown men straight and letting us help you pull weeds and toss out any unwanted snakes living in that high grass." He walked away before she remembered kneeling in that very spot.

CHAPTER 18

"Gosh Vic, all this stuff in here, where do we start looking?" Samantha and Victoria had asked to be excused after thanking the cheerful cook for their delicious mid-day meal and found themselves right in the middle of Victoria's big sitting room, filled with several old pieces of furniture.

"I think if we spit up and search in different rooms, we might move faster." Vicky looked around and then through to her bedroom, with even bigger pieces of furniture, like the tall chest of drawers, a large wardrobe, an elaborate antique desk with lots of drawers under its roll top cover. The old vanity with the magic mirror also had a row of drawers on each side and very unusual carvings along the sides. She'd let her friend decide which room she wanted to search for the hidden diaries. "Alright Sam, your choice. It really doesn't matter to me."

"I'll stick to this room, if you don't mind Vicky." Samantha looked past her beautiful friend and shivered at the sight of the magic mirror. "I'd rather not be near that mirror if it decided to become awake and sweep me away to another place and time!"

Vicky laughed as she patted her friend on the back. "You can relax, pal. That mirror only performs when someone summons it and asks it for help. Just start looking around and may I suggest feeling around that small library of books lining that shelf attached to the wall." She smiled when Samantha's eyes lit up with hope of making the discovery for once, instead of her sharp friend. "Many old homes have hidden doors in the book shelfs and some objects can be hidden in the wall, behind a portrait or a lovely painting."

"Great! I'll call if I locate the diaries or a secret door leading to an unknown place to explore later." Sam made her way over to the large bookshelf. "When you don't have a case to solve, there's more than enough good titles up here for us to read." She looked back at her friend. "Where are you looking first, Vic, the big desk? They're known to have a secret door, right?"

"And the reason for that is for hiding valuables, such as costly jewelry." Vicky noticed Sam giving her a raise eyebrow, a sign of letting her know most people find hidden papers or a personal diary hidden inside, perhaps love letters. "Yes Sam, I am aware that there are those who had personal things they don't wish to share with everyone else, like, love letters, or a personal diary, and that is why I think both the Victorias who lived in this room were too smart to hide the personal writing in a secret compartment, but someplace where I was sure to find it, yet stump everyone else, who had searched before I arrived."

"Then, where do you think they hid them? The high chest, maybe the top drawer, or possibly the bottom drawer, thinking most people wouldn't stoop down that low." Sam snapped her finger when she thought of something. "Suppose each woman hid their dairy in two separated places?"

"My guess is that both books are in the same hidden place and it is in neither the high drawer or the low drawer of the high chest. As a matter of fact, I believe those diaries are hidden somewhere on that magic mirror. That's the one thing that was here for both Victoria's, so it just makes sense."

"But, what about the high chest? I'm sure that dates back to Victoria Rose's time, so it was here for Victoria Bell. The desk is obviously old, and had to belong in the Stanford family before they built this manor house, agree?"

"I would agree about the roll top desk being here for both Victoria's, but I instantly ruled that out because it would be too obvious." Vicky smiled when her friend brought up the possibility of the tall chess being the hiding place, perhaps a middle drawer. "Sam, you can forget the tall chest. Charlotte informed me, while she was putting away my things, that Miss Victoria Bell had purchased the wardrobe and tall chest to give her more room for her clothes and personal things. Now, start looking and I will do the same."

"Alright, I will search, most likely for a hidden door or a vault behind that painting of horses!" Sam smiled finally, always excited to do detective work with her best friend. "Just don't touch anything you shouldn't, on that magic mirror, Vic!

I'd hate to beg my reflection inside that mirror to give you back, pronto!"

Victoria chuckled over her friend's statement and went straight to the mirror to begin her search. Her slender fingers trace over the unusual carvings on the mirror's frame and the one on the very bottom made a clicking sound when she turned the carved arrow down, causing an invisible drawer to slide out, then open up. Vicky took a deep breath as she reached into what appeared to be an empty space and moved her finders slowly around the smooth service until she felt a tiny lever. Pulling it ever so gently, the drawers' bottom clicked open, revealing two, rather thick diaries, one with a blue cover, the other with a lavender cover. Taking the cherished old books out, she noticed instantly Victoria Rose had her name on the lavender diary, and Victoria Bell's name was done beautifully in script, on the blue one.

Glancing through each book, Vicky noticed each woman mention several unsolved mysteries and had written each one like a separate short story. Both women had even thought about placing a table of contents in the back of their writing. To Victoria's happy discovery, Zechariah Castleton was listed in both books, at great length. The need to read just a small part concerning the man she loved so deeply, she found the page in her aunt's blue diary.

"How does one express their true feeling for a man who has no interest in you as a woman and just prefers being good friends. Of course, I had to agree with our friendship, so to keep him in my life. Zechariah Castleton appeared first in the Castleton Hotel, while I was preparing for bed, after attending a ball at Castleton Mansion, owned now by James Castleton's son, Reed and his wife, Jeanine, who had their son James, named after his grandfather." Vicky thought about Delores Castleton, the last Castleton to live at Zechariah's home, now owned by Marshall Maxwell, whose ancestors never got along with the Castleton family. The Maxwell's most likely envied the Castleton's great wealth and sought to make it their own, at least that was the impression Vicky had gotten with the obnoxious new owner of Castleton Mansion. He had bragged about owning a painting of her and Zechariah had informed her the painting belonged to him, along with one of himself, where he had paired them together. Now, the painting of Zechariah had been hidden somewhere in that huge mansion. Most likely the attic. Victoria's thoughts were interrupted by her friend's exciting shout.

"I found it! Hurry, Vic, come and see!"

"A secret passage! Most likely an escape route in case of an invasion." Vicky smiled at her excited friend. "Great find, partner!"

It suddenly hit Samantha what her friend had said the hidden passage might have been built for. "What sort of invasion could one have on a plantation?"

"Sam, are you forgetting that this plantation saw two American wars in her lifetime? It wasn't long after the first Stanford's built this house that the revolutionary war started and it had been rumored for years before that first shot was heard round the world in Concord!" Vicky laughed when her friend rolled her eyes up and made a face.

"I remember it well! To this day I can quote the Concord Hymn by good old Ralph Waldo Emerson! 'By the rude bridge that arched the flood, their flag though April breeze unfurl… Samantha dip down and waved her arm in front of her for Victoria to continue the long poem.

"Here once the embattled farmer stood and fired the shot heard round the world!" Vicky laughed and walked over to check out the dark tunnel that was hidden behind the middle bookcase. "Good old Mr. Shelton had a thing for minorizing long poems and had us, the seventh graders, either recite them in front of the class or have us write it down while he clicked on his time watch for twenty minutes. Nice guy!"

"You can say that again!" Samantha made a face, then pointed to the wall candles, next to wall torches. "Looks like they had plenty light in the tunnel. I just hope it was ventilated to the outside.

"I'm not sure they knew about dangerous fumes back then. Besides, it was just a means out to someplace safe if the British troops or the fellows in blue, Union soldiers, came in to take whatever their armies needed. Fresh horses, food to eat, like the livestock and anything eatable growing, usually stripping everything in sight!" Vicky looked around at her beautiful surroundings and said, Thank God, Stanford Hall Manor wasn't burnt to the ground like many of the big plantation houses, when the civil war raged on!"

"Maybe hot-foot Sherman didn't make it out to this part of the south." Samantha knew her history just like her friend, living in a historic town all her life. "I guess you will find the answers in those two diaries, if you ever find them."

"If I find them?" Vicky laughed when her friend made an 'I'm sorry face'.

"I know you won't give up until you find those well-hidden diaries, that no one around has been able to locate."

"It wasn't so hard, if you know all the tricks to finding secret places." Vicky chuckled at Samantha's wide eyes of surprise. "I must say, this secret drawer was well hidden and even had a double hiding place to find the blue and lavender books, packed with many mysteries. But the most personal thing for me to read, is what each lovely lady had to say about my Zechariah."

"Were they in the magic mirror's vanity?" Samantha was always impressed with her best friend's detective skills. "A drawer hidden behind another drawer or a completely invisible drawer, built cleverly in perhaps the side of the cabinet?"

"Two very good guesses, Sam, but I'm afraid both are way off." Vicky held up her hand before her friend could question her reasoning. "I know what you are thinking Sam, that there cannot possibly be anywhere else on the vanity for a hidden drawer, unless of course, it was somehow hidden on the top."

"Oh! Of course, it had to be the top!" Sam laughed. "No one would ever think to look on top of the vanity, where you keep your personal things." She studied for a moment and looked at her smiling friend, completely puzzled. "Just how can a drawer open on top?"

"It can't!" an even more troubling face came on her friend. "Relax pal, I did not find the hidden drawer on the vanity. I found it on the frame of the magic mirror, the first place I looked."

Joan Byrd

"Oh. The frame around the mirror, with all the carvings!" Samantha sank down into a big chair, feeling relieved to finally know the location. "So which carving was it behind?"

"It wasn't behind any of the carvings, dear friend, it was under the carving of an arrow on the bottom." Vicky knew she had her friend's attention, so she revealed her find. "I started feeling slowly around each carving and when I came to the arrow, it came to me that it just might turn, so slowly turning, to see if I was right, I heard the arrow click and when it faced completely down, the drawer popped out! I saw that it was empty, but I concluded it was just a trick, and felt around and found a small lever. After carefully turning it, the bottom of the drawer came open and the two books were lying side-by-side, in the bottom."

"Well, three cheers for the best detective in the south!" Samantha jumped up to hug her friend. "The best in the states! The very best in the entire world!"

"Better stick to the best in the south, Sam!" Vicky laughed. "I'm not sure fans of Sherlock Holmes would agree with you, as the best in the world."

"They would if they knew you and your rare special gifts for knowing things before they happen or the ability to call up spirits through a magic mirror!"

"Well, I just as soon they don't know about the magic mirror, Sam, so please do not tell anyone about its power." Victoria pulled her friend into her bedroom and pointed at the very old and unusual mirror. "I would hate for this beautiful old friend to get into the wrong hands. Someone like Marshall Maxwell! If he ever figured out the secret to finding the past or even the future, think of the destruction he could create!"

"Golly jeepers! I never thought of that, Vicky, but you're right!" Samantha let her hand run gently down the powerful old frame. "As far as we know, this mirror has only brought good things out. The old gypsy seemed to be a good person and found the secret of the mirror and according to Zechariah, helped others with it, finally leaving it to Zechariah, whom he had grown close to."

"Yes, like I've told you, Zechariah said Delmarrio had even

138

learned the secret to the channel of life and brought back that girl name Grace, who is still alive, after two-hundred-years!" Victoria stared into the mirror. "Oh, dear mirror, there is still so much to learn about you and I just pray I can learn your deep secret to the channel of life, so I can bring my dearest Zechariah back to life, so we can share a life together."

"Jumping catfish! Can something like that actually happen, Vicky?" Samantha backed away from the old mirror, suddenly afraid of its power. "What has me puzzled, is what gave this mirror its magic in the first place? I cannot believe our Creator zapped this mirror into existence! It just doesn't make sense!"

"That is one mystery we may never know, Sam. When the old mirror was found abandoned in some London dump or some backstreet ditch, where people threw out their unwanted junk, the young boy took it home and cleaned it up. He then built the vanity you see it attached to. It was very old when he found it, so who knows just how far back it really goes. Maybe the mid-evil times, when witches and warlocks practiced witchcraft and someone had the magic to enter the mirror and was trapped inside for the ages."

"But wouldn't the mirror perform only evil things if it was a wizard's spell that created it?" Samantha couldn't believe anything good could come from someone practicing witchcraft.

"Who said there couldn't have been good witches, maybe even some fallen angel that regretted following Lucifer and going against God and wanted to make amends by doing something good and helping others."

"I think you may be on to something, Vicky. I can see why a fallen angel might regret getting thrown out of heaven, a beautiful place filled only with perfect love and peace and find themselves taking orders from the one responsible for his great loss." Samantha felt a little safer beside the old mirror, thinking it contained a repenting angel.

"That's exactly right, my friend! Lucifer was turning all the beautiful angels into demons, to become his servants, while he ruled the earth and this one angel wanted no part of his plan so he thought of his own escape plan." Victoria could finally see everything unfolding in front of her. "The angel, Exemplar, which means, to reflect as in a mirror or something to be copied or serving as a model! An example! He turned himself into a looking glass in order to do good and he escaped Lucifer's evil plan to win souls away from the Almighty God! In return, Exemplar hoped to save loss souls and bring love to those seeking, like Zechariah!"

"Victoria Stanford, you amaze me!" Samantha shook her head in amazement. "You just discovered a mystery that has been buried since the fall of the angels! If you can unearth this mystery, Vic, you can surely find that channel of life." Samantha walked up close to the mirror. "Now that you know what the mirror's name is, surely he will help you bring your loved one back to life!"

"You're right, Sam, and I think I may know just how he does it!" Vicky sat down at the mirror. "Exemplar lived in heaven, so he knew Jesus. When Jesus came to earth, he raised the dead and taught his followers to do the same, through His name. I believe this angel's loving heart and true believeth in the One he knew in Heaven, then followed on earth, is how he raises the dead and brings love ones back!" Vicky turned to face her friend, the truth finally hitting her full. "The channel is the tunnel to heaven, where the lost souls are still wondering and Exemplar has learned how to go there and collect ever who is called out!"

CHAPTER 19

"Dear magic mirror, I know you far better than you think, unless of course you can hear conversation between friends, while standing in your angelic presence." Victoria was seated in front of the old mirror smiling. "What I wish for now is to see Zechariah Castleton, if you might be so kind to bring him back from wherever he waits at the moment."

Vicky had started looking at the fireplace behind her to see if the portrait was changing from Victoria Bell to Victoria Rose and to her delight, it did.

"My heartfelt thanks, dearest mirror. Please know, I am aware of your importance and the reason you should always be protected from falling into the wrong hands." Vicky traced the frame with tender gentleness. "Never doubt my loyalty to such a dear friend as yourself and I promise to keep your secret safe and only share it with those I trust most in the world."

"I hope I count for one such trusted, my darling Vicky." Zechariah touched her soft silky hair. "I do believe my dearest keeps getting even prettier each time we are together."

"Your good looks never cease to make me feel a million butterflies, Zechariah." Victoria turned to look up into his loving, alluring blue eyes. "Tell me, my darling, is it possible for a heart to grow bigger, for my love for you seems to grow bigger with each passing day?"

"I think you are just catching up with the amount of love I have felt for you for centuries!" Zechariah took her hands and lifted her up, then lowered his head and kissed her. "Now that I have you Vicky, I shall require many kisses from your sweet lips to make up for all the time I have longed to do so."

"Then, that is a requirement I will gladly permit you to have, as it also brings me much satisfaction." Knowing his time was always short, Vicky had many questions she needed to ask Zechariah. "Shall we have a seat on the sofa. I have a few questions regarding my very real dream when I was sixteen."

"You were at my grave this morning." Zechariah led her to the sofa and waited for her to sit, then he joined her. "You are wondering how you came to me and I had been dead for two-hundred and fifteen-years."

"Yes, I am totally confused as to how you managed that, but I know the magic mirror had something to do with it." Vicky had figured out some of what happened, so all she needed was the how. "I know little Rose had disappeared from the house on the night of Christmas Eve and you had been asked to find her. Those frightened parents knew you had connections with the magic mirror and it was their only hope in reaching their lost daughter, out in the freezing rain and snow."

"I ask to be left alone for a few minutes to find her, the mirror spoke to me so sadly, I thought at first we were too late and little Rose was already gone but that wasn't the reason for his hesitation in telling me." Zechariah took Vicky's hand. "The mirror told me, if I found the child, she would live, but I must die."

"Why, my darling, why would the mirror say such a thing? Surely he didn't expect you to let that child die." Victoria could not control her tears. "Rose was dreaming about Santa and his reindeer and heard their bells and got up to find them. In her sleep, she walked out the door into the freezing night and hearing the bells disappear into the forest, she followed. And all she had on was her nightgown, but you would have no way of knowing she was sleepwalking. You just thought, little Rose was too excited to sleep, knowing Santa was coming and thought she heard the bells and put on her heavy wool coat, scarf, hat and snow boots, just like her parents had taught her."

"My wise, beautiful woman! Yes, Rose had told me as she was going up for bed, that she was so excited she might never go to sleep, so if she heard the reindeer's bells, she might try to have a peek." Zechariah smiled as he recalled her big hug she gave him and whispered she would wrap up for the storm if she had to go outside. I told her to try and go to sleep, because Santa was sure to know if she wasn't and pass her house. With big eyes, the precious girl promised she would try real hard."

Zechariah looked over at the mirror. "I told the mirror I had to save the girl's life, even if it meant losing mine, but I had one favor to ask of him. He said, because of your good heart and your willingness to give your life for a child of God, I will grant you whatever you wish." Zechariah turned back to the woman he loved. "I ask him how I would die and he said the germ living inside me from the Yellow Fever would spark to life when I was out in the cold freezing rain. I knew I would die alone, maybe taking two days like my friend, Delmarrio, so I asked the mirror to reach out to the future and bring you to me, so your face would be the last face I seen before closing my eyes in death. The gentle heart of that mirror promised he would not only bring you to me, where I would find you waiting outside the old cabin and follow me, to remain until after my burial, but he would place my soul in a holding place until you came to own Stanford Hall Plantation and learn the secret of the past through him. He said, if your Victoria Elizabeth is as clever as she can be, she will also learn the secret of the channel of life and bring you back to live with her forever."

"Zechariah, I have learned the secret of the channel of life!" Vicky jumped when he grabbed her laughing.

"Tell me! This is the best news I have ever received since the day I heard you were finally coming to Castleton to get your inheritance!"

"And I shall tell you, my darling, as soon as you clear up a few more facts!" Vicky touched his excited face.

"Cannot all your questions wait until I'm free of that place of nothing!" Zechariah pleaded.

"Very well, Zechariah. I would not wish for you to suffer any longer in this strange place, but there is just one thing that has bothered me since that very real dream." She waited for a rebuttal from the man she loved, but he merely nodded for her to go ahead with her question. "When I woke up from what I thought was a dream, I had a white rose in my hand. I can remember your casket had a bunch of red roses covering the top, and as I lay weeping over it, I felt a hand place one of the roses inside my closed fingers. When I opened my blurry eyes to see who had given it to me, no one was standing close by, all were outside the fence. I then looked down at the rose in my hand and it wasn't red, it was white as the freshly fallen snow, that lay over the graveyard. That's when I woke up and found the rose still in my hand."

"Darling, everyone wanted to be there, but were afraid to get too close, because of the Yellow Fever." Zechariah tried to make sense out of the white rose. "I do know the Stanford family always used red roses on their caskets when someone died around Christmas and they buried me Christmas day. I believe the white rose came from an angel, probably through the magic mirror, as a reminder that the white rose stands for life. I think the mirror was trying to tell you there's life after death and he did not want you to forget me."

"I carried your face inside me for the remainder of my life and that's why I thought your face was so familiar, even at twelve. And that is another question for later, but now, I promised just the one and to talk about the mystery of the channel of life." Victoria stood up and walked over to the old mirror. "Zechariah, you said the mirror spoke to you and you even know it is a male."

"That's right, Vicky." Zechariah joined her in front of the mirror. "I overheard Delmarrio having a conversation with the very intelligent man in the mirror, so I just informed him one night, I knew he could speak so I would appreciate to hear his wisdom."

"Delmarrio seemed to know a lot about this mirror and he even found out the secret to the channel of life, so I guess he knew what it really was." Vicky noticed Zechariah's questioning face. "He did know where the channel is, didn't he and the mirror's name and who and what he actually is?"

"Gosh Vicky, you have uncovered all of that?" Zechariah stared with admiration. "You are one great detective, my love!"

"Just how much did your gypsy friend know about this magic mirror?" Victoria had a hunch she knew a whole lot more and never even knew the clever mirror could speak until this night.

"My friend knew all the secrets about reaching into the

future or the past, he even figured out how to draw Grace from the channel of life, but that was what he called it. "Zechariah once again stared at the mirror. "Vicky, did you say the mirror has a name and you even know who and what it is? My friend simply called him, magic mirror!"

"Maybe it's time to get our dear friend into our conversation, my darling." Vicky sat back down as Zechariah gently rubbed her shoulders, listening.

"Now that I too know you are a man of words, please, joined us in our little chat."

"Little chat? Such a modern term, my dear Vicky." The beautiful girl smiled up at Zechariah, who simply shook his head in astonishment "So, clever girl, you have found out my identity when no one else ever has. You are even more amazing than I foresaw, Victoria Elizabeth! It's good to hear you know the worth in protecting me from getting into the wrong hands. It takes a lot of smarts and bravery to outsmart Lucifer. Your strength comes from the Holy One, yes?"

"Yes, it does come from my strong faith, Exemplar, but of course, you would know of His great power." Vicky felt Zechariah's breath on her neck as he whispered.

"Vicky, who and what is Exemplar?"

"He is an angel, a very sorry, repenting angel, who escape the hands of Lucifer before he could be turned into a demon like his fellow fallen angels." Vicky looked sadly at the lost angel, hidden away from the time he was thrown from heaven with Lucifer and one third of God's holy angels who rebelled against Him to try and take over His throne."

"I wanted no part of hurting my creator anymore and once Lucifer turned you into his servant, his deadly demon, you would be doomed for all eternity." The fallen angel's voice held sadness. "Maybe, I will be doomed right along with them, but at least I can live what days I have, doing good and helping all those lost, wondering spirits find a close to their unknowing if they will ever find peace and justice. With you, dear Vicky, working with me, we can solve their unsolved cases and send them on through the channel of everlasting life." There was a hint of admiration in his next statement. "You claim to know

145

where the channel lies, Victoria Elizabeth and I assume you even know how I can bring a dead soul, long dead, back to life?"

"If knowing how you bring someone back to life is part of the test for getting my beloved here beside me permanently, then yes, I can reveal how you do the miracle." She felt Zechariah slide on the bench beside her.

"This I got to hear." He reached over and gave her a kiss. "Well, Exemplar, if my woman can give you all the right answers, can you send me to her side, never to leave."

"Of course, when you return, a complete and live man, you may remain with your woman once you have married her." There was a hint of mischief in the angel's voice. "Remember, she is a lady and a good Christian girl. If you wish to court for a proper time before you say your vows, I'm sure her parents and kin would understand a whole lot more, than you just dropping in and get married instantly. Zechariah, you have waited this long, what's a few more weeks, months, or even one little year?"

"I perhaps can wait a few weeks, Exemplar, but to ask me to wait any longer is quite impossible!" Zechariah felt Victoria touch his face.

"Relax my darling, we won't make it too long before we hear our wedding bells, but this wise mirror is right about my parents not understanding if we got married as soon as you arrive, alive! They will need time to find out about you and get to know you. I'm sure I can find a room right here in the manor house for you to stay until you join me in our rooms as Mr. and Mrs. Zechariah Castleton. I guess that will be quite a shock to everyone living here, come to think of it."

"Then listen to my wisdom, both of you." The mirror really loved this pair and he wanted everything to work out smoothly for them. "One of Zechariah's sisters left Castleton after she got married and had a son, whom she named Samuel Castleton."

"Why would she name him Castleton instead of her husband's last name?" Zechariah knew he was referring to his sister, Barbara Anne, who had married Eugene York.

146

"If you must know, your innocent sister got pregnant before she married Eugene York and he wanted no part of that child, so they put Samuel Castleton up for adoption. I'm sure you do not remember ever hearing his name because you never knew you had a Samuel Castleton as a nephew, did you?"

"No, I did not, nor did I know my saintly sister got herself pregnant with another man before she wed Eugene." Zechariah was stunned by the revelation, knowing how his sweet sister prized her innocents. "Even though I know Eugene York would have been my last choice for Barbara Anne, I just can't believe she would give herself to another man right before her marriage to this arrogant man."

"Then it's obvious you never knew your father arranged the marriage between her and Mr. York, giving the arrogant man, as you so cleverly put it, a huge sum of money and purchased them a large mansion on twenty acers of prime property in the state of New York, where Mr. York was born."

"Then I believe Barbara Anne was in love with this other man, probably not of much wealth so your father intervened, chose her a rich husband, most likely a man of high standing, set up the marriage and drove the poor devoted love one away, but not until Barbara Anne took her revenge and spent the night before her wedding with the man in her heart, and could never have again." Vicky thought how lucky she was to live in a new generation, where parents didn't have full control of their adult children, especially girls.

"My dear Victoria, you are 100% correct!" the angelic mirror stated, somewhat surprised by her great ability to read into the story and make a right conclusion. "After her wedding and honeymoon, Barbara Anne found out she was pregnant and intended to keep the fact that it was not Eugene's baby, from him after counting the days and secretly hoping it was her Robert's baby."

"But the obnoxious husband found out, either by counting the days himself, being one to never trust a female or the wonderful stud was incapable of having children and forgot to mention that little fact to his pushy father-in-law. My apologies Zechariah, darling." Victoria never liked arranged marriages, especially when true love was forfeited. "I am quite certain he failed to inform his new bride he could never give her a baby, either."

"It was the latter, my beautiful, clever young sleuth". The mirror laughed. "Samuel was adopted by his own daddy, Robert Castleton, your second cousin and there were sons born in every generation to carry on the Castleton name." the mirror grew very serious. "The last Castleton to have a son, from Robert and Barbara Anne's line, was a brilliant scientist named Gordon Castleton and he named his son, Zechariah, after you."

"Exemplar, I have a feeling this name was not all entirely Gordon Castleton's ideal!" Vicky glanced over at the man she loved. "Zechariah had been dead since 1800 and he was a far descendent of his. Second cousin to his grandfather Robert Castleton, so many greats back!"

"Vicky, what are you saying, darling? Someone placed that name inside his head?" Zechariah was confused as to what this had to do with his coming back alive. "Vicky, Exemplar, please, just tell me what this has to do with me."

"Zechariah, your woman is wise beyond her years and sees things most people could never see, not even this brilliant father who named his son, Zechariah." The magic mirror continued. "It was I that place the name and the seed inside of this man's head. We needed a body for Zechariah to enter into and I knew neither one of you would be satisfied to have a stranger's face instead of the handsome face belonging to one Zechariah Castleton, nor the same incredible blue eyes, that sets him apart from other men. So, I supplied the seed from the dust and sprinkled it with life, so the baby that grew in the dear woman who carried you nine months was 100% you, Zechariah Castleton, still a product of your dear mother, Isabell and your true father, of which you will learn later, through the wise woman you have chosen for your own."

"So, Joshua is not Zechariah's birth father?" Vicky reached over and gave her dear love a hug. "We will solve this mystery soon, my dearest, but now Exemplar has just informed us your earthly body must be joined to your spiritual body so you can live again." Victoria looked inside the mirror, wishing she could at lease see the falling angel's face, but perhaps the mirror had become the once beautiful angel. "I cannot believe Zechariah's body is somewhere moving around at this moment, not knowing who he really is, so, please tell us what state can we find Zechariah's body and where I must go to retrieve it, so it can be reunited when we bring him out of this 'channel of life'."

"Let me get this straight! My earthly body has been brought up from the grave and placed inside a new body?" Zechariah felt nervous about what must happen to come back. "Then my woman has to travel to wherever he...I mean, wherever I wait and bring me back here before she can contact you and get me out, alive?"

"For starters Zechariah, this is not a new body you will be entering, it is your body. The body that was buried on Christmas Eve, 1800, had already turned to bones and dust, so I needed to combined those fragments into one perfect seed and breathed new life into it, not of my own power but His!" The magic mirror, spoke with sincere love. "This lovely couple who called you their son, loved you so much they had the hospital keep you alive on machines for years and the handsome thirty-year-old man just lies there waiting for the day of uniting soul to body. The day that it happens, your spirit will reunite with your body and the doctors will noticed all the vital signs spark up with new life and the moment Victoria Elizabeth kisses your still lips, you will awake to your new life together." Seeing their smiles for one another, the mirror breathed with joy. "It's at Mercy Hospital, in New Orleans, a short distance."

"Then we simply come back, telling everyone here that I met the love of my life while on my little business trip, and we just knew we were meant for one another." Vicky laughed with happy joy.

"And I simply inform all the staff, as well as curious town folk, that I am a relative of Zechariah Castleton, a descendent from Zechariah's cousin, Robert Castleton." Zechariah felt the plan was sound and would work out for him and Victoria. "I have been told that I even look like my name's sake, although I would have no way of knowing this, but I do like my name,

149

Zechariah Castleton. It's a good strong name from the Holy book."

"You kids catch on very fast!" the mirror laughed softly. "And before you ask, no one will say anything about you leaving with Victoria, because they know her name well."

"You have sent letters, supposing to have been sent by me, in regards to my loving affection for this man lying in a coma since birth." Vicky smiled when Zechariah nuzzled her neck. So, when the mysterious woman shows up and kisses the sleeping handsome man and he wakes from his long dream, he just magically wants to leave with me."

"So, wouldn't the caring parents wish to keep their son with them after finally having him alert after thirty years?" Zechariah remembered how they had paid all those years to keep him alive and now the son was just leaving with a stranger to them."

"The loving parents gave the hospital all they had in their will to keep you alive before they died, two years apart." Exemplar knew Zechariah's good heart regretted he could never thank them for their part in helping him live again. He also knew, the brave man, had hoped the bad virus that took his life wasn't the reason for their early passing. "All the Yellow Fever germs have been destroyed, son. This couple did not catch the fever from you, they simply died from old age, having you late in life."

"Zechariah had asked earlier about the channel of life and how I would get him out." Vicky noticed Zechariah sat up with interest. "You avoided that statement, Exemplar because the fact is, Zechariah cannot know how I help him out and what you do for him. But I will tell my darling about this channel of life where you will send him, so he will know what to expect. It isn't as bad as he has imagined it, actually it will be far better than the place he's been waiting in."

"Then tell him only what you know you can, Victoria Elizabeth." Exemplar spoke boldly. "If you give him too much information, it will be almost impossible for you to draw him out!"

"I know my limits, my clever friend." Vicky turned to

150

Zechariah and caressed his face. "Darling, the channel you will find yourself will be briefly dark, then surround you with rainbow colors that fill you with total peace. My dearest, it is not a bad place and that is all that I can share with you, at least for now."

CHAPTER 20

"Exemplar has everything set for Thursday night, so I'm returning to New Orleans first thing in the morning." Vicky had met her friend in the breakfast room and had filled her in on the previous night's events, except the extra-long kiss Zechariah had given her before he had to go into the tunnel of life. She smiled to herself when she recalled his last words before vanishing.

"Vicky, my darling, the next time I see you, I will be a living, breathing, man. My heart has long for this so very long, the joy in knowing it is finally happening is my greatest happiness."

"Vicky to earth, did you hear me?" Samantha reached for another hot muffin and watched her friend look up and smile. "I ask you if I was tagging along to New Orleans? Everyone here will expect me to go with you, since we do almost everything together."

"How else could I manage driving two cars to New Orleans? It appears the rental is still here and I need to return it."

"I wonder what sort of car Mr. Hancock bought you to drive?" Samantha made a sour face. "If it's as old fashion as the rest of this place, it might be a jalopy! One of Henry Ford's first Model-T's!"

"At least we will be getting lots of looks when we drive up to Mercy Hospital and blow the Model T's horn." Victoria laughed along with her friend at the funny sight.

"How about the priceless look from the bellhop at the French Quarter Inn when he steps out to retrieve our luggage from the old Model-T Ford!" Sam stopped laughing when the serious butler walked in, keys dangling from his white gloved hand.

"Hardly a T-Model Ford, Miss Samantha but nevertheless a priceless antique." Thornton had been listening just outside the breakfast room. "You said you would be needing it Friday morning, so I took the liberty of having it serviced, filled with gas, and cleaned and buffed to a perfect shine."

"We were merely joking about the type of car waiting inside that closed garage. There was never a doubt that you would chose something attractive for the owner of Stanford Hall Plantation."

"Indeed, madam, we must set a good example, not only for the plantation but for the town of Castleton." The proper butler handed her the car keys. "Would you care to see your car this morning, Miss Victoria?"

"Yes Thornton, I would like that very much." Vicky stood up and was joined by her friend, Samantha. "Will you be showing us the car, or will we meet Reginald at the garage?"

"Mr. Myers is expecting you, so you may go anytime." The butler bowed gracefully. "The small Honda rental has been serviced as well. We want you to arrive safely and enjoy your shopping trip. Perhaps you might try Libby's dress shop, down town Castleton, the next time around. I totally understand the need for returning the rented car. It can get pricey just sitting parked."

"Thank you for your concern, Thornton." Victoria moved to the front door, Samantha by her side. "It's a pity Anthony and Jefferson had to scrap their plans in taking it back, but I'm sure they had a very good reason why they could not leave town."

"Yes, Miss Victoria, the fact that their court case in New Orleans had been settled out of court and the need to go there was canceled, the two gallant gentlemen were going to take your car back anyway when Mr. Maxwell called with an important case they could not turn down."

"So, the two 'gallant' gentlemen chose a high-paying client over a promise made to another client, one with higher morals than the latter." Samantha faked a smile. "I'm sure Victoria Bell left them enough money for handling her case and would have appreciated a small amount of that large check to be spent on a couple hired men to return the car for her niece, they treated like royalty."

"Sam, just give them the benefit of doubt. I'm sure the great and powerful Marshall Maxwell has his way of convincing people to do his bidding, much like the devil." Vicky gave the shocked butler a beautiful smile. "Relax Thornton, Mr. Maxwell is not in hearing distance, unless of course, you would care to share my opinions with the screw."

"Share your words with that jackal? No madam, I'd just as soon have my tongue cut out than to give that gigolo anything to use against you, fair lady!" The butler opened the door for the girls. "Speaking of the stealing bandit, there was a letter brought late yesterday afternoon, after you had retired to your chamber. I recognized the carrier as one of Maxwell's servants and he insisted the letter be placed in your hands only. He did say it was of a personal message and he would appreciate an answer as soon as possible."

"Thornton, why am I just now hearing about this letter?" Victoria knew Zechariah wanted her to wait until he was there beside her before accepting any invitations from Marshall Maxwell, from the family his people despised for generations.

"I suppose I had tucked it far back inside my brain, Miss Victoria, because of the distrust I feel for this vulture!" Thornton gave her a weak smile. "If it pleases you, my dear, I will go fetch it straight way."

"It can wait, dear friend. I have more important matters to attend to than to read a dinner invitation I will have to turn down. Hopefully, he will understand my reasons, but if not, it really is no concern of mine. Thornton, to be perfectly frank, I'm not just going to New Orleans to return my rented car or shop the day away, I am meeting someone I met, who means the world to me and who has stolen my heart."

"Congratulations Miss Victoria, this is very surprising news and I just hope he doesn't intend to take you away from your new home!" the butler looked disturbed over the thoughts of this brilliant young woman abandoning Stanford Hall for the love of a man.

"Take me away from Stanford Hall? My beloved would never ask me to leave a place he too feels apart of, Thornton." She smiled when his worried face melted into a big smile.

"When I found out he was a Castleton, I was overjoyed, then to learn he was named after a distant relative, I knew destiny had brought us together."

"What is the young man's name? Perhaps I have heard Zechariah speak of a cousin or some close relative by your boyfriend's name." Thornton was excited over the news and was anxious to hear the young man's name.

"Oh, you have heard his name many times, Thornton." Victoria stepped out on the porch and turned smiling. "His name is, Zechariah Castleton, tall, black hair and the most alluring blue eyes I have ever looked into." The girls left the butler, standing with his mouth wide open.

"It's not just any big black shiny old Rolls, it's been parked inside a dust free garage since it came off the showroom floor in 1950." Reginal Myers had pushed open the garage door for the car's new owner to admire. "Isn't she a beauty?"

"That is one sharp looking automobile, Reginal. I would be proud to be seen anywhere inside this handsome car."

"Miss Victoria, I'm aware of your plans in traveling to New Orleans. You will drive one car and Miss Samantha will take the other one, but if you will permit me, I have been preparing ever since your arrival was announced, to be your personal chauffeur." He pulled a chauffeur's hat from behind his back. "If you permit me to take you, then bring you both back, I would not only be honored but someone with your high standing in society needs a driver to take you around, especially over one-hundred miles away."

"Vic, That's not a bad ideal. For one thing, you might be recognized now as the new owner of Stanford Hall and it wouldn't be the same as when we arrived in New Orleans, two young women headed to the small town of Castleton." Samantha smiled over at the groundskeeper. "I hope there's room for one more rider, Reginal. Vic, is picking up her future husband at Mercy Hospital while we're in New Orleans."

"Did you say...future husband?" Vicky's new chauffeur, groundskeeper, looked perplexed as he fumbled with his cap." Is he a doctor, working at this hospital?"

155

"Nowhere close, Reginal, Mr. Castleton is a patient at Mercy Hospital and I am going to have him released and bring him home, where he belongs, with me." Vicky walked around the car, trying not to laugh at the man's confused expression. He jumped when she patted his back. "It's really very simple, Reginal, I met him some time ago, we fell in love, he caught a virus while in New Orleans, was admitted to Mercy hospital and now cured, waiting for me to come and release him. Having attachments to Castleton and Stanford Hall, Zechariah couldn't wait to see the plantation his distance cousin loved so much."

"Zechariah? He was named after…'the' Zechariah Castleton who lived here almost as often as he did his own mansion in town? The same Zechariah you wept over in the graveyard?"

"Yes, Reginal, all in the same." Vicky walked back out into the late morning sunshine. "It's as though the first Zechariah has been incarnated into the present Zechariah, who looks remarkably the same. Remember, I have seen his ghost. They could defiantly be identical twins."

"That explains why you were so attached to Zechariah at the graveyard, in your dream that is the exact same as the church records described." Reginal winked at her. "You can trust me, Miss Victoria. With everything we talked about in the chapel and now. I truly believe, somehow, someway, the man we will be picking up is the one and only Zechariah Castleton, somehow come back to life!"

"This grave is a mess, Vic!" Samantha tugged at a stubborn weed. "I cannot believe after two-hundred-years, these superstitious people still believe they can catch the Yellow Fever from this grave!"

"I think they're more afraid of the two spirits, coming to the top and making small talk." Vicky chuckled at the things people believed in. "I can hear them now, 'Zechariah, how's your coffin lay, mine is a little stale and could use a good airing out!', then Zechariah would answer, 'I'd settle for a puff of fresh air! It's impossible to breathed down there.'"

Samantha was laughing so hard she didn't hear the young chaplain walk up, carrying hoes, grass seed and paint.

"I'm sorry I was gone when you arrived, but I had to visit some of the field workers who just started getting in the first harvest." He walked inside the fence and held out the tools and paint. "Choose ladies, two hoes, for digging out those stubborn weeds or the paint brush, for painting a new coat of paint on this dull paint?"

"I'm great at painting, Joshua." Samantha stood up and wiped the dirt off her hands. "I'll have it looking like new in no time."

"Sam is the better painter. I'm afraid. I would end up with as much paint as the fence if I tackled that job." Victoria laughed softly as she heard her friend's soft humming. "But I've hoed many a weed out of my parent's garden." She watched the chaplain attack the weeds, tossing them out on a pile. "I see you're handy with a hoe as well, Joshua."

"Like you, Victoria, my years growing up on our family farm, taught me many skills that are helpful whenever needed." He smiled over at the beautiful woman, who was tenderly cleaning off Zechariah's tomb. "You really care deeply about that man, don't your Victoria?"

"I love Zechariah Castleton Reverend Whittington and he loves me." Vicky looked over and found him warmly staring. "Does this sound strange to you Joshua, after learning how I showed up here when Zechariah was dying and stayed with him until he took his last breath."

"What can become of this love, Victoria? He is dead and has been for over two-hundred-years." the chaplain reached over and touched her hand. "You are young and alive, with everything to offer a living man. You cannot spend your days thinking about what could have been and will never happen. Try to forget this dream and learn to love someone who can touch you, kiss you, and give you happiness."

"Joshua, I've already found that man, you just described and it's not a dead corpse lying in the ground. Very soon I will be in his arms, feel his touch, his kiss. He truly gives me happiness."

"Then I am glad you're not hanging on to the false hope of

having a life with Zechariah Castleton." The chaplain was depressed that Victoria had declared her love for another man and his hopes of winning her affections was all but gone. "There, the ground is ready for seed and Samantha looks almost finished." He handed Victoria some of the seed and they began scattering it around. "What's the lucky man's name?"

"You should know Joshua, it's Zechariah Castleton, and before you start thinking I have gone completely insane, I can explain. And what I tell you now shall remain with you, just like the real dream we discussed in the chapel. Do I have your word to keep this our secret?"

"I shall gladly keep this secret, same as the first one." Joshua gazed into her beautiful blue eyes as he thought. "At least this is something I can share with the woman I love."

"I cannot tell you who or what has made this miracle happen, but Zechariah's earthly body waits for me as soon as his spirit is joined back with it. Now don't go thinking it's just bones and dust, although these were brought up and formed into a living breathing man, who at the present is in a coma and has been since he was reborn." Vicky bit her lip as Joshua stared wide-eyed. "Just remember how I was brought to Zechariah before his death, over two-hundred-years apart. Can you explain that? Then how do you expect me to explain how this could happen, except to say, I was brought back in time, now Zechariah has been brought up in time!"

"Forgive me, dear Victoria. For a brief moment there I was living in a normal world. I keep forgetting this plantation holds mysteries unseen or unheard of by man." Joshua took her hands. "There are records in this chapel that cannot be explained, so if you say Zechariah has returned and is alive, I must believe you." He looked deep into her eyes. "I could never doubt someone who means so much to me."

"Dear friend, thank you for believing my words and for you undying trust." Vicky turned when she heard her friend blow out her breath and announce.

"I have finished!" Samantha had been listening and patted the chaplain on the back, before handing him the brush inside the empty can. "Joshua, we might as well get use to strange spirits wondering around with unsolved mysteries this great detective has to solve. I'm sure she already has someone in mine after she has finished solving the case on Zechariah and this who and what, she told you about."

"Well then, miss sleuth, you can always count on me to assist you in any way I can." He opened the empty grass seed bag and threw the can and brush inside, as he smiled at their perfect job. "I think Reginal wasn't needed after all and I'm sure his excuse for not helping was innocent enough."

"Very innocent, Joshua, same as yours for coming late." Victoria laughed as she walked toward the graveyard entrance. "Those part time field workers had to be given instructions before they could start gathering the harvest in." seeing his smile, she continued. "After all, that is his job."

"I guess one of your jobs will be to perform the marriage celebration between my best friend here and her true love." Samantha did not notice the smile vanishing from his face as she continued. "Of course, there must be a short courting time, introductions to Vicky's parents and a great big wedding ball in the grand ball room!"

"Sam, come down off that cloud." Victoria laughed. "The chapel is the perfect size for my guest list and either parlor will work perfect for the reception. The big Christmas Ball is the only ball I can handle, thank you."

"I'd be happy to marry you." He knew his words had a double meaning, and by Victoria's reply, he assumed her detective skills were kicking in when she said softly.

"Joshua, I'm not available, for my heart belongs to Zechariah. I am truly honored that you have feelings for me, but you must seek someone else." Vicky nodded toward her pretty friend, picking a handful of daisies. "Sam is truly a lovely girl, warm, charming, and witty. The best part is, she is a woman of faith. This should be important to a man of God."

"Victoria, it's hard to just cut off love, but I will be happy for you and Zechariah, as well as honored to perform your wedding here in Grace Chapel." He squeezed her hand, then smiled down at the sweet innocent girl picking off pedals, repeating, he loves me, he loves me not.

CHAPTER 21

"Exemplar, I am here to release Zechariah from the tunnel to heaven, were he waits." Victoria had finally sent Charlotte away, after the young woman kept insisting on doing things for her. Thursday had finally arrived and the day seem to drag by, even though she had pack some clothes for Zechariah to wear when he was released from the hospital. After reading some of Victoria Rose's diary concerning Zechariah, she had learned he kept clothes inside the wardrobe, folded in a brown box. When she searched the wardrobe, she was overjoyed to find a brown box with his name on it and inside was what looked like a new outfit. When she found the note on top with her name, she was amazed to read,

"My darling Vicky, when you find my clothes, please see that I get them. Hopefully they won't be too wrinkle."

"So, Victoria, you know he waits now in the tunnel to heaven. Does your sharp mind tell you why the one you love waits there?" the mirror waited for her to respond.

"Zechariah is waiting there just in case I fail to bring him out, knowing this is his last holding spot until the angels come and lead him to the light." Vicky answered with mixed emotions, knowing between the two places of entry, the wide path leading to the darkest tunnel where demons would grab hold and drag you down into the pits of hell, or down the narrow path to the tunnel of heaven, the later was always the best. "I realize if I fail, my chances of getting my love one out is gone forever."

"You just past the first test, clever one. Now, think before you answer the last question, for this will determined whether or not you won your devoted Zechariah's life." The mirror seemed to glow for a moment and as the glow vanished, what looked like an hourglass was sitting on her vanity table. "After I ask you the question, this five-minute time glass will flip over and began counting the seconds. Waste not a second, for your answer must be accurate."

"I understand Exemplar. I am ready! Zechariah is counting on me and his clothes are packed!" Victoria took a deep breath. "Ask your question?"

"To bring a man that has been dead for over two-hundred-years, back to life, is an impossible task, yet, his new body lies waiting to be united with his soul, his spirit. Victoria Elizabeth Stanford, can you tell me how this amazing act can be accomplished?" at those last words, the sand glass flip over and began sifting slowly out.

Victoria formed her answer carefully in her mind, for this was the most important case she had ever took on and her Zechariahs life or new life in heaven, depended on her answer. As soon as she saw the last grains fall through, she began speaking clearly.

"The answer to this amazing miracle is Jesus's healing and bringing back to life someone, even though he has laid in the grave for a long time. Exemplar, before you were created into a beautiful angel, there was Jesus, whom, after your creation, you admired deeply and loved beyond question. You were aware of his healing power long before he came to earth and started performing many miracles. Somehow, you managed to be there, to see him called Lazarus from his tomb where he had laid for four days. You will perform the uniting of spirit to body, through the name of Jesus Christ, who is the resurrection and the LIFE!" Vicky waited for what seemed like an eternity before the angel hidden inside the mirror spoke. Some people might start to question their answer, thinking they failed, but not the young detective. Victoria knew, without a shadow of a doubt, she was absolutely correct.

"And you are 100% correct, Victoria Elizabeth!" Exemplar laughed. Not only did you pass the first and second test, you past the hidden test."

"Hidden Test? That has to be, a test of the mind, going over what you just said in your thoughts and in my case, I knew my words were accurate. Others might start second guessing their response and get themselves into a tizzy, never knowing that angels can read minds. You can even speak spirit talk."

"No wonder He called you, the seeker of the truth, Victoria Elizabeth, way over two-thousand-years ago!" he sensed a question, but nipped it before it fell out of her beautiful mouth. "That is a mystery for another time, for now Zechariah is waiting. I leave you now to attend to his needs and you must get some much-needed rest. You have a busy day tomorrow and the one thing you don't need to worry about is returning a car to the airport rental department, so I've made alternate plans arise. With a small amount of coaching, I convinced Reginal Myers that he needed a truck and big wagon to help get the harvest in quicker. He will be informing you tomorrow that one of his workers, Harvey Pennywise will now be driving the rented Honda and return it, walk across the street to the Ford dealer and purchase the truck that will be waiting. Now, you are free to go directly to Mercy Hospital and collect a risen Zechariah, to the amazement of every doctor in the place."

"You see Exemplar, that speaking spirit talk into some one's mind, Reginal Myers, in this case, is something that can be used for good, even if the recipient thought it was their own brilliant conscious speaking." Vicky laughed, feeling relieved that she did not need to waste time taking the rental back, since she knew she would be driving it and Sam would choose to ride with her, letting Reginal follow in the big expensive car.

"I will see you and Zechariah tomorrow night to discuss his case, so you can start wrapping up a few more clues."

"Thank you, dear angel, dear friend." Vicky gave the top of the frame a little pat. "You are a good friend and I plan to take your case on next, although I may be learning things about you and from you for many years." She slid from the bench and stretch. "I'm off to bed now. Please tell my darling Zechariah, I will wake him up tomorrow with a kiss! Goodnight Exemplar! I love you dear friend."

"And I love you, Vicky! I have known millions of people, but you are the first person to tell me you love me and I find that…very moving and touching. I can truly see His light shining through you, sweet one." Victoria thought she heard a few sniffles when he concluded with. "Good night, my friend. Be sure to know, angels are watching over you!" the mirror grew silent and Victoria knew he was with her precious Zechariah.

Mercy Hospital, 12:00 Midnight, Friday Morning

The nurse had just finished reading the latest letter from the mysterious lady named Victoria Elizabeth Stanford to the silent man. She had begun her long shift of sitting by the coma-stricken patient. It would have been easy to fall in love with such a handsome man, had he not been born without a functioning brain. All the humming machines had kept him alive and breathing, but Gail Gilmore couldn't understand why anyone would wish this on another human being. Nevertheless, his devoted parents wanted to keep him alive in hopes that a miracle might occur and he would just suddenly wake up.

"What was going through their minds to even hope for any change in their son, when he had absolutely no brain movements at all?" she laid down the letter and picked up her book, ready for her eight-hour shift. Removing her bookmarker, she started to read when she heard a beep from one of the monitors. Her head flew up to check for any sign of lights flashing. Seeing none, she settled back down and started the book again, mumbling to herself.

"This job is getting the best of me! Now I think I'm hearing alive monitor, the sign of a brain in motion." Nurse Gilmore shook her head and gave a little laugh. "I might have gotten frighten if it was Halloween night." As she read, her eyes grew heavy and started to close when she heard the monitor beep again, but this time it grew louder as it continued beeping, turning all the monitors on full active mode.

"Oh my God! His brain is alive!" the excited nurse mashed down on the intercom, speaking loudly. "Call the doctor working the night shift! There is movement on the monitors! Mr. Castleton is alive!" she waited but got no response "Hello out there! Is no one awake at the nurse's station?" hearing confusion in the open door, Gail Gilmore looked around to find all the nurses, along with Doctor Wilson Turner standing in the doorway, each wearing a stun expression on their faces.

CHAPTER 22

Reginal pulled the 1950 Rolls up to the entrance of Mercy Hospital in New Orleans and stopped the car. His eyes went to the rearview mirror and noticed both girls checking out the old hospital. He climbed out and opened the door for Victoria, extending his hand to help her out.

"If I did not know you were a first-class groundskeeper, Reginal, I might think you have always been a chauffeur. All that practicing has paid off." Victoria smiled as she took his hand and climbed out, noticing she had drawn a few spectators, all wondering her importance. "I'm not too sure I like all this attention though. Perhaps we should have parked in the garage where I could walk in like everyone else."

"But you're not everyone else, Miss Victoria." Reginal Myers helped Samantha out after she slid over. "Did you not read the part in Miss Victoria Bell's diary about letters you had written to Zechariah to be sent to his bedside for the nurses to read to him while he lay in a comatose state?"

"I never had a chance to read that part yet, but I see Charlotte found the book on my bedside table and decided to have a peek." Vicky started to remember something about writing letters to Zechariah while he lay dying from Yellow Fever. Did he ask her to? While he was still alive, did, the man she love know this day would come and her letters being read to his still body would somehow keep him strong? "I guess what you are trying to tell me Reginal is, this hospital has been receiving love letters from a Victoria Elizabeth Stanford for twenty years to be read to Zechariah Castleton every night, one letter each month, repeated until the next one arrived always on the first."

"I guess you've become quite the celebrity Vic, the unknown, mysterious writer, sending words of affection to a man you've obviously never met, at lease to this hospital staff who has kept Zechariah's body alive his entire new life."

Samantha turned to smile at the gathering crowd. And notice several of them had taken out their smart phones and were snapping photos. She quickly grabbed her friend by the arm and gave it a tug toward the entrance doors. "I think it's time to get off the red carpet and go inside to mingle with the crowd."

The two friends walked through the main entrance and up to the front desk. A grey-haired clerk looked up and peered over her black rim glasses.

"May I assist you ladies in finding a patient?"

"You may, thank you. Which room would I find Zechariah Castleton in? I've come to get him discharged and take him home." Victoria noticed how silent those standing close by had become, but kept her attention on the clerk, who was obviously suddenly interested in this special request and from a total stranger.

"Excuse me Miss, but you must be mistaken, have the wrong patient in mind. The man you mention is in no state to travel with anyone." The receptionist reached over and pressed a button as she continued. "Mr. Castleton has been in a comatose state his entire life and is on state-of-the-art life support, which cannot be cut off, unless..."

"Unless a miracle happens?" Victoria smiled up at the serious male doctor that walked up to the desk, checking out his name tag, she, acknowledge him. "Doctor Davis, it's good to meet one of the doctors who have been keeping my Zechariah alive for twenty years. Now that he is improving, I have come to wake him up and take him home, where I can promise he will receive all the love and attention he deserves."

"Could you be Victoria Elizabeth Stanford, the lady behind all those beautiful love letters." He suddenly wished he were available and this beautiful young woman wasn't so in love with his silent patient.

"I am Victoria Elizabeth Stanford, the one responsible for writing the sixty love letters to my darling Zechariah when he reached sixteen until his twentieth birthday. Did not my last letter state, as you lie same as death, I will awake you with a kiss when 16 reaches up to 20!" Vicky recalled the last note she

165

had written after Zechariah had kissed her one last time before slipping away into death. She noticed her friend watching her with uncertainty, hoping Vicky hadn't just made the line up as a bluff, in hopes the doctor hadn't heard the nurse on call reading it. Samantha nervously watched as the doctor motioned for someone and had hoped it wasn't the hospital security.

"It is obvious you are indeed who you claim to be, Miss Stanford." Doctor Davis waved another clerk forward carrying a huge file and handed it to him. "I will take Zechariah's records up with us in case I need them for referral." Opening the elevator door, the cute doctor stood back so they could go in, then hit the button for number seven, the top floor. "At the presence, Zechariah is the only patient on the seventh floor. His parents had it added on just for their son and his personal care and privacy. They did not want a lot of nosey people calking at their handsome son. Should that kiss wake him up, which will definitely be a miracle straight out of a fairy tale, then this floor can be opened up for twenty patients."

"Twenty patients?" Samantha looked up at the doctor, still wondering if he knew what the real words were that were in that love letter. She just knew her friend had no way of knowing its contents no more than Samantha knew, herself, so it had to be a bluff. "The Castleton's must have been loaded to afford one entire floor and then pay for round the clock care for their son."

"That boy was their life and I can't explain how they could possibly know that he would miraculously wake up after his twentieth birthday." The doctor shook his head in confusion. "Never before has there ever been a case like his before. Very strange."

"There's nothing strange about a person who is comatose and on life support, Doctor Davis." Samantha had heard of many such cases. "What is so different about this case, except the fact the parents predicted when he might wake up?"

"Sam, I think what Doctor Davis is referring to is most comatose patients cannot develop strong bones and muscles or even grow to their proper height or weight." Vicky and Sam noticed the positive head nod from the doctor. "Zechariah is well developed, who's muscles look as though he did weights in a gym and even though he has never walked a day in his life, he has the strength to stand upright and walk out of here."

"You amaze me, Miss Stanford. You have never one time seen our patient and yet, you described his physical appearance perfect." The doctor waited for the girls to exit the elevator before getting off and taking them down the hallway to the nurse's station, where two women in white sat watching monitors carefully. "Tracy, Maybelle, can I pull you away a moment and introduce this charming lady and her lovely friend, Samantha. Ladies, this is the mysterious Victoria Elizabeth Stanford we've all been wanting to meet."

"Finally, we get to put a face along with all those beautiful words, each of us have shared with Zechariah since he turned sixteen." Tracy reached across to shake Vicky's hand. "Have you come to give him that kiss you wrote about?"

"It was such a romantic line I can quote it much like one would perform a play. It goes like this..." Maybelle cleared her throat as Samantha closed her eyes in total worry. "As you lie same as death, I will awake you with a kiss when 16 reaches up to 20! Isn't it lovely?"

Samantha's eyes flew open in total surprise as she blurted out "Vic, how did you know that?" suddenly she noticed all eyes were on her. "What I meant was, how on earth could she remember every single word she wrote after a month, but then, Vicky is extremely clever at remembering facts, even poems we learned from elementary school, she can quote them word for word."

"I guess you are anxious to see Zechariah and the amazing news is how the monitors came to life just in the last few days, Thursday to be exact, so there is movement in the brain now." Doctor Davis ordered the nurses back to watching the monitors and had the two friends follow him to a closed door, where two chairs waited just outside the room. "Miss Stanford, if you and your friend will wait here until Mr. Castleton's other doctor arrives and one of us will usher you inside." He smiled and walked away.

"Sam, Zechariah is just right through that door waiting for

Joan Byrd

my kiss to wake him up!" Victoria leaned over to check down the empty hall, finding it empty. "Oh darn, so close. I hope that doctor hurries up!"

"Anxious to kiss your forever mate, my dear Victoria?" Looking the opposite way, down the empty hall,

Vicky hadn't heard the doctor walk up next to them. She turned to see a very tall man with long blonde hair, unusually handsome in a strange way. "I hope I did not startle you. I do have a habit of making a quiet entrance. I suppose its from years of working in a hospital environment."

"Yes, I admit I never heard you approaching and I pride myself with knowing what's always around me." Victoria stood up, in hopes this was the doctor they were waiting for. "I hope we can go in now and see Zechariah. He has waited for my kiss long enough."

"Yes Victoria, Zechariah is more than ready to come back alive!" Vicky noticed how the man's eyes lit up when he winked and walked through the door. "There lies your beloved, kiss him quickly child."

Vicky had an unusual feeling regarding this doctor, with a twinkle in his bright green eyes, but it was a good feeling, a safe feeling, filled with hope as she made her way over to the bed and gasp at the handsome man lying asleep. Her heart beat with total love as she bent down and lovingly kissed the man she adored after saying his name softly.

A loud intake of breath jerked the young man into breathing on his own, a smile fell on his handsome lips as his eyes opened and looked up into those of the woman he had given his heart to over two-hundred-years ago. Then the familiar sound she had been waiting to here came clearly in the still room.

"Vicky, my dearest darling, you have brought me out of the tunnel to heaven, where my guardian angel waited with me."

"I think I have just met your guardian, my darling, for it was him who let me inside this room with you." She looked around to thank him and found the room empty, except for the beeping monitors. Once again, he silently disappeared. "I am glad Sam thought it best to wait for me outside so I could awake you alone darling, since the blonde headed doctor just disappeared."

168

"Tall man, strangely handsome, long blonde hair and bright green eyes?" Zechariah slowly sat up, switched off the monitors and pulled Victoria into his arms. "Yes, that was the angel that waited with me." The couple looked around when the door flung open and Doctor Davis raced in with the staff of nurses and another man in white.

"Oh my God! The patient is awake and sitting up!" the other doctor stated in total shock as Doctor Davis walked past him, staring at the couple.

"Miss Stanford, how did you manage to get into this room. We had the door locked, just in case you might decide to enter on your own. It is strictly forbidden for a visitor to enter without being accompanied by a staff member."

"I assure you Doctor Davis, I waited for a doctor and when one showed up, opened the door and took me inside, I did not hesitate." Vicky looked at both doctors before stating "Believe me, when the tall blonde-headed doctor told me to kiss Zechariah, I did not hesitate. He had waited long enough and we needed to be together after the miraculous occurrence took place."

"Miraculous is an understatement, young lady!" the name tag read Doctor Thomas Warren, as he marched up and stood within inches of the beautiful woman. "All I know is, when I walked up where Jeff and the nurses were waiting my arrival, the very active beeping monitors suddenly stopped and shut down. We all assume you had managed to inter the room, sneak over to the comatose man and unhook his life support, ending his death-like state, but we find right the opposite!"

"For starters, Doctor Warren, I would just as soon end my own life than to ever wish my beloved dead again!" Vicky stood her ground as Zechariah stepped forward and stared down at the shaken doctor.

"Do not talk to my woman like that ever again sir or I shall challenge you to a fight!"

The staff and doctors could not believe what they were witnessing and one of the nurses found the courage to speak to the patient who had suddenly awakened and could talk and make sense.

Joan Byrd

"Mr. Castleton, when we read you all those letters as you lay in a coma, could you hear us?"

"I was blessed with each and every letter my dearest wrote me and the last one, referring to the kiss, was my very favorite." Zechariah slipped his arm around Victoria's shoulders. "Now that I am better, I want to leave with my betrothed."

"This is a most unusual request, young man. We cannot be sure that you are ready to be released right after just waking up from a twenty-year coma." Doctor Jeff Davis walked over to check his blood pressure and found it perfect. "What if you leave and you suddenly have a relapse and fall back into a coma without any monitors and life-saving machines around?"

"You've never been outside this room, so you have been protected from all the common germs lurking around every day people! For them, it would be minor but for you, with no immune system it could prove fatal." Doctor Warren grew dramatic. "We promised your parents we would take care of you and by Joe, we will!"

"As I recall, the parents stated after their son woke from his death-like sleep, he must be released." Victoria knew the angels would not let Zechariah have the miracle of life again only to lose it from catching some virus. "That is what they requested, right doctors?"

"That's the way I heard it too, Doctor Davis." Samantha had walked inside to see what all the commotion was all about. "Surely you are not upset about Zechariah's inheritance going to him and your high paid salaries for watching him coming to an end guide your thinking! "Sam looked up at Jeff Davis. "Didn't you say if Zechariah woke up and left, the will stated you could use this floor for twenty patients? That sounds like a very generous gift to leave the hospital in gratitude for saving their son."

"Miss Samantha is absolutely correct!" the tall doctor appeared and presented the doctor in charge a legal paper. "I am Doctor Angel, the Castleton family doctor, and this paper gives me the rights to get my patient released at once. I do believe Victoria has brought a set of clothing for the young man to wear, so you can forget that excuse for delaying their exit."

170

He smiled at the loving couple. "I can guarantee the patient is healthy as a racehorse, all vitals perfect, immune system in topnotch shape. In short gentlemen, if I were a betting man, which I assure you, I am not, either of you would catch your death of cold long before this one!" having a pen appear from his pocket, he handed it to Doctor Davis. "Now, if you will sign my document, then take your fine-looking group back out and sign all the release papers, Zechariah can finally get back in his clothes and feel like himself again."

"I beg your pardon?" Doctor Warren stared in disbelief. "Did you just say, get 'back into his clothes' and feel like himself again? What does that mean?"

"Warren, forget it! This entire case has been anything but normal!" Jeff Davis smiled over at the couple. "Something tells me everything will work out for you kids and if you can find the time, drop us a letter and keep us informed on what's happening. You write a magic letter, Victoria Elizabeth Stanford and good luck Zechariah, we all will miss you. We watched you grow up into the special man you always were meant to be." The doctor wiped his eyes and walked out.

"I found your clothes where you left them, Zechariah, along with the note you wrote me." Victoria picked up the package containing the clothes and set it on the bed. "You had me write all those letters for you when I set by your bedside."

"I had been warned that this might happen to me if I made it through the channel of life, so that is why I wanted you to write so many love letters, then read them back to me so I would know they were yours I heard, while in a coma." Zechariah opened the box and smiled. "I think my Vicky ironed them for me. They're much too perfect." He kissed her tenderly. "I hope the heavy iron did not wear you out, dearest,"

"I must admit, I cheated and used the iron I packed, an electric steam iron, lighter and much faster than the old irons you had to heat over a stove." Vicky laughed and walked over to the door to where Samantha and Doctor 'Angel' were waiting. "We'll be waiting just outside the door, darling. I'd say, take your time, but I've waited far too long to have you by my side."

"I shall make with haste, my beloved and fly to your arms before you miss me, or, you may stay and help me dress, I am not shy when it comes to a woman's touch." He smiled, melting her heart.

"Tempting as it sounds, my darling, I must admit, I am shy when it comes to helping my man get dressed. I shall save that pleasure for our wedding night, when I help undress you." Vicky hurried out.

CHAPTER 23

"Exemplar, I cannot thank you enough for leading Zechariah to me. He is truly my eternal love and through some transformation, we were separated by over two-hundred-years and it was your genius mind that brought us together." Vicky never felt so happy as she did after leaving Mercy Hospital with her one true love, alive and healthy, despite his new body lying in a coma for twenty years.

"To finally get to meet the young lady who can start helping all those wondering spirits is a greater blessing to me, Victoria." She could hear relief in his voice as he continued. "Now I can began repenting for my part in the clumsy attempt to take over the throne of the Almighty God, Creator of all the universe and everything in existence! He might never forgive me, but at least I can feel better about my worthless existence by helping his children. If my fate is still to burn in the never-ending lake of fire with Lucifer and my fellow fallen angels, then it is God's just punishment for all of us."

"Exemplar, I will do everything in my power to help all the loss souls you seek to help." Victoria felt sad over her new friend's tragic situation and she knew in her heart she must try and help him, for she could see his good heart. "The way I see it my friend, these wondering spirits aren't the only souls that need help. Exemplar, I will make it a top priority to save your soul as well. We both serve a loving and forgiving Lord, who has given both humans and angels the gift of choice. Lucifer and all his other followers have sinned against God and Heaven ever since their fall, but not you Exemplar. You regretted your part in the battle for Heaven as soon as you landed in the dark water, which covered the earth before God made it into a living-breathing earth. Finding the bottom, you remained there, hidden away from Lucifer and the rest of your brothers. As the dry land began to appear, you could see light filtering in the water and you knew it was just a matter of time, someone

173

would spot you and your fate would be as theirs, to be turned into demons by the powerful angel of light, Lucifer who would be known as Satan and the devil."

"It was as though I could hear His voice warning me to hide myself and stay true." Exemplar took a big breath. "I told you I turned myself into a mirror, but fair one, I had no such power to transform my appearance into an object. Only the Creator can take a lump of clay and turn it into a vestal, a living-breathing body! One moment I was a scared broken angel, the next moment, I was a beautiful looking glass and that is when I saw Him, the Lord standing in front of me waving his hands over my oval head, filling me with His power to seek and restore, to heal and even make alive, in His Holy name."

"Don't you see, Exemplar, the Lord is giving you a chance to repent." Tears filled Vicky's eyes. "Such a loving forgiving Lord."

"I was hidden away in the Garden of Eden, then moved out when the angels were placed at the entrance to keep everyone out. I found myself in a cave until the first mirror was invented, then cleverly placed in a street market for my first owner to buy." Exemplar laughed softly. "I saw some pretty ridiculous faces over my existence and never talked to anyone until the young boy found me in the London ditch and took me home with him, where he cleverly built the vanity you sit at today."

"Who made the exquisite frame with the beautiful carvings around you? It had to be a gifted carpenter." Vicky ran her hand over the smooth wood.

"That is a story for another time, Victoria. You must finish your first mystery. The one about Zechariah. Who his real father was and what happened to him, why Delmarrio kidnapped the six Castleton children, but favored the oldest, Zechariah. Why do the spirits of the children come from the woods and what are they looking for? And last, to search and find the missing painting of Zechariah and reunite it with the portrait Zechariah had painted of you, currently hanging in Marshall Maxwell's bedroom."

"My portrait, in my bedroom, Exemplar!" Zechariah had walked in and overheard the mirror's long list of unsolved facts regarding him. "We will get my things back from that jackal, if it's the last thing I do!"

"Calm yourself down, young Zechariah. I did not just save your hide so you could do something foolish and loose it, leaving this beautiful woman a widow before your I dos grow cold!" the mirror scolded. "Patience and planning win the day, take it from one that knows."

"My darling, Exemplar is right. We must not rush into anything that could get you hurt. I just found you Zechariah, and it is my heart's desire to keep you by my side forever." Victoria stood up and he took around her lovingly. "Promise me sweetheart, you will not do anything dangerous or foolish."

"Forgive my temper, sweet one, but when someone messes with what belongs to me, I get upset." Zechariah looked deeply into her eyes. "I have waited a long time to have you belong to me and the thoughts of you being around that male gigolo sets me on fire."

"Darling, we both know the only way we are going to find your painting is for me to get inside your mansion and find where he hid it." Vicky ran her hand over his black thick hair. "I have a plan and I will need you to supply me with descriptions of your floor plans and where you think it may be in the large attic. Then we need a recovery plan and I have that problem almost solved."

"Tell me and maybe I can fill in the unsure part." Zechariah calmed down and was ready to do things the smart way instead of his usual rush in and take what was his, getting rid of anyone who might be in the way.

"When I except Maxwell's dinner invitation…" Vicky noticed the dark cloud fall over Zechariah's face and she gently patted it, then continued "so I can go in search of your painting and find some clever way to make him give me the one of me, I'll take Samantha along, making up some excuse for her coming with me. Samantha has a way of distracting a target when I need time for investigating, so while she is doing her thing, I will go in search of the painting. How do I get to the attic and where might he have hidden it, darling. The ruthless man will have no clue that the original owner is helping me

Joan Byrd

with the layout of the mansion."

"Vicky, darling, the center staircase climbs up three floors, then make a right on the third floor and go to the very end, you will see a set of steps leading up to the attic. Once inside, you will find a rack, most likely still containing old clothes, my mother's dresses and ball gowns. The painting is probably hiding behind them." Zechariah took her hands in his. "Dearest, the painting is large. How to you plan to get it outside. You cannot just prance down the steps with it. If Maxwell don't catch you, surely one of the staff will."

"Then it will have to go out the window, so I know I could never just drop it out from four floors up." Vicky started pacing around the room as she thought. "Maxwell wanted to send me a carriage, but I will insist on my driver bringing me and Samantha on my carriage. But, instead of Reginal driving the carriage, you will be the one behind the reins. Is there anything up in that attic I can lower the painting down on?"

"Not for lowering the painting on, but there is something up there that can bring me up to get it and carry it down." Zechariah grew excited, finally seeing their plan take shape. "You will find a large chest under the middle window, it contains a latter to attach to the window seal and the toss out, an escape route in case of fire."

"Darling, do you think the rope is still strong enough for you to climb after so many years? It could have dry rotted in that hot attic." Victoria had concerns for her loved one.

"Chains do not dry rot, beautiful." Zechariah laughed, along with the mirror, when Vicky arched her eyebrow.

"Chains? Will they not clang loudly against the house?" she tried not to laugh along with the two men, who continued their laughter. "I guess that's a no."

"Chains hitting brick and stone, don't make any announcements, darling." Zechariah grabbed her in a tight hug. "But, I don't see that jerk letting you have my portrait of you, dearest, and I'm not leaving without it!"

"Zechariah, we have discussed this. You cannot charge inside that house and demand your painting." Victoria laughed at the ideal of Maxwell believing he was seeing a ghost coming

176

in to claim what was rightfully his. "Although it does sound rather hilarious. I wonder if old Maxwell would turn white from fright."

"I am quite certain this devil of a man would not only turn white, but his hair would surely stand on ends." Exemplar laughed louder. "I regret I cannot witness all the action."

"There will be nothing to witness, Exemplar, because my handsome ghost is not coming inside that house and that is final." Victoria kissed him and started to walk away when he grabbed her, giving her a long romantic kiss, causing the mirror to blush

"I know when it's time to shut down for the night." Smiling in its heart, Exemplar whispered "Goodnight, loved ones!"

"Daddy, I received your telegram about coming for a visit and I couldn't be happier. There's someone here I want you and mama to meet." Victoria had called her parents as soon as she heard they had took some time off to pay her a visit and come see her new home.

"Vicky, is this someone a man, darling?" Irene Stanford had heard the excitement in her daughter's voice and knew it must be someone very special she wanted them to meet."

"His name is Zechariah Castleton and I love him very much." Vicky listened to silence on the other end, until her father laughed softly.

"I take it this Zechariah is more than just a good friend."

"You take it correctly daddy. He is the man I wish to marry."

"Then your mother and I look forward to meeting this very lucky young man." Steven Stanford paused for a moment. "Vicky, he is a young man, isn't he and not older than you?"

"At the present, Zechariah is twenty, same as me and Samantha. Speaking of my friend Sam, you are bringing her things with you as well, aren't you? We've had our clothes cleaned several times already and I was about to go shopping. Wearing the same outfits does not bother me or Sam, but some of the staff have brought it up every time they take in our wash, as they call it."

"Sounds old fashion, if you ask me, dear." Irene had to sit down when her only child mention marriage. "You may tell Samantha her mother brought what she asked for yesterday and it is packed in the S.U.V. ready for travel, first thing in the morning."

"Your mother was worried that you might not have room for us to stay over so if you prefer, we can book a room at the Castleton Hotel." Steven tried to imagine something built in 1770 when most of the mansion in Natchez was built in the 1800's.

"Dad, that won't be necessary, trust me. There is ample room in this manor house. The first floor has four spacious rooms, Two stately parlors, a massive library and a charming dining room. It also features its grandest room, the ballroom, large enough to sit two of our house in Natchez inside. There also a breakfast room and a large kitchen with a very large and filled walk in pantry." Vicky took a breath as she continued. "The second floor is furnished with ten guest or family rooms and the third floor is where I have my large space which includes a sitting room, luxury bath, once modern for its time in the late 1800's and a spacious bedchamber, as the staff refers it. There are two other family rooms up here, one where I replaced Sam and the other one belongs to Zechariah."

"That young man lives at the manor house? And on the third floor near you?" Irene spoke louder than she intended. "I mean, two single women on the same floor with a single man."

"That's right mama, along with six smaller rooms for staff members, most married couples." Victoria smiled at her mother's outburst. "You can relax mama, Zechariah is a true gentleman, you might say he is very old fashion in a charming way."

"That's good to know darling." Victoria's father chimed in. "Look for us in two days and don't worry, I am sure your mother and I will like your new boyfriend."

"Thanks dad, I'm certain of it." She laughed. "I look forward to seeing you both and should you see any children coming out of some woods on Carriage Wheel Road, don't start worrying about their safety. Let me just say, they made it home safely."

"Vicky darling, how would you know if children might be near a busy highway and have the knowledge of what they might do?" Vicky's mother asked, perplexed.

"For starters mama, Carriage Wheel Road is about the most boring road I've ever traveled on and let me say this one time, those children are mere shadows of the past, so they will not see you."

"The children are...ghost?" Irene stuttered

"Not exactly, they are just a vision of the past, the distant past." Vicky knew her parents would need time to process in their minds what unnatural occurrences were happening within Stanford Hall Plantation and the old town of Castleton. "I'll explain everything when you arrive and please don't worry, Stanford Hall is a lovely plantation."

"Vicky, my beautiful daughter, I am certain your mother and I will fall in love with Stanford Hall just like you did." Steven Stanford knew it was getting late and they needed to turn in early for their long trip to Castleton, Louisiana. "We've got to get up early darling, so we had better say goodbye for now. I cannot wait to see you and give my baby a big hug and kiss."

"Same here Vicky. Give Samantha our best and tell her we will see her soon." Irene blew a kiss over the phone. "This new fellow sounds serious. We are looking forward to meeting your Zechariah."

"He is looking forward to meeting you both as well. Be careful out on the roads. I love you both dearly and cannot wait to get those hugs and kisses, daddy. I will say goodnight and sweet dreams."

"Goodnight sweetheart and I know my girl will say her prayers." When her father hung up, she heard the butler clear his throat. "Yes, Thornton, do you have a question?"

"It's Mr. Maxwell's servant at the door, miss Victoria. He has given me this note for you to read and he insist on waiting for your answer." The stiff butler rolled his eyes up in discuss. "This is the third visit ma'am and I think his task master has given him the orders not to return this time with some kind of answer."

179

"The third time, Thornton?" Victoria took the note from his hand. "I was aware of one visit, but not a second."

"No ma.am, you could not have known, as you were off in New Orleans fetching your Zechariah when he showed up, all demanding and quite rude." Thornton remained straight face as he continued. "I told the brash young man he was wasting my time and to return to his master and tell him now is not a good time for a dinner invitation."

Vicky tried not to laugh as she opened the note and read it aloud when she saw Zechariah coming into the room. "My beautiful new friend, I was hoping you might be able to join me tomorrow evening around seven to dine with me. I will have my carriage sent to the plantation around six-thirty to pick you up. I pray your answer will be yes. Marshall."

"Even the overly confident serpent seems so sure of your answer, my dearest." Zechariah took the note and read it again, his teeth clinched tightly. "Send his carriage! Send his carriage in hopes of keeping you there. Over my dead body!"

"Zechariah, darling, we have already discussed this. You will be taking me and Samantha on our carriage, or the car if you prefer." Vicky noticed his frown. "Now what?"

"Better let me drive the horses Vicky, I have never driven a car and to be honest, up until you brought me home, I never saw anything remotely like that contraption before."

"Sorry sweetheart, I keep forgetting you lived in the 1700's. We will take the carriage, but for now, I need to go tell that young man I will except, only if I can bring my friend and have my own man bring us in my carriage." Vicky reached up and kissed him, "Then I and 'my own man' can put our plan in action!" she smiled when he winked at her, then followed at a safe distance to listen.

"I am truly sorry to keep you waiting, Freddy, it has been a busy time for me around here. I am sure you and your employer can appreciate how I must feel moving in a place as grand as Stanford Hall. It does take a lot of adjusting."

"Yes ma'am." He looked around at the big entrance hall, three times the size of Castleton Mansion. "I can see that it would take some getting use to. But Miss Stanford, it would get me out of a lot of hot water if I could have an answer from you, hopefully a yes."

"Then you may inform Mr. Maxwell that I will except on two conditions, that my best friend Samantha may join us and I insist on bringing my own carriage and driver." Victoria noticed Freddy's big smile.

"I am certain these conditions can be met, Miss Stanford. Mr. Maxwell has been beside himself waiting for your visit and has hinted at a possible invite from you, to dine in your elegant dining room." The man practically danced to the door, overjoyed by her answer. "I will go at once to inform him and ease his mind, get his response and return in about an hour."

"You could just call Freddy. There is but one phone in this house, besides my and Sam's smart phones, but it works perfectly well." Vicky could not get over everyone's refusal to go the modern way, especially if it was more convenient. "Do you want the number?"

"It's no trouble to come over Miss Stanford and I enjoy the quiet drive." Freddy Payne took every opportunity to get away from Marshall Maxwell, who could be demanding and extremely picky over little things. Before Vicky could intervene on his return, he made his way out the door whistling.

"It's obvious Vicky darling, Maxwell Marshall has been thinking about you a lot!" Zechariah came from his hiding spot, along with Samantha who had wondered up and started to ask the handsome man hiding who he was hiding from. Zechariah had grabbed her and held her mouth as he whispered in her ear about Maxwell's servant just a few feet away talking to Vicky. "Sam and I heard everything darling, even the fact that the jerk wants to come here to have a meal with you!"

"The jerk?" Vicky laughed at her 1700's boyfriend using that modern word.

"Samantha taught it to me, just moments ago, although I am not sure what it means, but it sounded proper for Maxwell." Zechariah finally smiled. "Dearest, you really have no reason to invite that woman chaser here! God, I should get you a ring so that jerk would know you are spoken for!"

"Zechariah, I have no intention of asking Marshall

Maxwell to have dinner with me. Should he bring up the undesirable subject, I will simply inform him, my fiancé would not approve me asking you over."

"And Zechariah, before you ask, if the 'jerk' questions why she accepted his invitation to dinner, it seems the neighborly thing to do, besides she really wanted to see that painting he claimed was of her." Samantha smiled when her friend nodded in agreement.

"Sam is right, darling, and that is all Maxwell needs to know, for now. Our plan to find your painting and retrieve it will be exciting, and somehow I will try and get that painting of me as well, before I leave your house."

"I will not leave without it Vicky." Zechariah put his foot down. "One way or the other, those two paintings will be reunited again, if I have to march inside my own home and retrieve it."

The telephone just off the kitchen rang out and Odessa waved off the young owner of Stanford Hall as she picked up the receiver. "Stanford Hall, Odessa Brown speaking. How might I help you?"

"May I speak with Miss Victoria Stanford. Tell her Freddy Payne is calling with a message from Marshall Maxwell."

"Is that a fact, young man. Lands sake alive, Miss Victoria just this minute went up to settle in for the night. Looks like you might as well give Odessa that message, Mr. Freddy, and I will see that she gets it first thing in the morning."

The group of three stood close by, trying hard not to laugh as the happy cook tried to get rid of the obnoxious man and he was speaking so loud they could actually hear him.

"Tomorrow morning? Could you not get a message up to her tonight?" his voice took on an excited high pitch. "I did tell her I would return with Mr. Maxwell's message, but due to it getting dark outside, I decided the telephone made better sense." Freddy bit his lip, hoping she didn't question how he knew their phone number.

"Tonight, or tomorrow morning won't make any difference in hearing what the gent has to say, so if you will just tell me before I lose my patience and hang up without either of us hearing it." the cook grabbed her mouth to hold in her chuckle when she heard the nervous man gasp.

"Alright, alright! Tell the lady Mr. Maxwell is very thrilled and extremely overjoyed by her visit tomorrow evening and he said he understands the need to bring her friend, Lady Samantha and she is more than welcome. Another pretty face at my table is always rewarding and if the use of your own carriage is what you choose my dear, feel free and I trust your driver will remain outside until you are ready to leave." Freddy took a big breath, glad to have the message out. "Madam, can you remember all that I said or should I repeat it for you, to write down, perhaps."

The cook placed her hand over the receiver and looked over at Victoria who shook her head no as she whispered, "We heard him." Giving them a toothy grin, she spoke up.

"I have it right here, written down, just as you said it. Now if you will excuse me, I got a kitchen to clean up before heading off to my own bed."

"You say, you wrote all those words down?" Freddy's voice grew tense. "Can you repeat it to me?"

"What? Did you up and forget what you just told me, not two minutes ago?" Odessa chuckled. "The way I see it, as long as I know it on my end is all that matters, Mr. Freddy, so don't you go losing any sleep over not remembering what you just told me."

"What? But—" she cut the nervous man off.

"Yes sir, it's a good thing Odessa knows shorthand. Gotta run." She hung up laughing and strolled off to the kitchen, leaving the three listeners laughing, until Thornton walked out of the shadows shaking his head.

"I know our Odessa can carry on with a continuous visitor and her quick humor can be refreshing, but are you overlooking the fact that constant thorn in our rear happen to know this phone number after he refused to take it from you, Miss Victoria?"

"As a matter of fact, Thornton, I did notice his blunder and how quickly he tried to cover it up." Vicky smiled at the serious face butler. "It's a good thing he didn't get the information about how loud the speaker was set at. It would appear Marshall Maxwell has a spy here on the plantation and by his unlimited knowledge within the manor house, this spy works outside this home, most likely a field worker needing extra money."

"Then I will start asking around tomorrow and see who might be needing extra finances enough to stoop to being a traitor to the best employer around Castleton." Zechariah lifted Victoria's hand and kissed it. "You, my dear. And for you, I shall not stop until I find the traitor and toss him out by his pant straps!"

"Zechariah, if my brave and courageous man finds this poor soul, please bring him to me before you kicked him out. We must give him a chance to explain why he chose to betray me. He may have a very good reason for putting himself out there."

"Vicky, dearest, you are a far better person than I. I say a traitor is a traitor and needs to face their punishment." Zechariah put his arm around the woman he had fallen in love with over two-hundred-years ago. "Since you are the rightful owner of Stanford Hall, I will usher the traitor to you for questioning, then I will take pleasure in getting rid of the bad apple."

"Darling, suppose this person was trapped inside a very bad situation and his only means of escape was to spy for the obnoxious rich man whose way with words can be cleverly covered-up to disguise his miss-deeds making everything sound up and up."

"This is why you are a detective, darling, and I am a fighter for what is right." Zechariah pulled her into his arms. "Your words are inspiring me to go at my task without pre-judging others before knowing the complete facts. Therefore, I will strive to be more, gentle when I manhandle anyone breaking the rules or the laws."

"Then we shall try out your new inspired way of approaching the enemy tomorrow evening, when you act as my chauffeur." Victoria smiled up into his serious face. "Darling, please don't tell me you already regret the ideal of striving to be more, gentle when it comes to someone who breaks the rules?"

"I was referring to a human person, not a low-down house thief, a clever woman slayer, who wormed his way into her lonely life, to get everything she had." Zechariah could not contain his anger for this man! Delores Castleton was my brother James's granddaughter, three greats backs, and I will not rest until I see this murderer punished for her death! Marshall Maxwell stole his way into her life, took everything she had, which is rightfully still mine according to the will that my father hid somewhere inside the mansion before his death."

"Zechariah, I do not mean anything against you when I say this, but how can someone who died and was dead for over two-hundred years, still be the legal owner of any property?" Samantha wrinkled her brow, trying to make sense out of his statement. "Do you know Vic?"

"Sam, I have never seen this will, so legally I would have no way of knowing, but..." Victoria touched Zechariah's handsome face. "Darling, your father loved you with all his heart and to him you would always be his first born, the apple of his eye. Remember what the mirror said about your real father, referring to another man being your birth father. Even though he never mentioned it to you or your mother, I believe somehow your daddy, the man that raise you and gave you more love than all his other five children, found out about your real father and wanted to prove to you just how much he loved you. I think Joshua Castleton met his lawyer in secret and poured out his heart to him asking for his legal help. The lawyer...I can see Shining, no...Shiver?"

"Mr. Silver, Shin Silver, my father's best friend and personal lawyer for fifty years." Zechariah looked at Victoria in total amazement. "You think Shin came up with a legal will making me owner of the Castleton estate forever?"

"Yes darling, yes I do!" Vicky grew excited. "And that makes another thing we must find a way to prove you are the owner. But until we find another opportunity to visit your home, we must act civil around the jerk, so he won't grow suspicious."

"I shall do my upmost best to act civil around Maxwell, but if he starts getting personal with you, I shall lay my fist in his fat jaw!" Zechariah gave Vicky a sweet smile. "Dearest, you cannot expect me to stand back while some man has his hands on what belongs to me, can you?"

"I appreciate my man standing up for me and defending what is rightfully his, but Zechariah, my love, I am not helpless when it comes to a pushy man. I can take care of myself, right Sam?"

"Vicky can defend herself when she is confronted with a flirty man or a would-be thief!" Samantha walked over between them. "Zac, I'm sure there might be times when you have to come to your woman's rescue, but in most cases, Vic's skills in the art of karate eliminates most of her aggressors "

"Art of Karate? Is this a new form of sword fighting?" Zechariah could not imagine his beautiful sweetheart stabbing some attacker with a sword."

"I have never learned the skill of sword fighting, although something tells me you are very good at it." she noticed his big smile and positive nod. "Yes, I thought as much. Karate is an old way of fighting, started by the Japanese for unarmed combat in which the hands and feet are used as weapons. When done correctly you can quickly throw your opponent down, even knock them unconscious."

"Vic earned her black belt, which makes her a legal weapon." Samantha patted her friend on the back. "She's quite the little fighter and the attacker won't know what hit them when they find themselves spalled on the floor."

"Great!" Zechariah gathered her hand in his. "Should Maxwell get too mushy you can cool him down on the floor."

"Shall I practice on you darling?" Vicky teased.

"We shall retire upstairs and while saying my proper goodnight with lots of kisses, you might try it out on me." His eyes lit up in mischief. "But, you might find yourself down on the floor with me, wrapped in my warm embrace."

CHAPTER 24

"You have a lovely home, Marshall." Vicky had ridden up the winding drive to the grand stone mansion seated next to her quiet boyfriend who was obviously taking in the familiar surroundings he had seen so many times when he lived here. She felt his emotions and reached for his hand when he stopped the carriage in front of the massive porch. Making sure no one from inside could see him, Zechariah lend over and kissed Victoria and told her to be careful and he would be waiting under the attic window. Marshall Maxwell had opened the door himself when he saw her being helped from the Carriage and called out to her driver, whom he mistook for Reginal Myers before ushering both girls inside and shutting the door.

"I fell in love with the place when I first saw it and declared it was the prettiest house around until I set my eyes on Stanford Hall." Marshall smiled down at her dress after his butler took their coats to hang up. "I must admit, fair Victoria, neither house compares to your beauty."

"You are most kind." She made a face at her friend after the flirty man turned his back to ask one of his footman to bring before dinner drinks, then took the girls in his parlor, somewhat smaller than Stanford Hall's, but nevertheless, an elegant room. Victoria knew why Zechariah loved it here. After taking their seats, the footman served what tasted like an expensive wine. "This is very good Marshall, thank you."

"I select only the finest wines, my dear. Price is no object when it comes to the very best, and that is what I always demand, the very best in everything." His eyes covered her as he took in her body, giving her the creeps. "Especially my women."

"I suppose that is why you chose Deloris Castleton and ask her to marry you." Victoria noticed the cocky man tense up at the mention of his dead wife. "I'm told she didn't live long after getting married to you. That had to be devastating to you,

Marshall." She watched him nervously drink down his wine and hold up the glass for a refill. "You're upset, poor man. I should never have brought up Zechariah's niece."

"Zechariah?" Marshall Maxwell swallowed nervously. "Are you referring to 'the' Zechariah Castleton who died from Yellow Fever over Two-hundred-years ago?"

"Is there another one?" Vicky laughed. "If I didn't know better, Marshall, I would think you were afraid of Zechariah's ghost."

"I've heard it exists and some have even sworn he has haunted these halls." It was obvious to Vicky and Samantha that Marshall Maxwell was terrified of the thought that Zechariah's spirit was roaming 'his' mansion, but to appear brave, he laughed nervously. "I think the whole thing is a bunch of made-up stories to scare visitors coming into the old town."

"I'm not so sure, Marshall." Victoria tried to keep a straight face as she recalled her visitor in the Castleton Hotel. "I believe the ones who have said they seen Zechariah's ghost wondering this mansion."

"You believe this ridiculous story?" he gave a chuckle before consuming the remainder of his wine and barely missed the table when he nervously sat down the glass. "Victoria surely you don't mean it. You are a fabulous detective who deals with facts not fiction."

"And That is why I believe them, Marshall." She smiled when his eyebrow went up. "I believe them because I too have seen the handsome ghost himself when I first arrive in Castleton and several times since."

"You actually saw Zechariah Castleton's ghost?" his eyes grew wide.

"I saw him, we spoke and the very romantic man has sworn his love to me before kissing me." Vicky took the last sip of her wine and waved off a refill. "I'll wait until dinner, thank you, Mr. Payne."

Marshall Maxwell was studying her words about Zechariah Castleton and he slowly stood up. "I never knew a ghost could actually kiss a person, Victoria. I was under the impression their spirit would just pass through a solid object."

"Looks like you have gotten all your facts from the movies, Marshall. I can assure you, I felt that kiss." She stood up.

"Vicky is right Marshall, that Zechariah is one very romantic fellow and he is totally devoted to my friend here." Samantha moved over beside of Victoria. "The affection goes both ways, but then who could blame Vicky for falling in love with such a gallant man, like Zechariah Castleton."

"Love? Surely you aren't in love with a ghost? A man who has been dead for over two-hundred-years?" his voice held strong envy for this dead man. "Victoria, you need a real man, one who is alive and can give you the love you need."

"Marshall, I am aware of what I need and I have found it, so just let it drop and go back to why Zechariah is wondering his home?" Vicky needed to slow Marshall Maxwell's real reason for inviting her to dinner, so she would give him something else to think about. "I think he is searching for what belongs to him and he will not stop until he gets it."

"You can't be serious!" He laughed out. "You think a spirit can just float inside my home and take something belonging to me?"

"No, I think Zechariah can come into his home, he did live here most of his life, Marshall, and carry out to the spirit world what he bought for himself." She looked around at the painting on the walls. "He did tell me he wouldn't rest until he got the painting."

"Painting? Which painting, did he say?" he walked over in front of her and took her shoulders. "Victoria, do you know what that ghost is after?"

Samantha brushed his hands away and gave him a faux smile. "I would think any lamebrain could figure that one out Marshall? He is in love with Vicky, totally devoted to her. Think man."

"I know!" Freddy Payne spoke up with excitement.

"Then speak up, for God's sake, Payne!" Maxwell face had turned a pale red, as a trickle of sweat ran down his face. "Which painting is he after? One of the priceless old masters?"

"You seriously don't know sir?" Freddy noticed the vein in his neck popping out and knew to speak up or get fired. "The

189

lovely painting in your bedroom sir, of Victoria Elizabeth."

"What? My painting of you?" he took her hand and led her to his bedroom, Samantha close behind. "There, on the wall in front of my bed. Did I not tell you I own it?"

"I'm sure the painting was in the mansion when your late wife, Delores moved in and I assume it was hung over the mantle instead of here where you have it." Vicky had noticed the wallpaper over the fireplace and two perfect bare square shapes were brighter than the rest of the wall where two frames had hung, side by side for many years, hers and Zechariah's. "Zechariah had told me he had commissioned the painting of me to be done for him, so that makes him the real owner Marshall."

"Correction, my dear, I now own the painting as well as everything in this mansion. My dear wife made me sole benefactor of her will." He was interrupted by the butler. "What is it Franklin?"

"Dinner is served, sir." The stiff butler stood to one side as they walked out, then he switched off the lights and closed the door. "Ghost! Poppycock!"

"That was a fine meal, Marshall." Vicky and Samantha followed the arrogant man back to the parlor for coffee and before they sat down, Samantha went into her distraction mode as she walked over to a chest board set up on a card table.

"Oh, chest? Do you play, Marshall?" She asked as he chuckled and walked over next to the table.

"I am a champion at chest, Samantha dear. Do you wish to challenge me to a game?"

"I certainly would! I consider myself somewhat of a champion at chest, wouldn't you agree Vicky?" she looked over at her friend and winked.

"You run circles around me when it comes to playing chest." Vicky smiled, knowing this would give her time to go to the attic and find Zechariah's painting. "If you don't mind, I will run to the bathroom, then come back to watch you both."

Sam quickly took the chair facing the room, so Marshall had to sit facing the wall. He glanced around before starting.

"Just find Franklin and have him show you the way to the bathroom darling."

"I can manage. I saw it just down the hall." She waved over her head. "Have fun."

Victoria made her way quickly up the dimly lit staircase until she reached the floor just under the attic. Following Zechariah's directions, she hurried down the hall until she came to the end and saw the steep steps rising to a smaller door. As she climbed up the light grew dimmer, so she pulled her trusty flashlight out of her pocket and switched it on and closed the old door behind her when she stepped in and felt a sense of reversing time when she noticed all the old clothes dating back to the 1700's.

"Zechariah was right! These have to be dresses belonging to his mother and sisters." Knowing no one had followed her and all the staff was inside the old mansion, Vicky searched for a light switch and, when she turned to look behind her face, ran into something ranging from the rafters. First, she thought it might be an old spider web but quickly learned it was a string attached to a light bulb. "Let's hope it still burns after it was installed when electricity was discovered." Vicky gave it a tug and a dim light shone over the dust covered floor.

"Now, to find the chest or trunk with the chain latter." Three big windows where near the center of the room and a big black trunk sat under the middle window. "Zechariah was right again. Some people can't remember what happened yesterday, but my darling man can remember everything about his home place and it's been over two-hundred-years. I just hope he remembers to be waiting under the window when I throw down the latter." She opened the trunk and noticed it was filled to the top with a coiled latter made of solid chains. "This should be interesting. I better find Zechariah's painting first, then tackle that heavy chain."

Vicky went back over to the row of dresses, hanging thick and no less with spiders making their home in them. "He said, behind the dresses was probably where the painting was placed to hide it. And I can see why it's such a great hiding place. A person would have to go through the spider guards to retrieve it" Vicky pulled at her sleeves, then reached into her pocket for another item a detective never leaves behind when investigating, a good pair of gloves and a cover for the head. "Now Spiders, I am ready to find what I came for, so stay out of my way if you don't wish to be squished!" Closing her eyes, Vicky made a dash through the old clothes and opened her eyes on the handsome face of Zechariah Castleton.

Victoria slowly raised the middle window and looked down to see her handsome beau smiling up at her.

"Vicky darling, just start dragging the chains over to the window and lower it out, the weight will take over so stand clear of it and the chains will do the rest. My father designed them that way."

"Thank God he knew the art of construction. They look super heavy." She smiled and held up the large painting for him to see. "It was where you said it would be, behind the row of old dresses and spiders."

"Spiders? Poor daring, you are my brave woman." Zechariah stood back smiling. "Throw that latter down and I'll be up it in a flash to reward you with a kiss."

"I could not think of a better reward, sweetheart." Vicky tugged at the heavy end and started pulling it over to the open window, then barely got it laid over the window seal when it picked up momentum and flew down to the ground. "She looked down and laughed. "I did it!"

"I had no doubt." Zechariah scurried up the latter so fast she could only blink twice before he had her in his arms. "I love you, Vicky Stanford!" the gallant man smothered her in kisses. "Now to get my painting of you, dearest one."

"And I think I know the perfect way!"

"It was a lovely dinner, Marshall. Thank you for asking us." Victoria smiled to herself, knowing the quiet house would not remain that way for long. "You mustn't look so down, poor man. I did tell you Samantha was better at chess than I was and I was the state champion for three years straight."

"You made it three years champion?" Marshall looked sick as he shook his head in defeat. How could Miss Brandon beat your record?"

"Sam studied chess one summer and went on to beat me and everyone in Mississippi for the last eight years." Vicky walked out the door and offered her hand in a shake. "Maybe you can beat her next time."

"Next time?" Marshall Maxwell suddenly stood straight and smiled broadly. "Are you suggesting we will be dinning together soon?"

"I noticed your framed certificates for first place in the Louisiana chest matches, four straight years." Vicky placed her hand on her friend's shoulder. "Now, that Sam is living here, she will be competing with you for first place, so I just assumed you would try to beat her so you can frame another certificate and add to your collection."

Suddenly a woman's scream came from somewhere in the big rock mansion causing the owner and his two visitors to jump. Not having time to fill Samantha in on her and Zechariah plan, the girl Friday stared in the direction of the scream, then looked at her friend which remained calm.

"Vic, what made that girl scream so loudly? A spider or mouse, maybe?"

"Could be or maybe it is the ghost of Zechariah, coming for his painting," Vicky stated, causing Marshall to twirl around, eyes wide, obviously frightened. "Marshall, I really don't think you have anything to worry about. The handsome ghost is not, dangerous if you do not disturb him from his mission."

"I could get my gun and frighten him off." He said tensely "I know I would not be able to kill him when I shoot the gun but it might scare him."

Samantha looked over at her friend nervously, but Vicky just laughed softly. "Don't be silly Marshall. If you attack him with a gun, that could never hurt him anyway, he would grow angry and I've heard an angry ghost can do a lot of harm when provoked."

"It might not even be a ghost, Marshall." Samantha knew it was Zechariah and somehow, they had come up with a plan to get the painting. "The girl could have seen a spider or a mouse after all. She stopped screaming."

193

"You're right, she did stop!" Mr. Marshall pulled Vicky back inside and shut the door. "You are the detective here, Victoria. That was Cassie's scream! The ghost might have her trapped!"

"Or maybe this Cassie is star-struck by Zechariah's charming appearance." Vicky's quick skills picked up Marshall's interest in this woman's safety, perhaps a maid he had taken for a lover. "You seem familiar with Cassie, Marshall. To recognize one woman's scream over every woman working for you."

"She…a…is my personal maid." He swallowed. "I mean, she does my laundry, attends to my room, fetches my coffee and paper in the morning."

"Sounds like the perfect little pet." Samantha winked at her friend when their host's attention was on the staircase. "We might as well go up and see what made Cassie scream. We will never know standing down here, especially if she is moonstruck over the gallant ghost."

"Well, I shall put an end to that nonsense." He led the way up to the first landing and stared down the dim-lit hallway to his open door. "I know Franklin closed my bedroom door when we left! I heard it click shut."

"There is only one way to get to the bottom of this." Vicky turned toward the door and called out. "Cassie, if you are inside Mr. Maxwell's bedroom, you had better come out and explain your scream."

"Who…who are you miss?" the nervous girl called out from Marshall's bedroom.

"Cassie, Miss Stanford is my dinner guest and we heard you scream out." Marshall Maxwell called out instead of walking down the hall to his room. Sam looked at her friend and shrug her shoulders in question, but the sly detective had picked up on the reason for Marshall's frozen spot and the real reason Cassie wasn't coming out.

"You're right about one thing Marshall, I am a great detective and I know why you are rooted in your spot and why the little personal maid refuses to come out of your bedroom."

"What reason could she possibly have except being trapped

194

by the charming handsome ghost." Mr. Maxwell forced out a weak smile for his beautiful guest.

"For starters Marshall, Zechariah has no intention of flirting with another woman. He is solely, 100% devoted to me." Vicky kept a serious face as she gave him her theory in the real reason his maid screamed and why she would not come out. "Let me refresh your memory, Marshall. Miss Cassie was undressed and waiting for you to come up for bed when Zechariah appeared in your bedroom for his painting of me, and it startled the dear girl, most likely recognizing the handsome ghost from family pictures hanging throughout the house. I would guess he would have mesmerize your Cassie with his gallant bow, his alluring blue eyes and his handsome smile, that captured all the ladies of his day." Vicky watched the cocky man tighten his jaw as he stared at the open door. "I think it's safe for you to go ahead Marshall. I'm sure while the lovely maid stared dreamily at the irresistible spirit lifting the painting down off the wall, she couldn't find the strength or will to call out to you to warn you and when I called out to her, she turned to face the door and Zechariah just disappeared with the painting."

"I shall soon find out! Marshall started down the hall when a shapely blonde stepped out of his room, in what looked like a man's bathrobe. She turned a bright pink when she noticed the two women standing behind her boss. "I…I had an accident while cleaning Marshall's shower. I…a…sort of cut the shower on me."

"Did you?" Vicky smiled knowingly. "Funny, you seem to be dry on your legs, hands and hair, still in place, especially after seeing the ghost."

"How did you know about the ghost, miss?" Cassie gave her boss a weak smile "I was…a busy working and the ghost just appeared, right in the middle of the room!"

"Is that when you screamed Cassie?" Samantha asked casually as she watched Mr. Maxwell coldly watching her.

"Why yes, wouldn't you if a terrorizing ghost was staring at you?" the girl shivered but Vicky assumed it wasn't Zechariah's so call ghost causing her shakes but instead the mean looks from Marshall Maxwell.

"Then tell me Cassie, why did you stop screaming if this ghost was so frightening?" the bold man grabbed her wrist. "The truth is you didn't scream because you were attracted to this dead man, just like Victoria here!"

"It's not quite the same Marshall, Zechariah and I are in love and have vowed to be together, forever." Vicky noticed the maid staring into her face when she recognized her from the painting she had seen so many times in her boss's bedroom. In a jealous rage, Cassie slung her head around to face Marshall.

"So, that's why you insist on placing that painting directly in front of your bed! It is you, Marshall, you're the one attracted to this woman and she's right about that Zechariah being in love with her! Why else did he take that painting of her?"

"So, he did steal it? The ghostly thief!" Marshall stormed inside his room to find the wall empty. "He could not have gotten far..." Marshall looked over at his guest for answers. "Could he?"

"You cannot expect to find that painting floating around in the air, carried by invisible hands, Marshall." Vicky and Samantha turned and started down the hall to the staircase, followed quickly by the upset man. "Marshall, the Castleton Museum is packed with information relating to ghost. One stat reports that some ghost lifts items of interest and carries them away into the spirit world, just as I told you. It's really a waste of time to look for it, Marshall." Vicky gave him a sorrowful look. "I'm really sorry for your loss, but cheer up, you might see me in town from time to time." As she walked down the steps she added. "And after I get settled in, I will have you out for dinner, one neighbor to another."

"Dinner?" His personality changed when his face lit up in a smile. "I would love to join you at Stanford Hall some evening for dinner." Stepping in front of the friends, he ushered them to the front door. "I see Myers is off the carriage waiting for you ladies. I will wait to hear from you Victoria." He called out to the driver. "Drive safely Myers. I wouldn't want anything to happen to Victoria and her friend."

Keeping his head down, Zechariah tipped his hat, then helped both ladies on the carriage before climbing on and driving away. He smiled over at Victoria and nodded to the back, rumble seat. No one would ever expect two big, framed paintings were hidden under the extra blankets.

CHAPTER 25

After the three returned to Stanford Hall manor house, they went up to her room to take the paintings, still wrapped in the blankets. Samantha looked at the perfect likeness of each face and was impressed with the artist that could paint someone so perfect it could pass as a photograph.

"Zechariah, who was the artist that painted these remarkable paintings?" she looked closely for a signature but found none. "Did he or she not sign it?"

"No, he did not, Samantha. He wished to be left anonymous. His people would not have approved of his wasting time with anyone outside their band." Zechariah had taken down Victoria Bell's painting over the mantle so he could hang up their paintings, side-by-side. "There, back together again, the way it should be."

Victoria wrapped her arms around his waist as she admired his painting. "I shall love looking up at your handsome face, my darling. Your gypsy friend Delmarrio was a very gifted painter."

"I suppose I gave the little detective enough clues to know who the artist was." Zechariah pulled her into his arms. "When we wed, I too can enjoy looking up at your beautiful face, Vicky darling, although I shall truly enjoy my real live wife far better."

"That goes without saying, sweetheart. A cold painting could never replace a warm body." Vicky smiled over at her friend and settled down in front of the mirror. "Sam, I know when there is something on your mind, so just ask."

"After I realized you and Zechariah had obviously come up with a plan for getting the painting of you, I thought you would probably use the ghost act since we had discussed it earlier with Marshall and it seem to upset the big brave flirt." Samantha walked over to Zechariah for her puzzling question. "the maid said you just appeared in the middle of the room. Now, I know

198

at one time you could have just appeared, but Zechariah, you are a living person now and it would be impossible to appear and then just disappear."

Vicky turned around to hear his answer, thinking she knew how he accomplished the feat. Knowing her talent for seeing the obvious, he bowed and waved his hand for her to figured out his magic trick.

"I could be wrong, but this is my guess. The bedroom that Marshall chose was yours when you lived at Castleton Mansion. The two perfect bare places over the fireplace mantle were where these beautiful paintings hung before the arrogant new owner took down the paintings, hid yours, my darling, in the attic with the spiders and hung mine in front of his bed, perhaps to admire me."

"Or other things!" Zechariah stormed out.

"We won't go there or I might get sick, darling." Vicky walked over and touched his handsome face, bringing out his smile. "You know that room like the back of your hand, so my guess is there is a secret entrance inside the room, near the middle. Most likely the bookcase."

"You are very clever my dearest, to figure that out." Zechariah gave her a quick kiss, only because Samantha was standing there watching. "Maxwell's lover had her head turned to get a glass of wine next to the bed she rested on, wearing nothing when I stepped out and spotted her. She turned and seeing a stranger standing there gave in to panic and the obvious reaction was to scream." He laughed remembering her sudden change. "That when I poured on the southern charm and as in pass experience, she was lost in a trance and just stared at me while I took down my painting."

"Oh, I get it now!" Samantha laughed as she imagined the naked woman reaction when Vicky called her out in the hallway. "Hearing Vicky saying her name and asking her to step out in the hall, Cassie panic, lying there with nothing on but an admiration smile for you, turned quickly to face the open door, she had foolishly left opened."

"My girl Friday is absolutely correct!" Vicky beamed as she sat back down. "With her attention on the door and another

199

woman's voice calling her, my charming southern gentleman slipped back inside the hidden opening in the bookcase and fled through the hidden passage to the carriage, where he hid the painting next to the one I found in the attic. This first case is almost finished. All we need to do is check in on our friend, Exemplar and see if he agrees with me on what cases will be next."

"Can I stay to hear what the mirror sounds like?" Samantha had mixed feelings being around such a powerful object, but with both Vicky and Zechariah with her, she felt safe. She would just stand back to observe.

"You have to meet Exemplar sooner or later, Sam. You might have to call him up someday and help me and Zechariah back, should our case call for us to go back in time to help solve the mystery." Victoria patted the bench as she slid over and reached out to pull another chair next to her. "Sam, on the bench with me, Zechariah darling, you can take the chair by my side." Vicky waited for her nervous friend and her brave fiancée to take their seat, then she called out to the angel inside the mirror. "Exemplar, my good friend, please appear."

The lights in the room flickered as the mirror seem to come to life. "Victoria, I see you and Zechariah have recovered the paintings and they are once again together. I can see this has made you quite happy, Zechariah."

"Extremely happy, Exemplar. To gain one thing back from that murdering thief is rewarding, but only a small start, as I'm sure you are aware." Zechariah stared into the mirror seriously. "Maxwell sits in my house like a proud peacock, acting as though he bought and paid for the estate, when in truth the bastard stole it!"

"Zechariah, patience will win the day, my son. You must not let your raw emotions get out of control as you did in your previous life." The mirror admired the raven-hair young woman next to him. "You have got the one thing that has always meant the most to you Zechariah. You cannot take chances anymore like you once did, now that you have Victoria to take care of. She will need your strength and protection when she takes on some of the cases waiting for her to solve. Ease up on your anger toward Marshall Maxwell and in time you will regain all that belongs to you."

"Zechariah, darling, Exemplar is right. We must move slowly where Marshall Maxwell is involved. If he finds out you are alive too soon, we might never have a chance to search for that will your father has hidden."

"Oh, now I get why you ask that overbearing man to have dinner here sometime!" Samantha had been confused as to why Vicky had told Marshall Maxwell she would have him out for dinner, now it made sense. "You would keep Maxwell occupied here while Zechariah looked for his father's will."

"Not exactly Sam, but you are close." Vicky was happy her friend finally felt safe around Exemplar to speak up, now, how would she take what she was about to hear. "I will, of course, dine with our obnoxious neighbor, along with you, pal. Then, my quick wit girl Friday will find the perfect thing to keep the flirty man occupied while Zechariah and I slipped over to Castleton Mansion in search for the hidden will."

"I have to think of something to keep Marshall Maxwell's mind off of you and where you disappeared for over an hour?" Samantha stared over at her friend. "Care to give me some good ideals here, Vic?"

"My dear Samantha, you have plenty of time before that unwanted dinner guest is invited to Stanford Hall." The angel in the mirror knew the man's real motives for wanting to come, and he was sure the young sleuth who figure it out before her jealous fiancée did. "That will be a part of your next case, my dear Victoria, and it will take some delicate planning."

"You are right, dear friend. My parents will be arriving tomorrow and I plan to spend some quality time with them while they're here and hopefully convince them to come back for Christmas to attend the big Christmas Ball, my very first to plan." Victoria made a helpless face in the mirror. "No one on the staff was living during the balls, so, it will take a lot of research to know what to do."

"Are you forgetting the very ones who had the balls can be reached through me, my dear?" the mirror chuckled when the beautiful girl lightly slapped the side of her head, recalling her

Joan Byrd

conversation with Victoria Bell. "Yes, both Victoria Bell and Victoria Rose can be called up from the past, and your Zechariah could offer you a tremendous amount of help concerning the Christmas Balls. I recollect you attended quite a few and kept the dance floor busy dancing with all the ladies."

"Exemplar, are you trying to get me into trouble with my Victoria?" Zechariah stared at the mirror before turning to see his true love observing him. "Vicky, dearest, I merely accepted every star-struck lady's request for a dance. I felt generous, it was Christmas after all and they all looked so hopeful, with their pleading eyes when they ask me."

"Oh. The ladies ask you for a dance?" Vicky laughed and reached over to give him a kiss. "I can't say that I blamed them for asking, my darling. I am sure you were standing there, dressed in the latest formal fashion, tall, dark, and handsome, the most gallant man on the dance floor."

"Oh, he was something to look at, Vicky, standing there in his white tucks with a silk royal blue shirt on under the well-fitting coat." The mirror could almost smell the fresh cedar hanging from the windows and balcony. "Perhaps I can bring the outfit back up for your man to wear this Christmas and find you and Miss Samantha the perfect gowns. Who knows, there may be that perfect beau at the dance for Miss Sam." He chuckled when the pretty blonde blushed.

"It's good to know I shall have a lot of good help and my best friend might find someone instead of her boyfriend back in Natchez, who she has written and called several times and she has yet to hear from him." Vicky never liked the boy that took her friend for granted, so if she found someone here who treated her good, she knew Samantha would be happy.

"I'm over Randy! Moving on sounds perfect, even exciting and what better place to meet my prince charming than a real ball." Samantha smiled at her friend. "What other mystery will we be working on next, besides the will search?"

"Finding out about Zechariah's real father and how he met Isabell, your mother. Why he waited so long to come back into your life, pretending to be just a painter your mother hired to paint the family portrait." Victoria reached for Zechariah's hand. "I know your father was the gypsy you grew close to, darling and that was the reason you didn't want him to be along when he was dying with Yellow Fever. But there's still a lot of unanswered questions that Delmarrio took to the grave with him. Why did he kidnap all your sisters and brother when he took you? Why did he decide to return years later and take your sisters and brother back home to their parents?" Victoria got up and walked to the window and looked out toward the cabin. "Why did he seek refuge here at Stanford Hall and leave the mirror here? How did he come by the mirror in the first place and why was the young girl Grace so important to him he brought her back from the channel of life?"

"All good questions, Victoria." The mirror admired her detective skills as he added "and the third part of your next case will be about me, will it not, my dear?"

"You are exactly right, dear friend. There are still many unknown things about you I will investigate, like what gifted carpenter built the strange, yet beautiful frame around your oval shape and one very important mystery concerning you, where did you get your magic powers? How was it Lucifer never remembered you were among the fallen and did not seek you out, either to destroy you or turn you into the demon you fled from."

"All good mysteries for sure, like the young man who found me in the London ditch, just a piece of discarded trash, or so it appeared, except to this one boy who saw something special, through blind eyes." The mirror smiled when he knew he had sparked a new question for the young sleuth. "I would say you have your work cut out for you, Victoria Elizabeth. But for now, prepare for your parents, take some time for getting to know Zechariah better, and we shall enjoy solving these mysteries together in the near future. Good night to you all." The lights flickered and Exemplar was silent.

Vicky gathered her friend under one arm and wrapped her other arm around Zechariah, as they stood looking at their reflections in the mirror.

"We've got our work cut out for us with the mysteries that lay ahead, but having both of you here beside me to help, will make each new mystery more exciting, maybe challenging, but truly rewarding."

"Rewarding, my darling? Why, just from solving the old mysteries and helping the loss souls find peace?" Zechariah ran his fingers through her long hair.

"Yes that, but our greatest achievement will be saving Exemplar from everlasting punishment in the lake of fire. If we are successful in solving all the unsolved mysteries hanging over our old friend's head, he will be forgiven by his Creator and restored to his angelic position in the realms of heaven." Vicky looked at Samantha and Zechariah, both nodding their head in agreement.

"Exemplar saved me and helped bring me back to life so we could be together." Zechariah declared "I will do whatever it takes to make sure these mysteries are solved, Vicky darling! You can count on me!"

"Count me in!" Samantha stood straight, ready to fight to save the angel who had made a big mistake then regretted it as soon as he was thrown out of heaven and swore to do good whether it saved him or not. "I've made my share of mistakes in my life and because of my faith, I can be sure of my salvation, but fallen angels aren't given the same forgiveness as humans so poor Exemplar is repenting the only way he knows and his fate does hang on all those loss souls being saved."

"Then together we will take on each case until every single loss wondering soul is restored and satisfied with finally being set free from their torment and the good shepherd can at last take them to their everlasting home."

www.ingramcontent.com/pod-product-compliance
Lightning Source LLC
Chambersburg PA
CBHW070926250626
47159CB00009B/3137